Caroline Fabre grew up in Kenya and was educated at Cheltenham Ladies College. She went on to live in Ireland where she worked as a model. She is the author of the novels *Our Father's House* and *Swan Season,* published by Random House, both of which have sold worldwide.

She is also the writer of two children's books, *It's Hard to be a Hero* and *Henry's Amazing Albatross.*

She now lives in Somerset with her French husband and two sons. She still models part time and is a qualified fitness instructor, who has run marathons in London, Dublin, France and Kenya.

Love On The Run

CAROLINE FABRE

Fen Books

FEN BOOKS PAPERBACK

A CIP catalogue record for this title is available from the British Library
ISBN 9780955182877

Fen Books is an imprint of
Willow Bank Publishers Limited
www.willowbankpublishers.co.uk

First Published in 2007
By
Willow Bank Publishers Ltd
16A Bunters Road
Wickhambrook
Newmarket
Suffolk
CB8 8XY

Author photograph by kind permission of Bob Whitfield

Printed and bound in Great Britain by CPI Antony Rowe, Eastbourne

This one is for Henry Fabre.

Acknowledgements

My love and thanks go to the following people – my husband and soul mate Philippe, to Robbie and Henry, my Mum, and my sisters, Sue and Anne who were at the finishing line, and to my brother Chris Going.

Finally a special thanks to my agent, John Pawsey

Other titles by the author

Our Father's House
Swan Season

For Children:
It's Hard to be a Hero
Henry's Amazing Albatross

— Prologue —

It begins innocently enough as a simple and relatively easy way to get fit, lose weight, become toned and energised – yet another grand plan filled with promise. Everybody seemed to be doing it, running through the city streets and country lanes, as if towards some better, brighter place.

For Fran Taylor, thirty-three, overweight and going nowhere, it was a last valiant attempt to change her life.

'I've started jogging,' she announces to Gela and Shelly as they linger in the car park after dispatching their children off to school. It's September, the start of a new school year, a time when Fran finds herself wondering where the past year and her life has gone. The shedding leaves and shrinking days fill her with melancholy; the one consolation being that soon she will be able to hide beneath her winter woollies again, disguise the lumps and bumps under layers of dark clothing.

Gela makes a face. 'Couldn't you just go to the gym and use the running machine?' Gela tends to go for the easy option – the why walk when you can take the car reasoning. She's also fortunate enough to be naturally thin with a racing metabolism that comes from a nervous disposition.

Fran shakes her head. 'All that pounding for hours and going nowhere! At least this way nobody can see the rolls of fat!'

Fran, who is the proverbial pear – narrow-shouldered and flat-chested, before ballooning dramatically at the waist, has tried every diet ever written, used free-weights to build up her breasts, a stationary bicycle to melt her behind and had three litres of fat sucked from her thighs. Yet she remains mysteriously Rubenesque as if it were somehow ordained. There had been anger, depression, and even a brief foray into spiritualism and a life of inner purity, whilst the fat clung stubbornly to the outside, like gristle on a piece of prime beef. She has read numerous articles on the subject by experts, claiming running was the most effective way of burning fat, and has decided to test the theory.

'… and you get out into the fresh air – back in touch with nature. Why don't you join me?'

Gela frowns. She can think of better ways of getting in touch with nature.

'What sort of distance are you doing?' Shelly demands curiously.

Shelly considers herself a fitness expert, although she hasn't exercised properly for years. In her school days she'd excelled at cross-country, and even considered becoming a personal trainer, only she'd never managed to get remotely fit enough. At five foot eleven she is a tower of a woman, with a thick torso and muscular legs. Her hair is coloured a dull aubergine, her eyes are dark and disturbing. She frequently goes on heavy drinking binges, arriving at school, bloated and baggy eyed, from too many Tequila slammers.

'Oh I don't know,' Fran replies, flustered now. 'I just do a kind of loop through the lanes, about a mile, if that. I've only just started.'

'I'm thinking of doing circuit training,' Shelly states. 'It's incredibly tough but you build up real muscle.'

'I don't want to build up muscle, I just want to demolish all this fat,' Fran wails, prodding her waist with disdain.

'Muscle burns fat,' Shelly points out knowingly.

'I need to do something,' Gela sighs, thinking what she really needs, is to get out of the house, away from the blank computer screen. She also needs to give up smoking and eating junk food, going to bed at all hours – the list is endless.

A willowy blonde with long legs and jutting hipbones, there is a brittle quality about Gela, as if those tapering calves might snap at any moment.

'Come and join me,' Fran urges. 'I could do with some

company, it might spur me on a bit. I've read that jogging for only thirty minutes three times a week can change your life.'

Gela raises her eyebrows. Her life has already changed considerably since moving to the country, and not all for the best.

But Shelly steps in saying, 'I'll run with you if you like?'

'Oh, I wouldn't be able to keep up with you,' Fran answers, gazing imploringly at Gela.

'I'll freeze,' Gela states, 'and I haven't got anything to wear and my hair will go frizzy.'

'There's a new designer sports shop on the High Street,' Shelly says dryly. 'And you could always wear one of your posh scarves to protect your precious locks!'

Gela's hand moves instinctively to her hair, which is already waving madly in the damp morning air.

'Well, all right,' she agrees, 'but I haven't been jogging since the boys were born and that was only the occasional trot around Primrose Hill.'

'We'll start on Monday,' Shelly announces taking control. 'I'll measure out a route.'

'How far?' Fran inquires suspiciously.

'Oh, not far. We need to get fit first.'

She can already see herself leading the way through the winding country lanes, towards some distant but as yet undefined goal.

'Sounds a bit serious to me,' Gela states.

'Look, when I said I was doing a mile I didn't mean I was jogging the whole way,' Fran says desperately. 'I walk most of it!'

'You just need to build up some endurance,' Shelly says dismissively. 'I'll work out a schedule for us with a proper carb based diet for energy.'

'Carbohydrates are lethal,' Fran cries, 'I'll turn into a whale!'

She is wary of Shelly and her wild schemes; the

excessive drinking and purging, the erratic mood swings and bursts of anger. Yet there is something compelling about her, which sucks Fran in. It is the almost fanatical belief that anything is possible.

'Believe me, in six months you'll be transformed.'

'We could give it a go I suppose,' Fran begins. She turns to Gela adding, 'you did say you wanted to tone up.'

'I don't even have a decent pair of trainers,' Gela states. She too, is aware of Shelly's habit of turning a cause into an obsession, always drinking one glass of wine too many, inevitably going too far.

Yet none of them could have dreamt how far. What had begun as an innocent plan would turn into a test of endurance, and nothing would ever be quite the same again.

— Chapter One —

'Didn't the guy who invented jogging drop down dead from a heart attack?' Gela groans, as they step out that glorious September morning. After a dismal August, the weather now seems set for an Indian summer.

'He had a weak heart,' Shelly replies, striding ahead. She has measured out a two-mile loop and now leads the way, swinging her arms in a jaunty power walk across the busy main road that cuts through the village of Charlton Haven.

'Me too...' Fran breathes, 'I was bright blue when I was born ... only weighed five pounds ... was a really skinny child believe it or not. Sickly, always in and out of hospital.'

'We'd better take it slowly,' Gela says, glancing at Fran anxiously. She recalls Fran talking in a jokey way about the hole in her heart nobody could ever fill.

'My heart's fine now,' Fran assures her between breaths, 'it's my lungs that are about to implode.'

'You just need to build up your aerobic capacity,' Shelly says. 'No offence, but the best thing you can do for your heart is lose weight – and running burns more fat than any other exercise, even sex!

Fran imagines the fat melting, streaming down her calves as if from the skewered leg of a roasted turkey. Then all she needs is a pair of implants, and she'd be transformed into a curvaceous creature of mermaid proportions – the embodiment of womanly perfection. Deep down, she suspects it may be too late and by now her body is already set in its immutable mould – that she's destined to go to her grave in the voluminous attire of the terminally overweight. (A dark floaty creation from *Evans,* perhaps) leaving her etched in the collective memory of family and friends as a woman 'larger than life'.

The truth is she's never managed to get on top of her

weight problem – like so many of those high hopes and dreams that hadn't got off the ground – since most of them had hinged on her getting thin. For instance, her desire to be a nutritionist, or learn about homeopathy and the natural ways to good health. Yet how could she possibly advise people on what to put into their bodies when hers was the size of an elephant?

'Francesca is not a self starter,' her P.E. teacher had written all those years ago, *'but if motivated can show great determination.'*

Fran has felt unmotivated for some time now, wallowing complacently in her comfort zone, like a hippo in a mud bath, her marriage smooth but dull, her daughter Chloe growing up fast – leaving Fran with that hole again, and even more time to wallow.

Shelly is breaking into a trot now, her shoulder blades moving like wings beneath a branded sports vest. 'Remember you should be able to talk when you're running,' she warns.

Fran forces her bulk along the uneven pavement, her breath catching in the air stream of a truck that whooshes past, leaving her badly winded. A man walking a lame Labrador, steps out of her path with alarm as she thunders past, her feet flapping against the tarmac. God I must look a sight she thinks, an image of her behind heaving and rippling like an ocean swell, coming to mind.

They are turning off the main road now, passing low stone walls, and neat cottage gardens ablaze with colour, towards the long sweep of the hill. Fran can feel the gap widening as she pushes on in grim pursuit, as if through a sea of glue. The hill, which she has driven up many times, has taken on mountainous proportions. She slows, struggling against a plunging sense of defeat, reminded of the mother's race on sports day (which Shelly won each year) whilst everybody else set off in a burst of speed, leaving Fran bewildered and alone having somehow missed the starting gun.

The memory of Chloe's stricken face, as she'd shouted,

'go Mum, go! Jesus what's the matter with you?' impels Fran on with desperate jerky strides like a car running out of fuel. Through a haze she sees Shelly doubling back, hears her shout, 'you can do it girl, don't wimp out, keep going!'

Fran wants to tell her to bugger off, but is incapable of speech. 'Gowan without me,' she emotes, weaving across the road.

'No way, we stick together,' Shelly breathes, one arm trailing, as if pulling Fran along on an invisible string.

'Go … meet … back … at … par cark …' Fran gasps. She feels drunk from an excess of oxygen, yet can't seem to get any air into her lungs.

Thankfully Shelly is pulling away, saying, 'we'll wait for you at the top.'

Fran sets off again in a determined walk, head high, hips swaying like an African tribes-woman carrying a heavy burden.

At last she reaches the brow of the hill where the road forks, and sees the others waiting in the umbrella'd shade of an ancient oak tree. Fran is struck by the fact that Gela's cheeks are only faintly pink, whilst hers are blazing as if from a third degree burn. Shelly, she notes, with some satisfaction, appears to be sweating copiously, the aubergine hair plastered to her scalp in damp strands, a dark vee of sweat staining the front of her vest.

'Holy shit …' Fran wheezes.

'Don't worry, it's downhill from now on,' Shelly grins.

'Maybe we should walk back,' Gela suggests. 'I mean we're all out of shape.' She has read numerous stories of the overweight and over-zealous keeling over on the squash court, of hearts arresting without warning. 'After all it's only the first day.' And probably the last she thinks taking in Fran's hectic colour with alarm.

'We'll intersperse some walking with a slow jog,' Shelly concedes.

To Fran's relief the road ahead is flat now, cutting through a village green, with clusters of thatched cottages on either side. A tall, bare-chested man stands in the garden of one of them, smoking and watching their approach through narrowed eyes.

'Keep going,' he calls out as they draw closer.

Shelly immediately lengthens her stride, shouting provocatively, 'why don't you join us?'

She and Gela are forging ahead again giving Fran time to take in tousled blonde hair, and a glorious expanse of nut brown skin.

He has dragged his gaze away from Gela's retreating figure now and to her horror is focussed on her with a look of amusement.

She slows in an attempt to control her wobbly bits, hears him say, 'well done! You'll catch them now.'

'Fat chance,' Fran breathes, pushing on blindly, to escape further scrutiny.

In my next life, I shall have men like that running after me bearing armfuls of exotic flowers she thinks, veering off the pavement and narrowly avoiding a cyclist, who shouts, 'watch out, for God's sake!'

The sun flashes through the gaps in the hedgerows like strobe lighting, dazzling her and dark clouds of midges swirl and rise in the air, as she runs past ditches choked with phlox and blackberry. As the lane dips she feels a wondrous sense of release, as if she's free-falling through the air like a giant rubber ball. The breeze cools her burning cheeks as she hurtles down the hill, arms outstretched – now a strange winged creature, too heavy to take to the skies. She can see the spire of the church and finally the rough stone walls of the village car park from where this tortuous journey began.

'Holy shit,' she breathes, as she stumbles through the gates. 'Jesus Christ,' she adds, having vowed to stop using expletives since Chloe's vocabulary was now peppered with them.

'You did really well,' Shelly says, in a voice so full of admiration Fran almost believes her. 'You have just run two miles girl, and look at you!'

Fran is not sure she ever wants to look at herself again, whilst Gela, she notes is bending down and squinting into the side mirror of a parked car, attempting to smooth her hair.

'God I look terrible!' she groans.

Shelly glances at her sports watch, saying, 'once you get used to the hill, we can start shaving off some time.'

'That wasn't a hill, it was a mountain,' Fran gasps. She shakes her head, causing drops of sweat to dance around her face, like a dog shedding water. '… and who was that guy … with the chest?'

'Gerry Ryan,' Shelly replies, raising her eyebrows. 'He used to drink at The Trout and Fly – always with a different woman. Likes them big, blonde and married. I think he's a gardener in his spare time,' she adds wryly.

'A gardener,' Fran repeats, dreamily.

'We could do with a gardener,' Gela puts in, still tugging at her fringe.

He's a serial shagger,' Shelly says in warning tones. 'Don't even think about it! So how are you feeling?' she inquires, keen to get back to the business at hand.

'Like shit,' Fran answers, flopping over like a rag doll, her long dark hair cascading to the ground.

'It will get easier,' Shelly promises, 'then we can start increasing the distance.'

'How far?' Fran groans.

'It depends how far you're willing to go! How badly you want to lose the weight, tone up?' Her eyes sweep over Gela's reed like frame, before settling on Fran again. 'Look, this will change your metabolism, your eating habits – your life.'

'Hmm,' Fran mutters, thinking about all those so-called 'life-altering' diets and exercise programmes that had changed nothing.

She had even followed one of them for three months

(some vile liquid shake and aerobics) only to end up losing a measly half stone. But as her heart settles, she feels a kind of heady optimism, no doubt chemically induced by all those endorphins racing through her bloodstream. All the same she sees her thin self, bursting free from its mantle of flesh as she runs through the leafy autumn days and into the spring.

Perhaps she's melting already, she thinks as a hot stream pours down the inside of her thigh.

'Shit, I think I peed on myself!' she cries.

— Chapter Two —

'We need a goal,' Shelly declares as they sit in the beer garden of The Charlton Arms that mild October day. The weather is still unseasonably warm – people are still wearing shorts and sandals – today a hazy sunshine filters through the trees, while drifts of copper leaves pile up along the pavements.

Over the last few weeks Shelly has led Fran and Gela up hills and down hidden country lanes, urging, cajoling, and pushing them onwards, until they'd almost doubled the distance. Fran's thighs were chafed and raw, Gela's feet were covered in blisters. Muscles that had lain dormant for years had been stretched to breaking point – Fran who had barely made it downstairs one morning had joked that rigor mortis had set in.

Only Shelly appeared impervious to the discomfort, dismissing the pain as part of the 'building process', assuring them they were growing stronger by the day. Now she's ready to push on to the next stage – announce the grand plan, which if at first seemed unattainable, now strikes her as a real possibility.

'… something to work towards,' she continues.

'My goal is to be a size twelve by spring,' Fran states.

Ten would be better, but unrealistic, she thinks. She longs to be able to wear lower waisted jeans that didn't cut into her stomach, sexy underwear that didn't slice her cheeks in half, to prance into the New Year in a clinging strappy dress. She has already lost nine pounds which is cheering, whilst being aware it always starts like this – a nine pound loss, followed swiftly by a ten pound gain.

'That will happen once we start putting in the real miles,' Shelly assures her.

'They're already real enough for me,' Fran states dryly.

This morning she'd peeled off after the first circuit, too exhausted to take another step. She'd left a note on Shelly's car promising to do the extra miles in the evening. (Anything to get the woman off her back).

'I'd just like to be more toned – and stronger,' Gela says. Mentally as well as physically she thinks. As to her main goal; to get to grips with the novel she's been planning to write for God knows how long – a long held ambition that seems to be thwarted by permanent writer's block.

'You're already stronger than when you started,' Shelly insists. 'We'll be building up serious muscle from now on, although we've got a lot more work to do.' She pauses, wondering how to announce the plan; a huge undertaking, but it could be done, she was sure of it.

'How about another round?' she suggests, glancing at her empty glass. After all it was Friday – she was looking forward to getting seriously hammered this weekend.

'I'll just have another diet coke,' Fran says. Fran doesn't drink claiming it's a waste of calories. 'We should order some food before it gets really busy,' she adds glancing anxiously at the next table, where an oversized family is tucking into hefty portions of battered cod and chips. She has been debating whether to have the Smoked Salmon Platter or the Pasta Bake (the latter is after all a good source of carbohydrates). Theoretically she should be able to devour half the menu after all the pounding she's done this week, but she knows from bitter experience it doesn't work like that. 'Have you two decided what you want?'

'I'm not that hungry,' Shelly replies, 'I'll just have a toasted ham and cheese sandwich, and another large glass of house red.'

'Same for me,' Gela adds, 'except I'll have a medium white.'

'Ah come on, have a large one – it's the weekend,' Shelly insists.

'I'm hopeless after too much wine,' Gela says, 'champagne is even worse – I tend to do – well, awful things.'

'Like what?' Shelly inquires curiously. She has come to the conclusion that Gela with her posh accent and expensive wardrobe is far too proper by half.

'Oh, you know ... just embarrassing things,' Gela replies evasively, cringing at the memory of that awful night.

'I'll go and order,' Fran says, scooping up the menus. She sets off along the paved path glancing towards a private garden at the back, her eyes immediately drawn to an enormous corset hanging on the washing line. Next to the corset is a massive bra of industrial strength, grey with age.

That will be me, she thinks grimly – yo-yoing into middle age, fighting the flab until the battle becomes too hard. She resolves to order the smoked salmon, which is after all a good source of *Omega 3* – and will help her aching joints as well as protect her heart.

She places the order with a waitress with a chest like a shelf. (No doubt the owner of the bra). In fact, all the waitresses are large, making Fran feel slightly cheered.

'Could I have a half portion of chips to go with the salmon?' she inquires, liberated by the sight of so much flesh.

'Don't do half portions,' the landlord calls from across the bar. He too is a human barrel of a man – bursting out of a rather grubby checked shirt.

'None of that nouvelle rubbish here! We're a proper eating house.'

'No wonder everybody is so bloody fat,' Fran mutters under her breath. 'Fine I won't have any chips,' she states stubbornly. 'I'll have a diet coke please,' (there's no way I'm going to end up a big pants woman) 'and a large red wine, and a medium white.'

She returns to the garden with the tray of drinks, pleased with her show of strength. 'I can see I'm going to have to carry on tramping the lanes,' she tells the others, before embarking on a description of the garments hanging on the washing line, followed by the landlord's policy of no half portions. 'Talk about a Fat Controller!' she mutters crossly.

'That's good,' Shelly grins, 'I mean the fact you want to carry on, because I've got a plan.'

Now, with the wine coursing through her veins it all seems eminently possible. 'I was thinking if we stick to the training we could be ready for the Marathon by April.'

There's a silence as the others stare at her, aghast.

'Or perhaps we could join the new Russian space mission,' Fran says finding her voice at last.

'Look it's not impossible.'

'Right! Only twenty four miles …!' Fran says.

'Twenty six point two,' Shelly states.

'You are joking aren't you?' Fran says wildly.

'I don't think she is,' Gela says shaking her head in disbelief.

Shelly lowers her voice, and leans forward. 'Look, I've been thinking about it for a while. We could do it, it's just a question of training – getting the miles under our belts.'

'Twenty six, point two,' Fran repeats, 'I'm glad you mentioned the point two – I mightn't have been prepared for that! Holy shit, Shell, do I look like the kind of woman who runs marathons?'

'People much fatter than you do it … not that you're that fat,' Shelly says swiftly. 'What I'm trying to say is, all sorts of unlikely people enter, even people with one leg,' she finishes.

'Maybe I could do it in a wheelchair?' Fran says wryly.

'We would all have a proper medical first,' Shelly moves on, 'make sure everything's in order, especially as you have that heart problem.'

Fran shakes her head. 'My problem is I'm just too damned fat!'

'You won't be by April,' Shelly states, 'trust me!' She turns her burning gaze on Gela. 'You'd be well up for it.'

'I wouldn't have the stamina,' Gela counters. 'I'd keel over, hit the wall or whatever happens to marathon runners.'

'That only happens if you haven't trained properly,' Shelly states. 'I've been reading up about it. Everybody is capable of running a marathon. It's nothing to do with size or build.'

'I wouldn't say everybody,' Fran murmurs as the waitress appears with the food.

Shelly orders another large glass of wine before continuing. 'This is a chance to do something for ourselves – show all those wimps out there what we're made of.'

'But I am a wimp,' Gela wails. She's always the last person to jump into the swimming pool, would stand shivering on the edge for ages rather than take the plunge.

'Imagine being able to say we'd run a marathon – how we'd feel afterwards,' Shelly says challengingly.

'Dead?' Fran suggests.

'It would be an incredible achievement,' Shelly continues, 'I know we could do it. Look how far we've come already?' She needs to convince herself it can be done – prepare herself mentally as well as physically. The daily runs have given her a new lease of life – the sense that whilst things remain frozen on the home front between her and her partner Bruce, she has embarked on a project that will somehow carry her forward.

She reaches into her handbag, saying 'look I managed to get hold of some entry forms. We could fill them in at least, start the training and see how it goes.'

Fran glances at the form in disbelief. 'Estimated time ... three days ... they'll have taken down the finishing post by the time I get there.'

Gela giggles. The second glass of wine has gone to her head making her long for a cigarette, but this is hardly the time to light up.

'Look we've nothing to lose by sending off the forms,'

Shelly persists.

'Credibility?' Fran suggests. She has a sudden overwhelming desire for a dessert – something wickedly rich and chocolaty, while Gela gives in to the nicotine craving and lights up.

'You are going to have to stop that, straight away,' Shelly snaps.

'I don't smoke that much,' Gela insists. 'Only socially.' Although capable of getting through a whole pack on a good night – she doesn't smoke enough on a regular basis to warrant giving up – she tells herself.

'What about the booze?' Fran says, as Shelly embarks on the fourth glass. 'I thought you said alcohol makes you dehydrated?'

'Wine is a good source of carbs,' Shelly states, with a grin. 'Anyway I'm going to give it up during the week. As I was saying, we need to get the forms off by the end of this month.'

'I suppose we could fill them in,' Gela says rashly. After all it's six months away she thinks. By then Shelly would have, no doubt, grown tired of the idea and started circuit training.

'How about I wait for you both at the finishing line?' Fran suggests, fighting the chocolate urge by summoning up an image of the giant corset on the washing line.

'No, we're all in it together,' Shelly states firmly. She can already see herself leading the others triumphantly across the line, to the wild applause from the crowds.

'No way, Shell.'

'Christ woman haven't you ever lived dangerously?'

'No, as a matter of fact,' Fran answers candidly.

Yes, Gela thinks – and I'm still haunted by it.

'We'd be doing it for charity – it would be for a good cause,' Shelly continues.

'Save the whale?' Fran suggests wryly.

'How about breast cancer,' Shelly says, pouncing on a cause close to Fran's heart. Her Aunt Lettie who had brought her up, had died of the disease five years ago, leaving Fran heartbroken.

'I could also organise another coffee morning, or a charity ball – get the PTA to support something new for once …' Fran begins.

'It would be a real adventure,' Shelly continues. 'I've heard it's an amazing event – more like a carnival, than a race.'

Fran looks sceptical.

'Look,' Shelly concludes, playing her last trump card, 'we'd have a laugh!'

'O.K, I'll fill the bloody thing in,' Fran says finally, 'but I have a horrible feeling the laugh will be on me!'

— Chapter Three —

S helly pushes the timer on her sports watch as they set off from the car park, that frantic November morning. The Indian summer is now a distant memory; the weather forecast warns of severe winds, which are already gusting wildly towards them with the force of an oncoming train.

'Remember to pace yourselves, we need to finish,' she warns Fran. 'You won't be able to stop half way on the day, say you'll do the rest some other time,' she adds dryly.

'I know, I know,' Fran snaps. 'I'll finish – just don't wait for me, I might be a while – like ages.'

Shelly suspects that Fran (and Gela for that matter) have no intention of running the marathon, although they'd both assured her they'd sent off their forms. Rather they were simply going along with the plan, assuming it would fold by Christmas.

Well they were in for a surprise, Shelly thinks. She desperately needs a focus – something to take her mind off the growing fear that she and Bruce had reached an impasse.

She had foolishly brought the subject up again, knowing she was venturing into thorny territory, but determined to point out that it was almost the anniversary of their first meeting seven years ago.

'We must celebrate,' she'd said. 'Do something special!'

'Like what?' he'd frowned.

'Well, we could get married?' she'd suggested casually.

His face had clouded over, making him seem all at once removed, inaccessible, someone she barely knew, rather than her lover of seven years.

'We don't need a piece of paper, to prove we're together,' he'd stated.

He was clearly puzzled by her conventional streak, which was so at odds with the free spirit he'd met that drunken evening in The Charlton Arms. 'Anyway nothing is permanent.' Here he was alluding to his ex-wife, who had walked out on him after eleven years of marriage, taking their daughter, Becky with her. Whilst Shelly had also been married and divorced, gaining custody of Gary who was now eight. 'Why go through all that grief again?' he'd argued.

'Because we know it will work this time,' she'd suggested.

And because I'm madly in love with you, she'd thought.

He was the antithesis of her ex-husband, Nick (or Nicotine) as she'd christened him – with his cigarette breath and mean spirit. Bruce was super-fit, partly from working on the moors, but also due to a recent fascination with rock climbing. A hobby Shelly didn't share, because of her profound fear of heights.

'I just don't want to be your girlfriend for the rest of my life,' she'd stated, 'your partner.' She hated it when he referred to her as 'his partner.' Lover, soul mate, other half – anything would be better, than that cold little word which conjured up a fleeting and tenuous alliance between two tennis players, rather than a life long commitment, she thought.

'Marriage is meaningless these days,' he'd argued, 'it doesn't bind people together – if anything it ruins healthy relationships. Look at us – we're both examples of failed marriages!'

Yet, in the practical sense, marriage meant a great deal. Right now she had no claim on anything he owned, or even the things they'd built up together; like the pub for instance. She was the one who'd suggested he buy the old Trout and Fly overlooking Charlton Lake, do it up and turn it into the cosy welcoming place it now was. She had set about re-furbishing it, working behind the bar for nights on end, putting up with beery breath and lewd comments from the local fishermen. It had literally driven her to drink, but the pub was now raking it in thanks to her.

She had lavished him with love and attention, hosted sumptuous dinner parties for his friends, been an insatiable lover, (has a different outfit for every occasion) yet she remains his 'favourite tart' (his jokey reference to her leather and lace ensemble) and not his wife.

It's becoming a burning issue, which Shelly is determined to resolve.

As she reaches the rise, where the lane winds away through a monotonous stretch of ploughed fields, it strikes her he'd be happy to jog along like this for the rest of his life.

She pushes on, against a vicious gust of wind tunnelling through the trees, feeling suddenly powerless by her inability to change things. The wind howls through the pylons, sending leaves and fallen twigs hurtling.

Gela is struggling against it too, calling anxiously, 'shouldn't we turn back – it could bring one of those cables down!'

Shelly shakes her head, wondering at Gela's habit of seeing danger around every corner. It strikes her the odds of a cable crashing down on them, was about as low as Bruce proposing.

'Keep going,' she shouts. After all, we've gone too far to turn back now, seven years, she thinks, her mind whirling with possible strategies.

An ultimatum is out of the question – Bruce hates being put under pressure, and the last thing she wants is to lose him. She could put him on the spot – propose to him on the radio, or on one of those reality shows. He could hardly refuse her in front of the whole nation! Perhaps she should try to conquer her fear of heights and go climbing with him – put it to him as they hang suspended from some rocky ledge – prove she's even willing to risk her life for him.

She takes a deep breath, preparing herself for the next circuit, knowing there is really only the one option – to hang on in there and hope he comes around.

The second loop seems to have doubled – the stump of the fallen Ash is further away than she'd thought. The hill looms spitefully, as if defying her to conquer it this time. Her hamstrings have seized in protest at this further assault, whilst the voice of doubt creeps into her head.

She recalls Bruce's reaction when she'd first announced her plan to run the marathon.

'It's a lot of miles,' he'd warned, 'you'd need to be really focussed.' He'd done a number of long distance runs to build up strength and endurance for one of his tougher climbs.

'I know that ... but with the right training.'

'You'll have to cut out the booze completely, get yourself in tip top shape,' he'd stated.

'I realise that,' she'd answered curtly, irritated by the fact he didn't believe she had it in her. I'll show him, she thinks, pushing away the doubts, and forging on in a show of power, up the sharp incline of the hill.

Gela is falling behind now, groaning about a blister, leaving Shelly to lead the way (she always feels better when she's ahead.) She grits her teeth, and focuses on the thought of a liquid lunch in the pub afterwards. After all, it's almost the weekend.

With the end in sight, the doubts evaporate – now she can see herself racing towards the finishing post where Bruce is waiting amidst a sea of cheering spectators. She's aware of Gela creeping up behind her and accelerates (she's damned if she's going to let Gela overtake now) and with a final agonising burst reaches the car park, the adrenaline pumping through her veins like a shot of tequila.

'Next week we'll do a five mile loop,' she announces as they gather in The Charlton Arms for a well-earned drink. The Fat Controller, as the landlord was now known, was used to them coming in soaked and windswept after a run and using the loo to change. He'd even joked about feeding Fran up with double portions since she was clearly fading away.

'I'll measure out a new route around the lake,' Shelly continues. 'We could do with a change of scenery.'

She shifts her gaze from Gela to Fran as if defying either of them to bow out now.

'It's just this blister...,' Gela begins, 'I can't wear any decent shoes anymore,' whilst Fran says, 'I'm knackered, Shell! I've no energy left to cook dinner in the evening – Brian's fed up 'cos he's not getting any sex!'

'Look I know you're both tired,' Shelly concedes, (she's exhausted too, although never too tired for sex) 'so tomorrow we'll have a day off. In any case we need to go shopping, get you both some decent trainers. We could have lunch.'

'Shopping ... lunch?' Fran breathes, as if such luxuries are a distant memory.

'I could do with something new to wear,' Gela says brightening.

'I need underwear,' Shelly states.

Fran raises an eyebrow. 'Planning something special?' she inquires.

'Yes, as a matter of fact – it's our anniversary.'

'But you and Bruce aren't married!'

'So? It doesn't mean we can't celebrate the last seven years,' Shelly says brusquely.

'No, but it's not quite the same.'

Shelly takes a slug of beer – a local brew, bitter and strong, like her mood. 'Why? Just because we didn't have some flowery wedding?'

Fran frowns. 'Well you're not bound together by law wondering if you'll make it to silver or even bronze. You don't owe each other anything,' she adds. Still reeling from an excess of oxygen, she's unaware she's hit a raw nerve.

'I reckon it makes it all the more romantic,' Gela adds swiftly.

'Yeah, well, both of us have done the marriage thing anyway,' Shelly says, putting an end to any further discussion.

She gives them both a frank stare. 'We're OK with the way things are.'

She drives home in a tense mood, rattled by Fran's comment about not owing each other anything – a reminder that should things go wrong she and Gary would be back to square one, homeless and adrift, having to start all over again.

She plans a special celebration – a three-course dinner followed by a night of all nights, which means buying a new outfit. Something sporty and sexy this time. She's tired of playing the harlot. It was time to throw out Bruce's 'favourite tart' ensemble and show off her newly toned body.

"I'll win in the end," she says to herself – "I always do."

— Chapter Four —

They trawl the High Street, dodging in and out of elegant shoe shops, until Gela finds the perfect pair, only the delicate straps with their jewelled clasps cut into her blistered feet like a saw. She gazes at them longingly wondering when she'd wear them.

'Too posh,' Shelly states. 'You live in the country now.'

'They are quite high,' Fran comments enviously, thinking they would never withstand the weight of her. The heel would surely break within minutes, followed by her ankle.

Gela dithers for a moment then fumbles for her credit card, thinking she would find an occasion – dinner at Ashlington Falls perhaps – the exclusive country hotel, where they'd stayed for a few blissful days before moving into Manor Farm.

Fran tries on a slinky black dress, claiming her arms look like rolling pins. 'Maybe I should try running on them,' she sighs.

Shelly sifts through rails of underwear, discarding all of them as too fussy. She finally pulls out a plunging velvet bustier, holding it against her ample chest for a moment.

'Try it on,' Fran urges.

Shelly shakes her head. Although not adverse to flinging off her top at drunken parties, she loathes communal changing rooms with a venom. 'Too many prissy women checking each other out in there! I'll take it – then we need to go to this specialist sports shop I've found,' she says.

'What about lunch?' Fran wails. All she can think about is food – barbecued ribs, chicken wings in honey and mustard sauce, warm Pecan Pie with vanilla ice cream (after all she must have run the equivalent of a marathon in the last few weeks.)

'First things first,' Shelly states. She leads the way down

the High Street turning into a wide precinct towards a sports shop with a sign saying NIRVANA.

'We need to invest in a decent pair of shoes – especially you,' she tells Gela, 'or you'll end up with black toe-nails as well as blisters. They should be a size bigger than your normal shoe size.'

The inside is dank and cluttered with shoe boxes piled high, the walls covered in posters of athletic men with carved legs, frozen in mid stride. There is a distinct smell of sweat in the air, Gela thinks, glancing at the rails of shiny tracksuits and branded t-shirts without much enthusiasm.

'They'll analyse your running style first, then fit you with the perfect pair,' Shelly states, pointing to a grimy pad on the floor which appears to be linked to a lap top.

'My trainers are fine,' Fran says hastily, a vision of her heaving behind transposed onto the screen for all to see. But Shelly is already conversing with the owner of the shop – a leathery faced man with the body of a whippet.

'We're training for the Marathon,' she tells him importantly. 'We need the best running shoes you've got.'

Moments later Fran is sporting a pair of high impact trainers, (no doubt designed for weighty runners) and being instructed to run across the pad, ensuring her foot lands in the centre.

'Looks like she's seriously pronating,' The Whippet says, glancing at the screen with a frown.

Fran hears it as ovulating. 'If only,' she mutters to herself. She is infertile – a barren wasteland, she sometimes thinks, since they'd removed her ovaries after Chloe's birth. She blames her weight gain on the operation and the long lingering depression that followed. But what The Whippet is trying to say is that she runs with her feet turned inwards like a duck. Whilst Gela, he proclaims, is neutral.

'She looks like a natural,' he says, apparently mesmerised, by Gela's endless legs.

'Needs to pace herself though, or she'll never be a good distance runner,' Shelly says immediately. Shelly tries not to dwell on Gela's potential, consoling herself with the fact that Gela lacked real muscle, would undoubtedly struggle once the going got tougher.

'What sort of distance do you do?' Shelly asks The Whippet.

'Ah, not enough these days,' he replies, 'apart from running to work and back which is about thirteen miles round trip and the odd triathlon.'

'That's serious mileage,' Shelly says, like one pro to another.

'Keeps me sane,' he grins, his face creasing like an old chamois.

Gela resolves to invest in the new, so called, miracle moisturiser with marine extracts if she carries on running.

'A marathon is all about the last six miles,' he says. He taps his forehead adding, 'that's when you need it up here.'

Armed with the perfect trainers they move through the shop searching for thermal tops and lightweight bottoms, Gela pouncing on a pink-cropped vest with matching lycra shorts.

'This is not some posh Pilates class!' Shelly reminds her sarcastically.

Fran tries on a special sports bra that squashes what little she has into tiny folded envelopes, concluding that the clothes, like the sport itself, is decidedly unflattering. She gazes at her reflection gloomily. She may have lost almost a stone but her bum is still huge - she might as well dress up as a rhino, with a sign SAVE MY HIDE on her behind. Nobody would know the difference.

They buy a special belt each, for carrying water bottles, and a tube of something called Sportslick.

'To prevent chafed nipples,' Shelly announces.

Gela groans. 'Frizzy hair, blisters, black toe-nails and now sore nipples – what next?'

'Aching hamstrings, shin splints, damaged knees,' The Whippet grins.

'So why on earth are we doing this?' Fran demands from behind the curtain.

There's a silence, then Shelly says, 'well there are lots of reasons ... why are we doing this?' she repeats. 'Because we need to do something!' she suggests finally.

Which just about sums it up, Gela thinks, a potential plot for a novel suddenly weaving its way into her thoughts.

Shelly pulls out a luminous vest and adds it to the pile – 'this is for when I take you across the moors. It can get really foggy up there, and I need to be seen.'

'I'll take one too,' Gela says, visions of being crushed to death by a farm tractor, arms and limbs severed, and lost forever in the bog ... but Shelly snatches it off her saying, 'one will do – as long as they can see me.'

'What if I just happen to be ahead?' Gela inquires, taken aback.

'You won't be,' Shelly states with an odd little smile. 'And if you are it means you're running too fast.'

'You said we need to find our own pace,' Gela reminds her.

'Yeah and you don't seem to be able to control yours,' Shelly reiterates tersely.

There's a strained silence. 'Look I've had quite a lot of experience of cross country ...' She recalls the pain of trying to stay ahead, the agony of being pipped at the post. 'You've got to learn to pace yourself – it's as simple as that.' She tries to keep her tone light, intimating it's all good sport, knowing deep down the race has already begun, but there can only be one winner.

'Anyway I've been doing loads of research – trying to tailor a programme that suits all of us, making sure we've got the right gear,' she waves her hand at their purchases as The Whippet rings up the items on the till.

This is my idea, she wants to add – I make the rules. 'I was the one who got us into this,' she says.

'Actually, it was me,' Fran points out.

'Fine then you lead the way ... or you,' she adds glaring at Gela, 'why do I fucking bother ... ?'

'This isn't a competition,' Gela says, bewildered. Or is it, she wonders?

The Whippet raises his eyebrows and smiles an ancient knowing smile. 'Running is all about competing with yourself,' he says, his gaze focussed on Shelly. 'Otherwise you're heading for trouble.'

***

Over lunch, Shelly sets about making amends – her good mood restored, after two tequila sunrises. 'Look sorry about earlier – didn't mean to offend – I've just got this well, bad temper – tend to lose it now and again – as you know!' Somebody had once suggested she do a course in anger management, which had infuriated her further.

Fran smiles. 'We'll let you off this time.' She knows all about Shelly's sudden flares of temper – which were invariably alcohol induced. She recalls a recent incident at a charity dinner when Shelly, fortified by too much cheap wine had grabbed Jasmine Fellows by the collar warning her to lay off flirting with Bruce. Jasmine, who ran the PTA and looked set to take over the running of the school, had since ostracised Shelly from various school events claiming she was 'bad news'. Fran's only regret was that Shelly hadn't strangled the woman.

'It's just that somebody needs to be in charge of the training ... but it doesn't have to be me!'

'I'm happy enough for you to lead the way,' Gela says warmly. Against all odds, she has become fond of Shelly, has already cast her as a woman with a big heart and generous spirit, tough yet oddly vulnerable, driven, but happy to help others along the way (as long as they didn't try to get ahead).

'Besides, I didn't like that luminous vest. Yellow's just not my colour!'

Shelly grins. 'To the three of us, getting to the finishing post,' she says, raising her glass.

"And to me finally becoming Mrs Bruce Wainright," she thinks to herself.

— Chapter Five —

Gela's mood is one of optimism as she drives home after a five mile run – the feeling all will be well no matter how bleak it sometimes appears these dark winter mornings. The tension has lifted – the earlier row with Marcus fading away now. She resolves to make some changes in her life, give up smoking for good this time, make a fresh start on the novel. Maybe these daily bursts of energy will free her from writer's block, the view of rolling hills, being back in touch with nature will (once she stops shivering) inspire her.

She has almost given up on the grand plan to write a novel – has re-written the opening scene thirteen times until her desk is littered with piles of typed script, covered in scribbled changes. She'd read each copy over and over, only to conclude the story was going nowhere – like the previous attempts, had died a death by chapter three.

She'd worked as an editor for a joint-publishing group before moving to the country, where frustrated authors paid large sums of money to see their work in print. She'd spent her days reading through those labours of love, knowing she could write a novel with all the vital ingredients that would make editors sit up. She saw it rising phoenix-like to the top of the best-seller list, followed by film rights and fame. Now at last she has the opportunity, only the story refuses to take shape – all those brilliant, illuminated ideas that kept her awake at night would somehow lose their glow by morning, leaving her staring dully at the computer screen.

She blames it on Marcus working from home, on the daily domestic chores, on Jamie who is hyperactive, on Matthew, who's a sickly child. While a part of her has started to question her ability to write a publishable novel in the first place, to keep the narrative suspense going and bring the story to its dramatic conclusion.

She turns up the long winding lane that leads to the seventeenth century farmhouse which Marcus had called the perfect retreat when they'd first driven down from London almost eight months ago. A day when the lanes had been white with cow parsley and the smell of wild garlic hung in the air. She'd taken one look at the old stone house with its swollen roof and ivy covered walls and said, 'it's paradise – but isn't it a bit off the beaten track?'

'That's what makes it paradise,' Marcus had replied.

Today the air is rank with the stench of slurry, or some vile fertiliser; Gela has taken to grading them from one to ten in order of foulness, this one ranks a number ten in the gagging order.

She switches off the ignition, catching sight of herself in the mirror, with a jolt. A black tear of mascara stains her cheek, whilst her hair is standing up madly on her head as if in protest. It strikes her, her legacy to the world will not be a best selling novel dedicated to nearest and dearest, but shelves filled with hair conditioners, straightening irons and serums.

Pushing open the faded oak door to the kitchen, her heart sinks at the sight of the mess; the table is still littered with debris from breakfast - discarded newspapers and toys are strewn all over the floor. There is a smell of freshly brewed coffee, indicating Marcus has bypassed the chaos and retreated to his study. The Growler, their ageing terrier, is curled up by the Aga fast asleep.

All her resolve and good intentions are evaporating now, the endorphins draining away, leaving behind a kind of prickling anger. The row they'd had earlier re-ignites and burns inside her. The sense of injustice as Marcus slept through the morning rush whilst she'd dashed around frantically, searching for socks and missing trainers, cursing as milk boiled over, toast burnt and Jamie and Matthew fought bitterly over the remains of the *Nutella*. The noise had reached a crescendo, causing Marcus to finally emerge from the bedroom, with the wary look of somebody who has entered a parallel world to find all order has broken down.

In the old days, he would have stooped to tie a shoelace, or kiss a sticky cheek before setting off to work in the company car to the calming sounds of Classic FM. Now he hovers in the sidelines like a referee, barking orders, 'Matthew you're dripping jam all over the table – Jamie you're eating like a pig! I thought we'd banned chocolate – no wonder the kid's so hyper!'

She normally managed to bite her tongue, anything to avoid the odorous atmosphere that lingered after a row, but a sleepless night (dreaming up yet another plot which now seemed farcical) made her snap, 'Oh, for God's sake, help him wipe it up! Can't you see I'm doing a million things at the same time?'

He'd shaken his head, as if questioning her organising skills, before striding towards the sink and looking around irritably for the sponge, which was sitting in a puddle of water beneath last night's egg encrusted saucepan.

'Here,' she'd said, throwing it at him, showering an arc of dirty water into the air, before storming out of the kitchen.

She suspects his decision to move to the country and work from home on a consultancy basis is not proving to be the great escape he'd hoped for. That he misses the corporate life he'd once claimed 'ulcerating'. He has started to spend more and more time on the phone talking to former colleagues as if he's still part of that vibrant team he once headed, and goes back and forth to London on a regular basis claiming unfinished business.

Yet he'd been the one bent on 'getting away from it all,' keen to leave the stresses and strains of city life behind. He'd dismissed her fears that he'd miss the social whirl, the restaurants and theatres, not to mention take-away food and their widening nucleus of friends.

'We'll do other things,' he'd stated, 'go for long walks

through the fields and eat in quaint little pubs.'

Only the quaint little pubs serving decent food were few and far between and the long walks had been thwarted by months of bad weather.

It strikes her they haven't really dug themselves into country life – she'd never even explored the back lanes until recently whilst Marcus it seemed had never left London in spirit. Yet the boys had settled in straight away, relishing the large garden with its stagnant pond, the surrounding fields and muddy ditches. Jamie had already made friends at the village school and the sickly pallor had started to fade from Matthew's cheeks. It was the right decision, she tells herself, trying to dismiss the uneasy feeling that Marcus is not happy.

She swings around on her heels, her trainers squeaking against the tiled floor, as she picks her way through an obstacle course of Lego, Jamie's remote control car, and the rubbish sack which Marcus has conveniently forgotten to put out.

She pushes open the door to his study, wishing she'd showered and blow-dried her hair before confronting him. She's always been insecure about her looks – however many times Marcus tells her she's a beauty. Her face is attractive inasmuch as there's nothing wrong with it – full lips, pert nose, eyes the colour of sphagnum moss. It's just her hair that doesn't belong – right now her fringe has curled into two perfect buffalo horns, whilst the rest has risen into a halo of honey coloured frizz.

Marcus turns around, his handsome face breaking into a contrite smile.

'Hello Angel, sorry about earlier, I was about to clear up when the phone rang. How did the run go?'

'Fine,' she replies shortly.

'How far did you go?'

'Five miles – we did the loop twice then added on an extra bit.'

'Only twenty one to go,' he grins.

When she'd first told him about Shelly's plan to run the marathon (emphasising it wasn't her plan) he'd said, 'why not? You could do it – I don't know about Fran or Shelly, but you've got exactly the right build – long sexy legs like a gazelle.'

She'd smiled saying – 'I'm not sure I'd want to put myself through that kind of misery.'

Now she says, 'Shelly's determined we're going to do it.'

'Shelly is driven by ego … it's not a good formula,' he says oddly.

He doesn't like Shelly, since one of her famous dinner parties when she'd boasted she could drink all the men under the table. She'd alighted on Marcus first, knowing he was unlikely to take up the challenge.

He worked in the wine business for God's sake – he'd told her icily, he wasn't prepared to drink any old plonk.

'You're just a snob,' she'd said, causing Marcus to say with a smile that didn't reach his eyes, 'and you dear woman are a lush.'

'She's a loose cannon,' he'd said as they'd driven home. 'Always getting plastered.'

'Bruce seems to take it in good spirits,' Gela had answered, thinking about Shelly's good-natured partner – a big bear of a man, who appeared to take Shelly's drunken antics in his stride.

'Until she goes too far,' Marcus had muttered.

'You'll beat her to the finishing post,' he predicts now.

He reaches for his pack of tobacco – he has started rolling his own cigarettes since downshifting, and taken on the slightly wild and unshaven look of somebody who works from home. 'Better get back to work; I've a load of phone calls to make.'

'Marcus we need to talk,' she says, before launching in clumsily, ' … I just feel we're not in this together … you get up when you feel like, then come barging in, trying to take control ... I mean we're meant to be a team ... it's like you're on a different schedule. I just don't want to come in after a run and have to clean up ... the kitchen's an absolute disaster, ...' she flounders.

She's never been good at getting her point across. She always comes off worse in a row, whilst he manages to floor her with counter arguments – the main one being that he has a stressful job (although that no longer applies) hence, he should be exempt from domestic duties. Yet apparently maintaining the right to control the running of the house.

But to her surprise, he says, 'I'm sorry, I've a lot on my mind right now, a difficult case at work ... decisions to be made,' he rakes his fingers through his thick brown hair. ' ... to be honest, I'd like to break away from the company completely, do something else.'

'What's stopping you?' she inquires. It was not as if he was short of ideas. He'd often talked about starting a business of his own, importing fine wines and speciality foods.

'We live in the country now,' he says.

'Everything is done on the internet.'

'I had a long chat with Paolo earlier,' he digresses, 'he's thinking of diversifying into up-market wine shops – stocking rare vintages. A bit like I was hoping to do.'

'Oh?' she says, her heart quickening.

Paolo Conti, is his confidante and now a multi-millionaire after setting up a chain of intimate wine bars called The Grape Escape. Gela suspects Paolo's success is part of the reason Marcus is so restless although Marcus has never admitted it. Rather, he concedes Paolo had the right idea at the right time. Yet there is something in his tone – regret perhaps, for lost opportunities – all those brilliant ideas he too has had, only at the wrong time.

The familiar dread is back, the memory of that terrible night almost five years ago, returning like a bad dream.

'... he wants me to help him set it up ...,' Marcus is saying. 'Which means spending time in London – meeting up with the key people.'

'How long for?' she inquires, with a thumping heart.

'However long it takes.'

'You're starting to spend more time up there than here,' she says, trying to remain calm.

He frowns. 'You should be used to me being away by now, surely?'

'It was different when we lived in London. It's just so isolated here. I don't sleep a wink when you're away.'

She could see the headlines – *WOMAN MURDERED IN REMOTE FARMHOUSE MYSTERY.* The boys would be spared though, found huddled together in one of Jamie's secret hiding places, whilst the forensic team searched the house for her dismembered body.

'You've got The Growler,' he says.

'She's getting more and more deaf,' Gela points out. She takes a deep breath, trying to quell the unease. 'Where will you stay?' Now he no longer had the generous expense account he tended to stay in a small hotel off Baker Street.

'Oh Paolo will put me up, until I get sorted – he's got loads of space. He's bought one of the new penthouses overlooking Canary Wharf.'

Gela feels as if a cold weight is pressing down on her.

She remembers a conversation all those years ago – Paolo talking about his dream of living high up – on top of the world. At the time he was renting a basement flat and working in the off-licence in Primrose Hill. Marcus would often stop by on a Friday evening after work to chat about Premier Crus, or the merits of the new Beaujolais. She would hover in the background, aware of Paolo watching her from time to time, a flicker of amusement in his dark eyes (eyes that didn't reflect the light) as if he knew she wasn't taking it seriously.

'Are you all right?' Marcus inquires. 'You're shivering –

come here and let me warm you up,' he adds holding out both arms.

'I'm all sweaty,' she protests, but he pulls her onto his lap, and buries his head in her armpit. 'Mmmm, divine,' he breathes.

He loves the musty smell of her, is forever protesting against her obsession with deodorant and body lotions. He pushes his hand under the thick band of her sports bra, making her stiffen.

The best thing about working from home, he often said, was they could have sex any time day or night. Gela, who often thinks back nostalgically to the early days before children – languishing in bed until noon, liquid lunches and love in the afternoon, wonders why she doesn't want it now she has the chance.

'I need a shower,' she says again. Her body temperature has plummeted, making her feel chilled to the bone. 'Then I have to clean up the kitchen, go to the supermarket, the dry cleaners.'

It's those daily domestic chores that take the edge off desire, she thinks.

'Why don't you ask Mrs Allen to come in three times a week,' he suggests, referring to the bossy old cleaning lady she'd found in the village after a long search.

'Because she drives us both mad,' Gela reminds him. Again it was fine to have somebody dusting and sweeping when you were out at work, but quite another when you were working from home.

He lets go of her reluctantly.

'How about we go out for lunch, then come back for dessert like the old days?' she suggests, trying to compromise.

'I still have a pile of work to do.'

'You can do it later. I'll pick up the boys from school, take them into West Charlton, so you can have some peace.'

'I'm expecting a couple of phone calls,' he states,

indicating the moment is lost.

She knows she should retract, fall into his arms, and onto the leather sofa, but her body seems to have shut down – as if shell shocked. She doesn't want him to coax it back to life, she needs to stand under the hot jets of the power shower and think about this latest turn of events.

Almost five years and her secret was still intact. Paolo it seemed had been as good as his word.

'I don't want trouble, Angela,' he'd said, when she'd plucked up her courage to walk into The Wine Cellar and confront him. Blurting out in a chaotic way that it had been a terrible mistake, she'd drunk too much – allowed things to get out of hand. Marcus must never know.

'I don't discuss my private life with anybody,' he'd said coldly. It was clear he didn't like being called a mistake.

Now she tries to blank out the image of him and Marcus, exchanging confidences over a bottle of Chateaux Lafitte as they sit overlooking Canary Wharf.

It had been a moment of madness, an aberration, something that never should have happened. She'd almost convinced herself it hadn't – rather she'd dreamt it up – she and Paolo were simply characters from a novel, a piece of bad fiction, enacting a love scene. She'd been drafting a novel at the time about a woman who risks her marriage for a night of passion and the next moment she seemed to be living it – high on vintage champagne, locked in an iron embrace with a man she barely knew. She had tried to extricate herself but it was too late – he would have none of it – had plied her with more champagne, dismissing her protests with urgent kisses, demonstrating a kind of intractable force, like a person who holds all the cards.

Time and time again she'd steeled herself to tell Marcus, but could never find the right words. She'd even attempted to write it down, only to conclude it read like one of those sordid confessions in a cheap magazine – *'I had sex with my husband's colleague – and now they're planning to work together* – she would have to add. *Should I tell him?* She'd rather lie her way out of it than disclose the shaming details of that terrible evening.

For months she'd lived in fear of Marcus finding out – there were times when she almost hoped he would, get it out into the open, but he never had, and soon afterwards Paolo had left the off-licence and opened his first wine bar in the West End. He and Marcus had kept in touch over the phone, whilst news of Paolo's success coupled with tabloid tales of his affairs hit the gossip columns.

Marcus had shrugged it off. 'That's what happens when you make it big. They knock you down.'

Gela has barely thought about it since moving to Charlton Haven, had tried to put it behind her – write it off like those discarded chapters. Yet apparently the story hadn't ended, rather it had re-emerged, waiting to be concluded.

Maybe she should just tell him over a quiet dinner, explain she'd drunk too much, didn't know what she was doing. Paolo had taken advantage of the situation.

She sighs, knowing whichever way she tells it, Marcus would be shattered, horrified, and in the light of a previous betrayal (a brief marriage to a Dutch girl who had had a final fling with her ex a month after marrying Marcus) more than likely the end.

If it should come out, she could deny it – after all it was Paolo's word against hers. '...you've got to be kidding,' she imagines herself saying incredulously. 'He's just not my type …' That was partly true – Paolo with his Mediterranean skin, inky eyes, square jaw, and glossy black hair somehow managed to attract and repel her at the same time. His was the superior and narrowed, inward looking gaze of somebody who doesn't see the world around them, so focussed are they on their own reflection. He was a caricature, whom she had cast as the rogue in a saga that would never get beyond the third chapter.

She comes downstairs, sleek haired and fragrant, to find Marcus has cleared up the kitchen. He's even cleaned the pan, and wiped the greasy puddle from the floor where the sponge had landed. She can hear him talking urgently on the phone, no doubt making arrangements for his trip to London.

She pours herself a strong coffee, grabs a bar of fruit and nut chocolate (to hell with healthy eating – she needs a quick fix) then makes her way to her study, planning to delete the twenty five page draft of her latest work. A love affair, or rather a triangulation of sex, lies and betrayal that would end in tragedy. It was a bit of a cliché, but considering there were only something like seven plots in existence, and the rest were simply a variation on a theme, it wasn't easy to come up with anything of startling originality. A marriage in crisis – when a couple decide to downshift and move to the country perhaps?

The Grape Escape ... she thinks her mind drifting back to Paolo and the irony of it all – the fact that Marcus was now planning to rush back to the city like a rat down a familiar drainpipe.

She forces her mind away from real life back to fiction. A friendship between three women who meet at university was another popular story line. She had considered this as she ran along the rise, with Shelly and Fran. She would forget the university and have them come together later in life at the school gates – three women poles apart, bound together by a common goal – to change their lives.

Fran certainly had an interesting story to tell – a mother who'd abandoned her when she was a baby and gone to live on an Ashram, a hippy father who Fran had never met, a strange dislocated childhood, living with her eccentric Aunt Lettie, who had died tragically from breast cancer.

Whilst Shelly was a complex character – a mass of contradictions, with plenty of layers to dissect.

"Write from the heart," she would tell all those aspiring

novelists – for as St Exupery says, 'it is only with the heart that one can see clearly what's in the mind.' She gazes out of the window at the view of sloping fields and hedgerows. The trees are losing their leaves now – thin branches etched like charcoal against a steel grey sky. Perhaps she should write about betrayal and the fear of being found out – about a woman running away from the past. She'd better not be too heavy on the symbolism, but it strikes her you can never really escape, no matter how far you run.

— Chapter Six —

'It appears to have been some time since you've had a thorough check up,' the doctor says, glancing at Fran's notes. Shelly had insisted they have a full medical before the training began in earnest.

Fran stares at her badge, which reads Doctor Janet Groper.

Surely not, she thinks. There is something decidedly odd about the woman, she concludes taking in the heavy jaw-line and angular body, the unnaturally high breasts. Even her voice with its low Scottish inflection is somewhat androgynous.

'However, your ECG shows everything is ticking over nicely,' she beams 'I gather you haven't had a flutter for some time now?'

'Never been much of a gambler,' Fran jokes.

The doctor smiles politely. 'And you're no longer on any form of medication for your heart?'

'No – only homeopathic, if I get stressed. Actually I've started running,' she adds, 'with a couple of friends, which is why I decided to have a full check up. Who knows we may end up running a marathon,' she says testing the response.

'Indeed,' the doctor replies with a light laugh. 'That would be a bit extreme. How far is it? About twenty six miles?'

'Twenty six point two,' Fran answers. Ever since Shelly announced it, she's been clocking up the miles in her head – measuring routes as she drives along, trying to imagine herself still jogging along at mile fifteen – and failing.

'Heavens, it should carry a government health warning,' Dr Groper says.

'But my heart problem shouldn't stop me from running long distances should it?' Fran inquires. After all we both know I'll never go the whole way ...

'No, as long as you're sensible. In fact, running or any weight bearing exercise is good, as it keeps your bones healthy which is important in your case now you're no longer menstruating. Just don't overdo it. We're not trying to win any medals are we?'

Fran raises her eyebrows. Actually, I'm aiming for the Olympics, she wants to say, a vision of herself ploughing up the steps in slow motion, carrying the torch for fat women all over the world.

'Why don't you pop on the scales,' the doctor says briskly. 'I'll need to check your heart and lungs, do a blood and urine test, breast examination and an internal.'

Fran nods heavily, trying not to dwell on those long gloved fingers feeling their way inside her.

She steps reluctantly onto the weighing machine. Fran only weighs herself first thing in the morning, stark naked having emptied her bladder. Now it's almost noon, and she's drunk two milky coffees, which doesn't bode well. However, she appears to have lost another three pounds, bringing the total to seventeen. Her heart leaps.

'Right ...' says Dr Groper – 'you're down four pounds since your last visit.'

Only four! Jesus she must have piled on even more than she thought over the intervening years.

She takes an enormous breath before exhaling into a machine that looks like an oversized bladder, remembering Shelly's joke about being breathalised. Shelly and Gela had had their tests done the week before – Shelly stating proudly that her actual 'forced vital lung capacity,' or some term like that, had been above the predicted score. Fran wonders how she answered, *how many units of alcohol do you consume per week?*

Gela too had come out well in spite of her penchant for chocolate and crisps, not to mention the 'social' smoking.

Fran's blood pressure is right down too, along with her

resting pulse, which means her heart rate is as it should be.

'Good,' Doctor Groper says, writing some figures on a chart.

She cringes as the doctor sets about prodding her breasts. She seems to be focussed on the right one, her fingers doing a complicated little dance around the nipple as if sounding out the territory. Fran is just beginning to wonder if the woman is some kind of pervert – a genuine groper when she hears her say, 'there is something just here … very small, about the size of a pea.'

Fran feels her heart quickening – like a gathering drumbeat announcing the arrival of that dark spectre forever looming on the horizon. After all it was in the family – her grandmother, a great aunt, Lettie …

'Here, let me show you.'

The Groper guides Fran's index finger to the spot, saying, 'it could be just fatty tissue, but I would like to be sure.'

Considering her breasts are the least fatty part of her body, Fran feels a kind of helpless injustice. This cannot be happening, she thinks, trying to locate the pea. She can feel something gristly, and fibrous, more like a string bean than a pea, but then she supposes it's relative.

'You're not going to tell me I've got cancer are you?' she says in jocular tones.

'Let's not start imagining the worst just now,' The Groper says firmly. 'But as there is cancer in the family, we need to be able to rule it out straight away.'

Fran thinks about Lettie, who had taken care of her from the day her mother set off for Pune in India to find herself. 'It's in twenty three of my lymph nodes, Frannie, the odds aren't great … '

She feels a lump welling in her throat – the guilty sense that out of the two sisters, Lettie should have lived, whilst her mother (a forty fag a day woman) should have died.

'I'd like you to have a mammogram this afternoon,' The

Groper says, as if it was a rather special treat. 'The radiologist isn't in until three o'clock – have you any shopping to do?'

'Shopping?' Fran repeats, thinking this is hardly the time to indulge in a slinky halter necked dress.

'Or there is a little café around the corner that does very nice rolls, freshly made.'

'I'm not hungry,' Fran answers, nauseated by the mere thought of food for once.

'Well, if you could be back here before three,' The Groper says.

Fran hooks up her bra with shaking fingers, and struggles into her elastic waisted trousers telling herself not to panic, but as she makes her way to her car, her nerves give way and she fumbles for her mobile to call Brian.

'Hi, I'm a bit tied up right now,' he jokes suggestively, 'but you can leave a message and I'll call you back if you're lucky.'

She doesn't bother, thinking it would only alarm him. Brian isn't good in this kind of crisis. Although supportive over the operation that had robbed her of the chance of having the large family she'd dreamed of, he'd been at a loss to deal with the depression that followed. He was a man who got on with the job (his was programming computers) he never dwelt on the worst scenario. Whereas she needs to thrash it out, write her obituary, choose the CD she wants played at her funeral (probably Michael Mc Donald) he would file it away until he had all the information.

She calls Gela's mobile next. Gela picks it up immediately. She sounds giddy and light-hearted after a short run with Shelly.They had kindly agreed to wait for her before doing the next long run. The two of them are now sitting in Shelly's newly decorated kitchen drinking freshly squeezed orange juice.

'It's me, Fran, they've found a lump.' Her voice wavers, visions of her crowning glory dissolving, as they pump her with chemicals. 'I have to have a mammal thing,' she can't get her head or even her tongue around it.

'Mammogram,' Gela clarifies. There's a brief silence then she adds, 'look Fran, you mustn't worry, it's probably nothing ... where are you?'

'... it's Fran,' she hears Gela mutter, 'they've found a lump in her boob.'

Shelly is now on the line. 'Fran, girl, listen don't panic – it's probably nothing. Look, call us when you're done, and then come over to my place ... I'll pour you a stiff drink ... yeah I know you don't drink but today's an exception.'

'All right,' Fran mumbles, trying to pull herself together. 'It's probably nothing, I'll be fine ... Jesus, shit,' she wails, 'what if they have to cut it out? There'll be nothing left ...!'

***

She winces at the sight of her right breast, which is now flattened between two transparent slabs, so it looks like a little mouse's snout. The perspex, or whatever it is, cuts into her skin so brutally, she fears it's about to slice the whole boob off, lump and all, which might be a good thing perhaps. Get the job over with so they can start rebuilding her. Give her a pair of swelling D cup breasts and a plunging cleavage. There's a pile of leaflets in the reception about breast augmentation and how to go about it. Perhaps they've got some kind of scam going whereby they cut you up on the third floor, so they can re-build you on the first. All the profits probably go into this swish new Health Centre with its glassy blue windows, plush waiting rooms and state of the art coffee machines on every floor.

At last the ordeal is over, the radiologist releases her and the flattened mammary – a mere gland that can enhance, diminish or even kill you, springs back to life. This is obviously some kind of retribution, Fran thinks miserably.

It occurs to her that health checks, which have become part of everyday life, make you ill, mad or both.

The radiologist tells her to get changed, and return to the waiting room to wait for the results.

Fran finds a seat at the far end, thinking if it's bad news they can bloody well come and find her. Perhaps she should just leave now, before they deliver the verdict. She flicks through a magazine pausing at an article headed, 'how I survived breast cancer.' The woman who had lost both breasts calls herself a "statistical casualty". Apparently the disease runs in her family too. Fran has read enough – she considers having another coffee, then remembers an article about a possible link between caffeine and cancer. Besides it will only set her heart racing.

'The ultrasonography shows a solid area rather than a hollow cyst,' The Groper tells her kindly, 'which means we do need to remove the lump and examine it under a microscope.'

Fran feels as if the lump is now lodged in the back of her throat. Last time they'd gone in, they'd taken out both of her ovaries – she can't go through that again.

'When?' she says, shakily, 'because I'm really busy at the moment – what with the training. I can't have an operation.'

Dr Groper smiles reassuringly. 'We should be able to fit you in next week. Don't worry, we'll give you a local anaesthetic followed by a needle biopsy. You won't feel a thing.'

***

'If I have to have a mastectomy, I'm going to tell the surgeon who does the reconstructive bit to make me a 38C,' Fran says, as they run along the rise. Shelly had insisted a long run would take Fran's mind off things, but it was still with her, a great weight in her chest, that turned her legs to lead. It was all she could do to make it up Charlton Hill.

'It's bound to be benign,' Shelly says, for the umpteenth time, 'you've got to stop worrying.'

Fran sighs, thinking easier said than done. The world has turned black since Dr Groper discovered the pea, everything taking on an awful significance. The sight of a heron lifting off from the pond this morning, carrying Chloe's carp in its beak had filled her with foreboding. She'd made Brian rush out onto the lawn to shoo it away, then shouted at him that it was too late.

'You should have put a net over the pond now it's winter,' she'd yelled.

I should have kept up my yearly check-ups, she'd thought darkly.

Unable to sleep she'd tried meditating, but her mind refused to be emptied. Rather she'd become possessed with visions of dying scenes, and all the things she still wanted to do with her life – that course in nutrition and homeopathy, travel the world. More than anything to have some time on earth as a thin person.

She'd even decided on the poem Brian could read at her funeral – "Remember Me" being one of her favourites. '... *when I am gone away, far far away from this distant land, and you can no longer hold me by the hand...*'

She has consoled herself that now she's lost some weight they could at least bury her in something reasonably flattering – a black shift dress perhaps, just above the knee.

'Maybe it would be better to cut both of them off and start again,' she breathes, as they finally make their descent towards the car park.

'It won't come to that,' Gela tries to assure her.

'You've got to be positive,' Shelly repeats.

The art of positive thinking – she'd tried that before, but it hadn't changed the outcome. They'd still whipped out her ovaries.

Still, she was fit now, could run five miles without stopping! She felt better than she had for years, which was somewhat ironic.

'You're right,' she says, feeling marginally uplifted, the endorphins are doing their work, plus the fact they are now running downhill. 'In any case no point worrying myself sick .... might be the start of something new! The new me ... you said yourself in six months I'd be transformed!'

'Yeah, absolutely,' Shelly says easily.

'It'll be fine, I know it will,' Gela adds, hoping her voice carries the same conviction.

As they reach the car park Fran notices a rusting Land Rover parked rather too close to her brand new Honda (Brian would have a fit if her car had got even the tiniest scratch). A tall, well built man was ambling towards it, cigarette in hand.

It's him! Gerry Ryan, she thinks, her racing heart going into overdrive.

Even in his winter attire of brown cords and a thick checked shirt, he looks wildly handsome, the dark blonde hair uncombed as if he'd just got out of bed.

Fran tries to control her ragged breathing, whilst praying her bladder holds up.

'Still at it?' he inquires, his eyes sweeping over the three of them and settling inevitably on Gela.

'We're training to run the marathon,' Shelly says immediately.

'Some of us are,' Fran amends between breaths.

'Hope there's a decent pub at the end of it,' he grins.

His gaze is now drifting towards Fran, no doubt sizing her up and concluding she's definitely out of the running, so to speak.

'Not me ...,' she emphasises. The idea he might think that she thinks she's up to it is doubly mortifying. Anyway I'll probably be dead by then, or at least horribly mutilated. 'I don't get out of bed for twenty six miles,' she grins, trying to joke her way out of it.

'Don't blame you,' he says. 'I wouldn't either.'

He turns to Shelly with a frown, 'Didn't you used to work behind the bar at The Trout and Fly, a while back?'

Shelly nods. 'We, that is my boyfriend owns the pub.' I

was just the bloody barmaid, she thinks bitterly.

'A couple of nights up there I won't forget in a hurry,' he states with meaning.

He is no doubt referring to one in particular, when fortified by half a bottle of gin, she'd almost punched one of the locals for calling her, "Bruce's piece of pie." Bruce had suggested she stop working there after that, since she was clearly consuming more alcohol than the customers.

When Shelly doesn't respond, he says, 'Anyway, nice to talk to you ladies and good luck with the training.'

He winks at Fran causing her heart to quicken. 'I bet you'll cross that finishing line,' he adds.

'Thanks for the vote of confidence,' she says, provocatively.

She watches him drive away, lost in a fantasy in which his mouth is pressing down on hers, his hands roving sensuously over her body, searching for her breasts … not being able to find them ….

She hears Shelly say, 'fancies himself as the village stud!'

'Seems decent enough to me,' Fran says, suddenly exasperated by Shelly. 'Why are you always so damn cynical?' No doubt he'd witnessed one of Shelly's drunken episodes, she thinks to herself.

'Bit sensitive aren't we?' Shelly frowns.

'How about we go inside?' Gela says hastily. 'I'm freezing out here – I could do with a coffee.'

'Good idea, come on I'll buy you both a drink – it's the weekend,' Shelly adds.

Fran hesitates, torn between going home for a long hot wallow in the bath, and staying to find out more about Gerry Ryan.

Shelly is now putting a heavy arm around her shoulder saying, 'sorry if I pissed you off, but I could see he had his eye on you.'

'Oh yeah right! Give me a break, – you know he fancied Gela,' Fran says, slightly mollified.

'Absolutely not,' Shelly states, assuredly.

'I agree with Shelly,' Gela says, relieved all is calm again – 'it was definitely you Fran.'

***

'You're worrying about something that might never happen,' Shelly insists as they sit at their usual table by a smoking peat fire. 'The test will be fine – you're fit now, thanks to all the training.'

Fran's mood has plummeted again. According to Shelly, Gerry Ryan was seeing a woman from West Charlton called Rose (married and overweight) and has another on the side (a single mother, blonde, voluptuous with big breasts).

'Don't go down that road,' she'd said in warning tones as if she could read Fran's mind – had somehow guessed that Fran had, on a number of occasions, taken a detour home past the thatched cottage, hoping for a glimpse of him.

Fran has a sudden desire for a Ploughman's – a thick slab of crumbly cheddar on soft warm rolls, sweet brown chutney, followed by a calorific dessert – Death by Chocolate – she might as well be prepared. Even the memory of the giant corset on the washing line doesn't deter her.

'I mean if it is something,' Shelly continues, 'which we know it isn't, and say you hadn't had the test, it might have developed into something really worrying.'

'Yeah ... ? So what's your point?' Fran's aware she sounds aggressive but she's fed up of Shelly's obsession with the training, (as if having conquered all those miles, she would never be struck down by something as trifling as cancer).

Gela shoots Shelly a warning look, but Shelly is well into her third glass of red wine, there's no stopping her.

'My point is if we hadn't decided to train for the marathon, and have a medical then you might not have known.'

'For Christ's sake Shelly, would you shut up about the

bloody marathon … I'm never going to do it anyway, not now. I'm sick to death of talking about it!' God there it was again, that bleak word ... death.

There's a strained silence. Shelly stares at the remains of her wine with a hurt look. 'Just trying to help,' she mutters.

'Well it's not bloody helping …,' Fran hesitates, her eyes filled with mortified tears. 'God I'm sorry, Shell – you're right, I am really sensitive right now – if it wasn't for you two, I'd probably fall to pieces.' She attempts a wobbly smile. 'Maybe you're right. Running could have saved my life!'

— Chapter Seven —

Gela limps into the house after running six painfully slow miles, to find Marcus back from London early, talking rather urgently on the phone.

'Catch up with you later,' he says, glancing up.

'I didn't expect you until tomorrow,' she tells him, scooping up a pile of newspapers from the floor.

'I wanted to surprise you – catch you in the arms of your lover,' he says, with a wry grin.

Her heart skips a beat. She examines his face carefully, looking for signs that he knows about that fateful night with Paolo, but his expression gives nothing away. That was the trouble with Marcus – she never quite knew what he was thinking.

'I did call earlier but you must have been out running. How's it going?'

'Oh not great, we're all a bit demoralised at the moment what with Fran's scare.'

She had told him about the lump on the phone but sensed he hadn't taken it in. 'How is she?' he inquires now with a frown.

'Worried sick. It's the waiting that's so awful – the not knowing. Brian's not much help – he's so mechanical.'

Still at least he was there, Gela thinks, tidying up after her, making her cups of tea.

'It'll be fine, these things usually turn out to be nothing.'

'The worrying thing is, that her aunt and grandmother died of cancer.'

'You're looking at the bleak side as usual,' he says, lighting a cigarette.

She notices he's exchanged the roll ups for a smart packet of *Benson and Hedges*, now he's back in London mode.

'They've found a lump,' Gela emphasises. 'It is scary.'

'It'll be nothing,' Marcus repeats with assurance.

'So how was London?' she inquires, spooning coffee into the expresso machine.

'Busy, hectic, more crowded than ever.'

'No regrets then?'

'There are always pros and cons when you decide to change your life,' he states, gazing away through the mullioned windows, towards a sea of muddy fields.

'And how's Paolo?' she inquires after a pause.

'Good form – very busy with this new venture. He's thinking of buying a house in the South of France, and there's a new woman of course – another leggy blonde from S.W.1. Married, although that seems to be falling apart since she started seeing Paolo. Bound to end in tears,' he concludes.

Gela hands him his coffee with a thumping heart.

'And the new penthouse?'

'Nice in a nouveau kind of way. I didn't spend much time there as we ate out every evening. And you? No dramas this end?'

'Nothing major,' she answers, carefully. 'Jamie's been a bit hyper – he and Matthew have been at each others throats as usual.' She doesn't go into the details of how Jamie's teacher, Miss Baine (the bane of all their lives) had threatened to move him to a desk at the front if he continued disrupting the class. Or how she'd found him trying to set fire to the mattress to find out what *Highly Flammable* meant. She knows from past experience it would only make him defensive and they would end up arguing. 'I need to unwind first,' he would say, pulling her towards him and burying his face in her neck, claiming he needed to smell the essence of her.

'I knew you'd cope,' he says now, glancing around for today's paper. He sits down with his coffee, adding, 'I'm sure you want to have a shower and relax.'

She hovers for a moment wondering why he hasn't

suggested she sit down with him – have passionate sex on the sofa. He hasn't even kissed her properly, she thinks ominously.

When she comes downstairs forty minutes later, smelling of three different scented lotions, about to suggest they go out for lunch, catch up with one another then spend the afternoon in bed, he's standing by the fridge munching on some left-over pizza.

'Starving,' he says, 'I skipped breakfast.'

We have become out of sync, she thinks with a pang. Like a couple working on different shifts – meeting up at odd hours to catch up with each other's lives.

'I'll go and do some work on the novel then,' she says.

'How's it going?'

'I've started something new – it's early days.'

She prays that this new draft, a story of an unlikely friendship between three disparate women, bound together by a desire to change their lives will get beyond chapter three.

'Maybe you'll let me read some of it?'

'Oh, it's a mess at the moment – totally illegible,' she says hastily. She thinks about the main character, the rather doom laden Donna, a woman haunted by a previous affair with her husband's best friend (a bit close to the bone perhaps). But then it was a work of fiction and to use the standard phrase "any likeness to real life events was of course purely coincidental."

***

The following morning Marcus announces he wants to take her out for dinner that evening.

'It's a bit late to find a babysitter,' she points out.

'Try,' he says impatiently. 'I'd like to have an evening alone with you so we can talk.'

'About what?'

She waits for him to say, "about us and the fact you cheated on me five years ago."

'Whatever we normally talk about,' he answers, looking puzzled.

Get a grip, she mutters to herself.

'There are a couple of things I need to discuss with you,' he says moments later. Again his expression is unreadable, the pale blue eyes revealing nothing.

'We can talk now,' she suggests – she can't bear being kept in suspense for five minutes let alone a whole day.

'Later will do.'

She manages to persuade Amy, (Jamie's riding instructor) who lives in the farm along the lane to baby-sit, with the promise Jamie is on best behaviour. She'll have to bribe him with a bar of chocolate and pay the price later.

She spends ages getting ready, using a new conditioner that promises sleek, glossy, manageable hair, plus a serum called, 'Get It Straight.' If this is the moment of reckoning she needs to look her best – to be able to hold her head up, without her hair standing up on end too.

She hasn't even asked where they're going. Knowing Marcus it will be somewhere special – a lavish country hotel, with a four star restaurant, or maybe he plans to drive the thirteen miles into the city to Chez Gerard or Ricardos.

After discarding half her wardrobe as too 'city' she settles on a pair of tan suede trousers and a cream cashmere sweater, then pulls out her new shoes, wondering if she dare wear them. Her feet are still covered in blisters in spite of her new trainers, but the shoes look fabulous, even though she feels as if she's walking on hot coals.

Marcus drives with practised ease through the winding dark lanes she has come to know so well recently, past The Charlton Arms which is lit up invitingly, the scattered farm-holdings and isolated cottages, deeper into the countryside.

'I managed to get a table at Ashlington Falls,' he tells her.

'That's a coincidence,' she replies.

'Oh?'

'I was going to suggest we go there for dinner.' At least there's still a meeting of the minds, she thinks.

'Well I've done something right,' he says, in the slightly martyred tones he's adopted recently.

He turns down the long tree-lined avenue which is artfully lit up, bathing the trees in an icy winter hue, towards the square Georgian country house where they'd stayed for a week before moving into Manor Farm.

Taking her hand, he guides her over the cobbles (she should never have worn her new shoes) under an arched stone gate, towards the main house.

'Drink first?' he suggests, waving towards the bar.

She nods, thinking she could do with a stiff gin and tonic and a cigarette – the first of the week, but her nerves are on edge.

The bar is packed with noisy Londoners lounging on the leather sofas. In the background a wide screened television is showing what appears to be a video of cows grazing in a field. Marcus orders a gin and tonic for her, a vodka and coke (an old favourite) for himself.

'So what did you want to talk about?' she inquires.

'How about we go to our table?' he says, 'it's too noisy in here.'

She follows him into a low-beamed dining area with a marble fireplace stacked high with wood. Conversely, an artificial fire burns brightly in the grate.

The menu is a gourmet fantasy – Wood oven baked partridge with morels, Angel hair pasta with truffles but she can't take anything in – she won't be able to eat anything either unless she gets a hold of herself.

'I'll have the Linguine with Porcini Mushrooms,' she says at last.

'Nothing to start with?'

She shakes her head. 'Maybe a dessert.' (If the evening hasn't disintegrated into tears and recrimination by then).

He spends ages choosing the wine. She loves his attention to detail (that is most of the time) loves the way his hair curls at the nape of his neck, the smell of his skin, the way he manages to chase away the demons. He finally settles on a bottle of *Chateaux Lafitte* (she would have been just as happy with an Australian Chardonnay) then sits back and lights a cigarette.

'You look ravishing tonight. Country life seems to suit you,' he ventures.

She smiles. 'I still think it was the right move. Matthew hasn't been ill since we came down here, Jamie's definitely calmer.' You're the only one who's restless, she thinks.

'So you don't miss London, too much?'

'I miss certain things, like the health club, and Thai take-aways but not the underground, the crowds, those excruciating company dinners.'

'I can't replace the take-aways, but you might like to know we are now officially members of the Health Club here.'

She stares at him, in surprise. The exclusive club with its outdoor swimming pool had a year long waiting list. 'How did you manage?'

'Oh, I have my contacts,' he says airily, 'but it should fit the bill. They even have a hair salon!'

She shakes her head in surprise. 'And I thought you were going to tell me something awful, like you'd decided to abandon me and the boys!'

'There is something,' he says, making her freeze – a forkful of linguine poised mid air. 'I've had a long chat with Paolo.'

She waits silently, almost calm now the moment has arrived.

'He wants me to go into business with him, work with him on this new venture as an equal partner. Which would mean investing quite a bit of money into it.' He pauses before adding, 'it would also mean I'd be working in London during the week.'

She stares at him speechlessly. There seems to be no air in the room suddenly – as if all those logs have sapped the oxygen.

'I don't have to decide now. In any case I can't do anything until March when my contract ends, which gives us time to think about it.'

'I don't believe it,' she breathes at last.

'What don't you believe?' he asks briskly.

'I thought you wanted to get out of the rat race! It was your idea to up-sticks and move down here – live a stress-free life in the country. We haven't even been here a year, for God's sake!'

'An opportunity has arisen,' he states. 'I can't pass it up.'

'It's not as if we need the money,' she emphasises. His father had died a year ago and left him a substantial fortune, hence his decision to take a step back, and work on a consultancy basis. Yet he was still driven it seemed, determined to make it big like his highly successful father who had made his millions but lost his family somewhere along the way.

'I've always wanted to do something like this and Paolo has provided an opportunity.'

'You told me once he's completely reckless?' she says desperately.

'Maybe when it comes to women!' he answers.

She lets out a shaky breath. The desire for a cigarette is overwhelming. She helps herself to a *Benson and Hedges* and lights up guiltily.

'I think you've always been envious of Paolo,' she says moments later. 'It's like you can't beat him so you've decided to join him.'

His mouth tightens. 'That's bullshit! You're the one who seems to have a problem with him! You shouldn't believe everything you read, you know.'

'Look, I thought you wanted a different life,' she argues, 'watch the boys grow up? Spend more time with us as a family?'

He pushes his fingers through his hair, which springs back accommodatingly, unlike hers.

'The timing wasn't right after all.'

'Now you tell me! We made a decision Marcus, I gave up my job!'

'You were fed up with editing! You wanted to write a novel remember? Look, it's just the weekdays. I used to go away for weeks on end.'

'Yes, but I had a job then, a busy life, there were street lights outside our front door.'

'You managed very well without me! Let's face it I don't help much around the house. Last time I tried, you threw the sponge at me,' he reminds her.

'But at least you're there – to empty the mousetraps, and cope when bits of the house fall down. The boys need you around, Jamie's already getting into trouble at school. He nearly set fire to the whole house whilst you were away!'

'You've coped with worse,' he points out.

She'd never forget it as long as she lived – Matthew's haunting cries and stiff body, as he strained his head away from the light. The sudden violent retching. By then she'd suspected the worst and been right for once. She'd bundled him into the car and driven him straight to the children's hospital where they'd diagnosed meningitis. She'd sat beside his inert little body in an agony of fear and dread, cursing Marcus for not being there. The crisis had passed, Matthew had recovered but she'd never forgiven Marcus for not having gone through the horror she'd gone through that night. He'd been in Paris, at a board meeting and hadn't picked up her frantic messages until the evening, by which time fog had descended over Heathrow and his flight had been cancelled.

'What if Matthew gets ill again in the middle of the night?'

'There are ambulances in the country,' he points out. 'Look we could sell up and go back to London, only I'm not sure it's the right decision either.'

She puts down her fork, defeated by the mound of pasta. In spite of the mud, the foul smells and bleak wintry evenings she doesn't want to go back to her old life. She wants to be here in the spring when the lanes are white with cow parsley, to spend the long summer evenings in the garden, amongst the lupins, writing the climax of her novel.

Marcus has stopped eating too. He sits back and lights a cigarette.

'I thought it was too good to be true,' she says, helping herself to another one. To hell with it – she might as well smoke herself hoarse tonight, and give up again tomorrow. 'No more roll ups, back on the vodka and coke ... even this place.'

It strikes her Ashlington Falls has become an oasis for Londoners – where tired city traders come to watch videos of cows grazing, rather than get their feet muddy. 'It's like you never really left Primrose Hill in spirit!'

'It's work, Angela.'

'You have the consultancy work,' she points out. She hates it when he calls her Angela.

'Until March, and then I'll have to start looking around for something else.'

'Well you could have done something from home, taken up gardening – I don't know.' She has run out of arguments. Marcus would never be happy pottering around the garden. He was too fired up, too ambitious, forever on a quest for new ways to make money.

'It was Paolo who got us membership here wasn't it? Doesn't he hang out at Sheldon House?' (The sister club in London where anybody who was anybody belonged).

'Yes it was as a matter of fact, but I don't see the issue. You seem to have some kind of bug bear about Paolo.'

'He's an opportunist,' she says, 'plus, I think he's dishonest.'

'In what way?'

'Lots of ways,' she flounders, 'what about that business in the papers a few months ago ... you know when he tried to sue that guy. The one who helped set him up? What's to stop him doing the dirty on you?'

'That was unfounded,' Marcus states. 'Alan Jacobs was a crook.'

'I just don't like the way he operates – always getting involved with married women.'

'Maybe they're the ones whose morals are in question,' Marcus states with irony.

She meets his gaze directly, wondering if he's guessed, has gleaned it by some form of osmosis.

'Paolo has changed,' he says finally, 'in fact I forgot to tell you, he's also training for the marathon. He gets up at five every morning and does up to ten miles on a running machine.'

For some reason this only adds to her misery.

'Look,' he continues, in his reasoning voice, 'if you're really unhappy, I'll think again. I shan't be signing anything until March. I need to clarify a number of things. Who knows? It could all fall through.'

Tell him, says a voice in her head. Just say it.

She opens her mouth, but the words refuse to form. Leave it, argues the other voice – confessing now would be premature. Especially as it might fall through. Yet how on earth would she get through the next four months wondering whether it would go ahead?

'Are you all right?' he frowns.

She sighs. 'It's just I had this romantic vision of family life in the country.'

He reaches for her hand. 'It won't be forever – if it does happen that is. I could rent a decent flat in London, so you and the boys can come up whenever you want. We'll find a way.'

'I've got a bad feeling about this,' she says after a silence.

He smiles and squeezes her hand. 'You and your bad feelings!' he replies.

— Chapter Eight —

Shelly sets about preparing a sumptuous anniversary dinner – little towers of fishy mousse sitting on a bed of rocket leaves to start, followed by seared skate wings, served with a special hollandaise sauce. A *Baileys* cheesecake is chilling in the fridge, along with a bottle of champagne. It's actually sparkling wine, but has the same effect. She pours herself another glass of wine – 'cooks perk' as she calls it, and checks the mousse, which is setting nicely. She has lit the fire in the living room, bought scented candles and is sporting her new black bustier which is a bit tight, but will probably be ripped to shreds by the end of the evening. She's even organised for Gary to stay at his friend Sam's house so she and Bruce could have the weekend to themselves. She checks herself in the mirror, still unused to the transformation; the aubergine hair is now a vivid strawberry blonde, the same shade it had been when she'd first met Bruce. She remembers how he'd called her 'Bomb Shell', adding that she was the sexiest woman he'd ever met. Afterwards they'd driven straight to The Old Foundry and had wildly athletic sex on the kitchen table.

She's embarking on stage one of the sauce (the recipe advises clarifying the butter to prevent curdling) when the phone rings. It's Bruce, on his way home from the peat moors, calling from the Land Rover.

'There's a session on at the Old Fighting Cock tonight,' he tells her. 'Some country rock band – followed by Karaoke, should be a good night!'

Shelly's heart sinks. 'I'm cooking a special dinner, it's a celebration.'

'What are we celebrating then?'

She hesitates. 'Being alive, and together ... having the whole weekend to ourselves.'

'Sounds all right! But I fancy a bit of music as well as

your ass,' he jokes.

'We could go to the pub after dinner,' she suggests after a pause. 'The band will just be warming up by then.'

She loves a good session, especially when she can sing along, prides herself on having a deep, powerful voice – has spent many an evening wailing into the microphone, Patsy Cline style.

The dinner turns out to be a bit of a fiasco. Bruce had stopped off for a pint on the way home which meant the sauce had curdled in spite of the clarified butter, the tower of blended salmon collapses, which she hopes isn't a bad omen. But Bruce is his usual appreciative self, wolfing it down with gusto. She might as well have given him steak and chips, come to think of it.

She opens the bottle of sparkling wine sending the cork flying. 'To seven passionate years,' she says raising her glass.

He raises his glass dutifully, 'to us. Great nosh Shell! And great bum,' he adds, squeezing her leather clad behind. 'All that running seems to be paying off.'

She grins. 'We're going to start putting in some serious miles, once Fran gets the all clear.'

She'd tried calling Fran last night, and again this morning but there'd been no answer on the landline or her mobile. In the end she'd left a message, saying, 'it's Shell. Just checking you're OK. I know you're going to be fine. Look how fit you are! You can run six miles!' God she was back to running again, Fran would think she was really obsessed now. 'Anyway if you want to chat, I'm here all weekend.'

'She was doing so well with the training,' she tells Bruce now, 'she's lost a load of weight.'

A dreadful thought flashes across Shelly's mind. 'You don't think there's a connection do you?'

Bruce does one of his famous shrugs. 'Nah, on the other hand, who knows?' he says, unwilling to commit himself as usual.

Shelly empties her glass, and stares at him intently. 'You

just never know what's round the next corner. You've got to seize the moment.'

All that melting butter and blending salmon has killed her appetite, whilst the wine on an empty stomach soars to her head.

'*Carpe momentum*, or whatever,' she says effusively.

He nods. 'You're right there. People worry far too much about the future. Waste of bloody time.'

'You've got to have a few plans,' she points out, 'otherwise what's the fucking point?'

'Not sure there is one,' he states.

Yet he'd had plans once, she thinks – had committed himself to a woman who had ultimately betrayed him. Surely the fact he'd backed the wrong horse (or in this case, fat cow) didn't mean he couldn't try again?

He turns down the *Bailey's* cheesecake, saying 'got to get into shape by April if I'm going to do Helter Skelter.' Climbing to the summit of the treacherous, and rather phallic looking tower of a rock in Wales had been his ambition for months and was now planned to take place a couple of weeks before the Marathon. She dreads those climbing trips, imagines him falling thousands of feet to his death, leaving her literally bereft. The Mantis (his ex-wife – a real praying mantis who had already devoured most of his savings) would claim what was left, leaving her and Gary with nothing.

The sparkling wine is making her morose. She needs a top up but the bottle is empty, she's drunk nearly all of it.

Seven years of unswerving loyalty only to end up on the street, she thinks. No deal ... something had to be done. If Bruce wasn't prepared to marry her, she would have to start thinking about herself, insist he put The Trout and Fly in her name, let her take over the running of it again. She would try not to hit the bottle this time, which wasn't easy when everybody else was having a good time.

She was hardly drinking at all during the week now, what

with the training. Surely she deserved to break out from time to time. Like tonight, in celebration of the last seven years ... and in the hope of putting some kind of seal on the future.

***

The car park of the Old Fighting Cock is choked with sleek looking cars and four-wheel drives. The pub, which has recently changed hands, renamed The Cock and Bull now attracts people from the city as well as the nearby villages and towns. Instead of scampi and chips, they serve fragrant Thai curries, exotic salads, and cocktails with weird names, becoming famous for Bullshots – an unlikely mixture of clear broth, vodka and spices.

'I'll try one,' Shelly says impulsively as they weave their way to the bar. The band is already playing an old Willie Nelson song, lightening her mood. *'On the road again...'* she sings along, an image of herself striding powerfully up Charlton Hill – on and on through the twisting lanes, pushing her body to the limit and beyond.

'Order a couple of drinks so we don't have to queue up again,' Shelly suggests. 'I'll have a Bullshot and a large glass of red wine. (Better not get too carried away if she is going to do a distance run on Monday). She looks around for a table but the place is heaving, there's barely room to stand.

But Bruce has spotted a couple he knows and is forging his way towards them. The man, who is blond and tanned, with rugged outdoor looks, turns out to be one of his rock-climbing mates. They immediately get caught up in climbing anecdotes, leaving her with the girlfriend, who strikes Shelly as a bit of a prima donna – a woman who relies on her beauty (which is of the dark mysterious kind) to get what she wants.

She sips her drink, which is surprisingly good, hot and spicy, more like a meal really. She's beginning to feel a bit peckish now so drinks it rather quickly, wishing she'd ordered two Bullshots instead of the glass of wine, but not wanting to face the bar again.

The dark beauty smiles politely when Shelly tells her she's training up a couple of friends to run the marathon, and how they'd run a total of twenty miles last week.

'The worst thing is the hills,' she says, embarking on the red wine. 'I was seriously stiff this morning!' She's aware she's failed to engage this snooty cow who is far more interested in what Bruce and Ian are talking about so adds, 'could barely get my leg over ...'

The girl smiles thinly saying, 'I know what you mean.'

Ah, a jogger, Shelly thinks, doing what half the world does, donning her flashy trainers for a Sunday jog in the park. She knows the type.

'We've just come back from a climb in Patagonia,' she informs Shelly.

'Rock climbing?' Shelly inquires nonchalantly.

'No, mountaineering. We did the Vanishing Trail.'

'Ah,' says Shelly wishing the woman would vanish right now.

'Bloody hell,' Bruce says, overhearing this. 'That's an incredible achievement!'

'So what's the next project?' Shelly inquires lamely. 'Everest? Mounting the ogre?' The evening is beginning to seriously piss her off.

The dark beauty, whose name turns out to be Marissa, laughs throatily. 'Actually, Ian and I are getting married. He's a bit of an ogre – aren't you darling?'

'You can mount me any time,' Ian grins.

The three of them roar laughing.

'I'm going to get a drink,' Shelly says. Or maybe two, she thinks.

She stands by the bar for ages whilst the band sings an old Merle Haggard song, then drinks the Bullshot at the counter, thereby delaying going back to the table.

Nobody talks to her, which suits her fine. The music is enough, filling her head, blanking out images of Ian and

Marissa, exchanging nuptials on some icy summit.

Bruce is behind her suddenly. 'All right there, Shell?'

'Oh fine, as happy as a sandpiper or whatever ... bring me a dream ...' she sings.

He frowns. 'Take it easy eh! Remember you're in training.'

She notices he's still sipping the same pint he'd ordered ages ago. 'Have another one,' she urges. 'Go on! Get arseholed for once!'

'Who'd take care of you?' he inquires, raising a thick eyebrow.

'We'd get a taxi. Or just run home!' she grins. 'I'm up for it!'

'I'm enjoying the evening too much,' he states with meaning.

***

Some time later, she doesn't know how long, she and Bruce are sitting at a table with a group of people they have never met, singing along to a brilliant version of Islands in the Stream. It slowly dawns on her that the band has drifted away, the gutsy voices replaced by recorded music, whilst one of the barmen sets up the microphone for Karaoke.

She goes to the loo to check her makeup, her heart thumping in anticipation of getting up on the stage and showing them what she can do, but when she emerges some time later – with scarlet lipstick, somewhat clumsily applied – there's some old crooner up there hogging the microphone.

'I just want to feel real emotion,' he wavers.

'That was for my lovely wife, Lisa,' he concludes, 'who has put up with me for twenty brilliant years. Thank you Lise.'

The crowd cheer, people are ready for a bit of soul baring now.

Shelly approaches the stage from the back, thereby avoiding Bruce who will undoubtedly try to restrain her, making a beeline for the microphone. By some miracle of chance (some things are meant) Patsy Cline comes up on the screen.

'*Crazy...*' she yodels, catching sight of Bruce's alarmed face below. '*...crazy for being so lone...lay . . crazy for being so blue oo oo...*' she hangs on to the last note dragging it out plaintively long after the original has ended. The next verse goes like a dream, her voice hovering shrilly, on the word *do...* before plummeting again. She wiggles her hips and sinks seductively to the ground, her breasts swelling over the tight band of her new bustier.

The crowd cheers as she straightens up, ready for the final verse, her voice soaring above the dead Patsy – the living embodiment of raw new talent. She may not be able to climb mountains but by heck she can reach the highest notes in the whole spectrum. Bruce seems to be giving her a standing ovation – at least he's standing rigidly by the stage, his face set, but she hasn't finished her party piece yet.

'That was for Bruche,' she breathes into the microphone. She tries to fix him with her most seductive gaze, but his face keeps shifting out of focus. 'Who I'm crazy for ... I've an impotent ... oops, I mean impudent question for you big boy...!'

There is a hush around the room, as the crowd holds its breath.

'Will you marry me?' she says.

The silence is deafening, punctuated by the sound of several clearing of throats.

'Well...? Don't tell me you still can't dechide?' she adds petulantly, as if it's just a bit of a game – a reality show in which the audience can join in.

'Well, Brucey?' somebody shouts.

Bruce simply stands there shrugging his huge shoulders a weird look on his face – reminding her of his passport photo.

Shelly feels as if something is squeezing her chest,

squeezing the life out of her. She considers unhooking the bustier and flinging it into the crowd, show them what Bruce is turning down. She reaches behind her back, squirming sexily, as if there is something caught down her cleavage.

'It takes him forever to make up his mind,' she slurs as somebody shouts *'get it off girl!'*

'Sheven years to be precish ...'

'Come on Shell,' Bruce is saying, holding out a hand, as if trying to help her down a treacherous rocky slope.

The game is lost, she's about to be voted off the stage and out of his life.

The barman is taking over, grabbing the microphone off her, saying 'looks like we'll have to wait to hear the outcome of that! Now who's up for the next song?'

She registers Marissa grinning and nudging The Ogre and has an almost overwhelming urge to walk over and punch the woman in the face. But the memory of that famous dinner when she'd almost flattened Jasmine Fellows stops her.

That and Bruce's gruff tones as he says, 'time to go home.'

'You didn't shay anything,' she cries, as they stumble out of the pub into the freezing night air. 'You could have just said yesh, then told me to fuck off later.'

'I wouldn't do that to you.'

'What you did was worsh ...' she is wild with fury and from the shame of it. She wants to punch somebody – go back inside and flatten that smug-faced Marissa. The cold air hits her chest, but does nothing to dispel the burning anger.

'It's not what I did Shelly! It's what you did! I would have stopped you going on the stage in that state if I'd known.'

'Yeah, just do nothing – that's your spechshiality...' she slurs.

'Take it easy,' he says firmly, steering her towards the Land Rover.

She registers stars spinning, the world tipping, as she falls into the back seat.

'Why don't you just tell me to pisssh off ...?' she slurs as they rattle up the bumpy drive to The Old Foundry.

'Because I care about you,' he answers.

'Not enough to marry me,' she replies.

'You're obsessed with bloody marriage,' he says. 'It's just a bit of paper. It doesn't mean anything.'

'Don't worry, I won't never mention it again ... ever! Gary and I can manage. We don't need any fucking favours from you!'

'Ah, leave it out Shelly,' he says tightly.

Back at the house, he carries her upstairs to bed, brings her a jug of water and some pain-killers then makes his way to the door.

'Where are you going?' she calls.

'To the spare room so you can get some sleep.'

'I don't want to shleep. We could have sex ...', she drags herself upright, and stares at him wildly then staggers towards the wardrobe, searching for his 'favourite tart' outfit – the little leather micro mini, the fish net stockings and high heels, forgetting she's thrown it out. She wouldn't have been able to manage the suspenders, anyway, she thinks pouncing on a pink frou frou skirt and cropped top. 'Limbo Lucy,' she slurs, 'jush need to find my balanch ...'

'For God's sake Shell, you can hardly stand.' He shakes his head in disgust. 'I thought you were going to stop drinking, run the marathon!'

'I have,' she hiccoughs. 'Tonight was an excepshon. It's shupposed to be our annivershary ... I am running the marathon.'

'Well good luck,' he says, 'you're going to need it, up here!' he adds, tapping his forehead, reminding her of The Whippet in the sports shop. She hears the door close sharply behind him.

She lies there, wide awake, heart pounding, whilst the ceiling see-saws alarmingly above her. At last she sinks into semi-consciousness, only to wake an hour later with a raging thirst and thumping head. She gulps back a tumbler of water and two pain-killers, her mind racing – the knowledge she's reached a kind of crossroads – or more likely an impasse in her life.

She's still too drunk to register the full impact of the evening. Tomorrow the shame and humiliation (not to mention the embarrassment) will kick in. Now what hurts most, apart from her head, is the fact Bruce has no faith in her.

'I'll fucking show him,' she mutters, the Bullshots still coursing through her veins.

She falls asleep at last and dreams that she's ploughing her way through some weird gluey substance in pursuit of Gela, who is slowly inching away from her, becoming a dot on the horizon. The road ahead is curiously empty for a marathon, the crowds appear to be shouting for her alone as she tries to forge through the glue, but when she looks down she realises she's running on the spot. Now she's in a Portaloo, straining urgently whilst time ticks away and the rest of the competitors thunder past. The cheers of the crowd have turned to gales of laughter now – she can see them pointing at her through the walls of the Portaloo, which to her further horror have turned to glass.

— Chapter Nine —

Fran tries to meditate as the needle is inserted into her right breast, focussing on the metallic blue rays of light filtering through the window. The Groper is right, she can barely feel it. As soon as it's over, she glances down expecting to see her boob wizened and deflated like an old balloon, but apart from a slight redness where the needle had gone in, nothing appears to have changed.

All weekend she's been prodding and poking, but still hasn't located the pea. Maybe all that fondling has broken it down, turned it to mush. A mushy pea, she thinks queasily.

She thinks about her mother suddenly. Gwen had never gone through the indignity of having her boobs squashed by a giant press she'd informed Fran smugly over the phone.

'Yeah, well it might have saved Lettie,' Fran had pointed out.

She'd rashly mentioned it to Gwen expecting the usual response – a long list of ailments far more sinister than a mere lump. There were the dizzy spells ('I came over all weird like in Asda') the abdominal pains (of which test after test had been carried out, but no cause found) and more recently memory lapses. Alzheimers perhaps? Fran puts it down to too much dope during those years on the Ashram.

But this time her mother hadn't mentioned any of the above, rather she'd said gruffly, 'so what they going to do about it then?'

'They'll do a biopsy,' Fran had answered, keeping it brief.

'Are you saying they're going to cut you open?'

'It's done with a needle. They just remove a few cells.'

A bit like liposuction she'd imagined, trying not to dwell on the pink frothy liquid they'd sucked out of her thighs.

'I hope they know what they're doing,' Gwen had

muttered ominously.

She'd called five minutes later, suggesting Fran get a second opinion, since most doctors were 'out for your money' especially in the private sector. 'All those posh health centres with their fancy equipment,' she'd added. 'And guess who's paying for them ...'

Not you, Fran had thought, irritably.

'I don't need to see another doctor. I'm not ill! If anything, I'm fitter than I've ever been in my life. I'm training to run a marathon.'

God what had possessed her to blurt that out?

There was a shocked silence, then, 'You're having me on! How long is that then?'

'Twenty six miles, and a bit.'

Another silence, followed by a sharp intake of breath. 'Bleeding hell Francesca, you're not designed to run! You're a big girl. You've always liked your food!' A line from one of Fran's childhood books had suddenly come to mind '... fill up the pan says greedy Nan ... let's sup before we go.'

Gwen, ironically was stick thin, almost emaciated. 'And what about your heart?'

Fran could hear her mother dragging hungrily on one of her interminable fags.

'My heart's fine,' she'd snapped. 'Look, I've got to go ... something in the oven. I'll call you next week once I know the results.'

She'd put down the phone, but seconds later it had rung again.

'Frannie, luv, I don't like the sound of this, especially after what happened to Lettie. I'm not saying you're going to die or anything, I mean they'll give you chemo. But what about your hair? My poor sister lost the lot! You've got such beautiful thick hair.'

'Mum, please – I'll be fine.'

'I hope so because all this worry is bad for my blood

pressure,' Gwen had stated, coughing throatily.

Fran had stopped answering the phone after that, letting the messages pile up – one from Gela, two from Shelly and a series of breathy silences, no doubt Gwen keen to deliver more of her worldly advice.

She had dispatched Chloe off to her friend Clare's house, and spent the weekend slumped in front of the television, eating and watching World War Two movies, whilst Brian rallied around making tea, re-stacking the dishwasher – putting spoons, knives and forks into their proper compartments.

'I could end up deformed,' she'd said gloomily on Sunday evening as a wintry darkness seeped into the house. Brian was now busy at his computer, installing a new program.

'It wouldn't change anything for me,' he'd answered loyally.

'It would for me, I'd feel like a freak. No ovaries, and only one boob – might as well have a sex change,' she'd added with a bitter sigh.

'Ah come on love, I didn't marry you for your boobs.'

'Obviously,' she'd replied. Yet she'd often noticed him gazing wistfully at big-breasted women in the street, or from behind his newspaper as they lay on some crowded Mediterranean beach. 'You married me for my child bearing hips,' she'd suggested. Another cruel twist of nature it seemed!

'Come to think of it, I was quite thin in those days. Then it all went pear shaped, literally.'

'I think you look fine the way you are,' he'd said. 'You worry far too much about your weight! I'm not convinced all that pounding the road is good for you. Doesn't seem natural to me.'

It wasn't the first time he'd questioned this new obsession with running.

'I certainly couldn't do it,' he'd said patting his stomach, which had expanded if not proportionally to hers, then substantially since they'd met. He was comfortable with it, comfortable with her and with their marriage. They were a unit – albeit a rather solid one.

'Maybe not, but all I know is running made me feel so much better about myself, more intensely alive than I've ever felt. It was as if I was finally getting somewhere,' she'd concluded.

***

'You can get dressed now,' the nurse tells her. 'Then make your way back to the consulting room where the doctor will be waiting for you.'

Fran pulls on her fat clothes – 'tracky' bottoms and a voluminous sweatshirt that covers most of her bottom. She must have consumed more than ten thousand calories over the weekend, sending Brian out for freshly made donuts, tortilla chips and dips, bread and butter pudding with clotted cream. She'd felt a bit like a prisoner on death row ordering the last supper before the dawn execution.

She vows to herself that when all this is over she'll drink green tea and eat her five portions of fruit and vegetables a day. She'll take fish oils and selenium – and run that bloody marathon after all. She'll do it in aid of breast cancer, in memory of Lettie who had left such a huge void in her life.

She sets off down the corridor, finding herself lost in a maze of unfamiliar passages, lined with identical consulting rooms. She pushes open a door, stopping short at the sight of a young woman in a flowery hospital smock, tears streaming down her face. The woman is quite bald apart from a few remaining wisps at the nape of her neck. A man sits beside her, attempting to mop up the flow. He is crying too, saying, 'we can fight this Sam ... we have to try.'

Neither of them appear to notice her standing there. It is as if they are removed from the present, from this cruel world with its random twists and turns, and are now waiting in the antechamber of the next. Fran feels her throat constrict, whilst her heart is fluttering bizarrely as if detached from its moorings. She takes a slow deep breath and holds the air in, following her old family doctor's instructions... *'pretend you're blowing up a balloon, if you feel an attack coming on.'* She counts to twenty, sucking the air downwards, but to no avail. Her heart is accelerating alarmingly, like a runaway train about to crash against the siding of her ribs. It's been a while since she's had a flutter. She'd almost forgotten the awful dry mouthed fear of it all. She fumbles in her bag for her homeopathic drops – Nux Vomica for shock, but it's empty. She must have swallowed the whole phial over the weekend. She sets off blindly along the padded corridors, towards the lift, stabbing the buttons in her haste, ignoring a nurse who asks if she's feeling all right.

The lift sinks soundlessly to ground level, where Brian is waiting patiently to drive her home. (He had balked at the idea of sitting beside her during the procedure.)

He stands up with a look of concern as she bursts through the swing doors.

'Get me out of here,' she gasps.

'You don't look well – maybe we should consult the doctor?'

'Too much coffee,' she mumbles, although she'd only had one cup. 'Be fine once I get out of this place.'

She's panting wildly now as if she's just run up Charlton Hill.

'Don't you think ...?' he begins. But she's heading towards the exit, barging past a hospital orderly, out into the chill November air.

'What happened?' he inquires, as they cross the car park.

Her heart is slowing, thank God, but she feels shaky and nauseous and her arms are tingling as if she's had an electric shock.

'They stuck a needle in my boob,' she snaps. 'That's what happened!'

'It's over now,' he says calmly. He helps her into the car, saying 'when will you have the results?'

'Don't know.' She remembers she was meant to go back to the consulting room and talk to The Groper.

I'm as bad as Gwen, she thinks. Doing a runner the moment things get too grim.

'What do you think triggered it?'

'How should I know?' Fear no doubt. The sight of a young woman in a hospital smock, being told there was nothing more that could be done for her – the memory of Lettie's swollen and ravaged body?

'Odds are it's all that running,' Brian states grimly.

'Running has got nothing to do with it,' she fumes, 'in fact the doctor said there was no reason why I can't run a marathon if I want.' She doesn't mention The Groper's comment about it carrying a government health warning.

'I'll call the doctor when we get home,' he states.

'I'd rather you didn't! I'll call her when I'm ready,' she answers, wishing he wasn't so bloody methodical. 'In fact I'd like to go away for a few days,' (anything rather than waiting around for the phone to ring with the verdict) 'if I can find somebody to look after Chloe.'

'I'm sure Marcia or Jasmine would have her for a couple of nights,' Brian suggests.

'I can't ask Marcia again, and Jasmine isn't talking to me since I've started running with Shelly. She's a stuck up cow anyway!' Everything seems insurmountable suddenly. 'I suppose Gela might do it.'

'Where would you like to go?' Brian inquires gently.

'I don't care. Anywhere.'

'You need a good rest,' he says decisively. 'No more running up hills for the time being.'

***

Back home, Fran fights against an urge to crawl into bed and stay there until further notice, only the last time she'd done that she'd put on a stone.

When the phone rings she snatches it up, expecting to hear The Groper's deep confidential tones.

It's Shelly. 'God Fran, I've been calling and calling for fucks sake! You must have switched off your mobile. How did it go?'

'Fine,' she replies, after a pause. 'Put it like this, it was far less painful than liposuction! Shame they can't pump in a bit of silicone at the same time!'

'When will you have the results?' Shelly inquires, after a pause.

'Oh, sometime this week. How did the run go?'

'We didn't do it in the end,' Shelly tells her, sounding sheepish now. 'Gela had to drive Marcus to the station. He's going to be working in London from now on. She's really stressed out about it. And, well I had a bit of a heavy weekend.'

'The anniversary! How did it go?'

'It went really well,' Shelly replies shortly.

Fran notes the hesitation in Shelly's voice, the way she shifts the conversation back to Gela. 'She'll go nuts alone in that big house! You know how paranoid she is. Thinking somebody's going to break in and murder her!'

'What brought this about?' Fran inquires, thinking she'd better not ask Gela to have Chloe after all.

'Apparently Marcus has been restless for a while. Big ego, wants to make it big time, God knows why? It's not as if they need the money!'

'I thought he was the one who wanted to move down here?' Fran says.

'He did, but he's had an offer from this self-made millionaire who Gela loathes! I get the distinct feeling something happened there. He and Marcus are setting up this wine business together. That's men for you – it's always on their terms.'

Fran catches that note of discord again.

'Anyway, she's keen to get on with the training. Says she needs to get out of the house. But we're not doing it without you.'

'You must,' Fran insists. You might have to. 'You're both well able for it. In any case I'd only hold you back.'

'No way,' Shelly states firmly. 'We're all in this together.'

— Chapter Ten —

Shelly puts down the phone after talking to Fran, with the sinking feeling everything is falling apart. Without Fran on board, she's reluctant to go ahead with the training, recognising somewhere deep down, that Fran's weakness is her strength. The knowledge of Fran plodding along behind keeps her going, whereas Gela's sudden bursts of speed unnerve her, cause the doubts to come flooding back in.

Then there was her relationship with Bruce. It was almost as if the two things had become linked – that the training would somehow bring them closer and he would see her as a woman of strength and determination, rather than the binge-drinking, sodden mess she'd been lately.

The memory of that drunken proposal still makes her cringe, yet Bruce had been sweetly forgiving the following morning, bringing her a tumbler of orange juice and more pain-killers, telling her she was one 'Crazy' woman.

'That was a heck of a show,' he'd stated wryly, 'for a moment there I thought you were going to take your kit off!'

She'd wanted to point out it wasn't a show (had she really almost taken her top off) that she was fed up of being his 'favourite tart.' But she'd held back sensing an undercurrent beneath his surface calm, the feeling everything was suddenly poised in the balance, about to come crashing down around her.

Later he'd announced he was meeting up with Ian and Marissa and another couple at the Climbing Centre and wouldn't be back until the evening.

'I thought we were going out for lunch,' she'd said, the memory of Marissa's amused expression as she stood beside her 'ogre' of a fiancé, causing a sick feeling in the pit of her stomach. Besides it was a Sunday ritual – hair of the dog at The Carpenter's Arms, several *Bloody Mary's* and a roast lunch followed by a walk across the moors, weather permitting. 'Gary's not back until six.'

'Don't you think you've had enough booze for one weekend?' he'd said shortly. 'I thought you were in training! At this rate you'll never cross the starting line.'

That had stung more than his decision to abandon her for the whole day. She'd lain there listening to him revving the Land Rover, feeling herself descending into that dark spiral – a bottomless pit where all she wanted to do was drink and forget. She felt alone and adrift, a bit like a climber, whose rope has been partially severed, leaving him hovering over the abyss. Even Gary seemed to be drifting away from her, spending more and more time at Sam's house, or withdrawing to his room to play violent games on his *Playstation*.

She'd dozed for a while then dragged herself downstairs and wolfed down a hearty breakfast of bacon and eggs followed by two slices of toast – the only hangover cure as far as she was concerned. Feeling marginally better, she'd put on a Waylon Jennings CD (it was going to be a while before she could listen to Patsy) and settled down on the sofa to read through some training manuals she'd bought back in October when it had all begun. There were hundreds of books on the subject – *Slow Burn, Fast Pace, Runner's High, Run For Your Life,* but she'd been drawn to *Marathon Madness*, written by an eccentric, straight talking, ex-marathon runner who called himself Phil Dippides, after the original runner – Pheidippides, who'd set off to Athens from the battlefields of Marathon twenty six miles away to announce victory to the Athenians (and subsequently dropped down dead). The book was full of wacky remarks that made her laugh out loud, beginning with, *'Welcome to the sweating, spitting, swearing, defecating masses – embrace them as your fellow kin as that is what you will be doing by mile twenty one.'*

Now she embarks on the first chapter, which is headed

REASONS TO RUN A MARATHON.

Because you can't run your life...
Because you need to focus and be the focus of others for a while (believe me people will be knocked out by your efforts, and so will you)...*
(note asterix indicates just kidding!)
Because you need to know you can do it to satisfy that massive ego of yours that secretly believes you are special – only nobody else seems to realise quite how special you are...
Because you've never done the distance, or come close to reaching the finishing post.

She'd continued reading until it was dark, feeling inspired and uplifted. It was a far better read than any of those self-help books preaching how to be happy. She'd resolved to give up the demon booze completely and get back on track. She would fuel herself with carbohydrates, and build up muscle mass with the help of some supplements. Make sure she looked the part.

Bruce hadn't returned until well after dark, by which time her spirits had plummeted again. He'd turned down her offer of dinner, a crabmeat quiche followed by the untouched *Bailey's* cheesecake.

'We stopped at the pub for a bite on the way home,' he'd explained.

She'd nodded, feeling as if all those rocks were now tumbling down on her, crushing her to a pulp.

'We're going to be doing some serious training from now on,' he'd warned, as if already planning his escape route.

'That's fine, because I'll be busy training too, once Fran gets the all clear. I've been reading up about it. I know I can do it.'

'It's a big commitment,' he'd stated.

Something you're incapable of, she'd thought, with irony.

'I realise that,' she'd said, meeting his gaze.

'I'll be watching out for you at the finishing line,' he'd said at last.

— Chapter Eleven —

Brian informs Fran that he's booked two flights to Dublin on the net and found a hotel right in the city centre.

'No point taking you to a country hotel, when we live in the country,' he states. 'Besides it's a really good deal. And there are some great restaurants and bars all around the area,' he says, producing a small map.

He seems to have dismissed the fact she doesn't drink and is meant to be on a diet.

Fran, who had envisaged a luxurious hotel, complete with swimming pool, sauna and steam room to sweat off the excess pounds (she seems to have piled on another ton since this whole nightmare began) says, 'what about Chloe?'

'I thought you were going to ask Gela to have her?' he says.

'She's got enough on her plate with Marcus away.'

If only Gwen was a normal grandmother who drove a car and did normal things, she could have come down to look after Chloe, driven her to school, to the cinema, they could have baked a cake together. The thought of Gwen baking anything is too bizarre to contemplate.

'Shelly would do it. She's not likely to go on a bender during the week.'

Brian frowns. 'I don't think it's a good idea.'

He'd always had reservations about Shelly, and now more than ever, claiming her training schedule was excessive. She was not qualified to act as a coach. 'If you ask me she's bloody dangerous,' he'd stated.

'I didn't ask you,' Fran had replied sharply, 'besides anybody who manages to galvanise me into running six miles deserves a medal.'

Now he says, 'she'll probably have Chloe running round the garden fifty times.'

Which wouldn't do her any harm, Fran thought. It could no longer be dismissed as puppy fat, Chloe was becoming decidedly chubby.

'Fine I'll ask Marcia,' she says at last, although it was the fourth time in a row. But to hell with protocol.

She needs to get away and think about her life or what might be left of it.

***

The hotel at the top of O'Connell Street is comfortable but characterless, the weather cold and drizzly, but the city is teeming with life, the hotel staff so welcoming, Fran feels slightly uplifted. Brian has organised each day down to the last detail. A visit to St Michins to shake the leathery hand of an 800 year old crusader, to Trinity to see the Book of Kells, the Kilkenny Design Centre to buy local pottery. They eat in expensive restaurants recommended by the Good Food Guide. Fran goes along with it all – eating and drinking everything that comes her way. She tucks into a full Irish breakfast, munching her way through baskets of crumbling soda bread, thick with butter, for lunch, platters of smoked salmon and more soda bread. In the evenings, a three-course dinner accompanied by copious amounts of potatoes. She even tries a pint of Guinness in a run down pub close to the Halfpenny Bridge full of old men with tweed caps and weathered faces.

It's very atmospheric – one of them obligingly plays a tin whistle and Brian chats away to the barman who asks if they are on their holidays. Two men wearing oversized suits introduce themselves as pig farmers up from the country. Brian shakes hands with them and asks about farming in general, explaining how he lives close to a pig farm across the water.

Fran sips an Irish coffee and listens with one ear, feeling pleasantly woozy. She has given up on the Guinness, which tasted vaguely sulphurous as if it had come straight out of the turbid looking River Liffey running along beside them.

'I've had a really lovely time,' she tells Brian, who is now consulting his Good Food Guide for the final dinner. She kisses his round familiar cheek, adding 'It's taken my mind off things a bit.'

'That was the idea,' he smiles, patting her thigh fondly. 'No point worrying until we have all the information.'

Only at night, does she start feeling for it again beneath the sheets, imagining a tingling ache deep in the core of her. Perhaps it was already spreading to the rest of her organs, eating away at her. It certainly had plenty to feed on, could take years to munch through all that flesh. Come to think of it she might end up the only fat cancer patient on the planet.

The man on the tin whistle is coming to the end of his hectic jig, the last strains fading into the air. A thick silence descends on the pub. Fran gets up to go to the loo, feeling as if she's floating after the double shot of Irish whiskey.

Maybe I'll take up drinking she thinks to herself, aware of the two pig farmers watching her slow progress up the stairs.

'Jaysus that's acres of a woman,' one of them announces, in the booming tones of the partially deaf.

'Fine looking woman all the same,' says the other.

Fran holds herself in check until she gets into the loo. And then she starts to shake with laughter, bending over with mirth, tears streaming down her face, until she's not sure whether she's laughing or crying.

***

Back home there's a message on the answer phone asking her to call Dr Groper on her private line.

'Here goes,' she says to herself, only this time I decide when and where they operate. A private clinic this time with the best plastic surgeon on stand-by. 36C perhaps. I don't want my cups to overflow like Shelly's.

'Yes, it's Francesca Taylor returning your call.'

'Mrs Taylor, how are you?'

How the hell do you think I am you freak of nature? she thinks nastily. That was the trouble with fear, it turned you into a monster, angry and resentful, full of loathing for the world in general, particularly the medical profession.

'I'm fine,' she says briskly, 'I've been in Ireland, on holiday.' Away from groping hands and needles, from surgeons wielding their scalpels.

'I've had the results of your tests back.'

'Yes well the thing is, I'm tied up for the next few months, with the training, and in any case I'd like another opinion.'

Might as well test Gwen's theory after all.

'No need, no need at all. Your tests have proved negative. You will be getting confirmation from me in writing.'

'But the pea? What the hell was it then?' Fran says weakly. Wasn't she like the woman in the magazine – a statistical casualty?

'Fibroadenoma or benign tumour,' The Groper states levelly.

Fran feels a mixture of relief, and fury surging inside her. 'Do you mean to say I went through all that worry ... sleepless nights ... all that misery, for nothing?'

Gwen was right – the tests and X Rays were all a scam, a way of buying more expensive coffee machines, more silicone for all those flat-chested women.

'I haven't slept for days, I must have put on a stone from all the stress,' she adds furiously.

She wants to ring the woman's scrawny neck suddenly, stick a needle in her perfectly shaped boob, and see how she likes it.

There's a silence, then The Groper says, 'I understand how you feel, but it's not always as straightforward as you think. I've had to call two patients back this week, one of whose condition is too far advanced for treatment.'

Fran has a vivid image of the bald young woman in the

hospital smock, imagines the pain and fear, the terrible helplessness of knowing nothing more could be done.

'Nor was I quite so lucky as you,' The Groper adds. 'I lost both breasts, but I still have my life.'

Fran feels hot with mortification. So they weren't real after all. 'I'm sorry,' she begins.

'Don't be. The trick is not to run away from it. Have regular check ups. Oh and talking about running – certainly keep it up. But don't overdo it. A marathon is a significant undertaking.'

'Not for the faint hearted, is basically what you're saying,' Fran says with irony.

'You are carrying excess weight,' The Groper says without beating around the bush, 'which means you'd be putting undue stress on your heart.'

'I'll lose the weight,' Fran says resolutely. 'I can do it.'

Only this time it will be for good.

— Chapter Twelve —

'Now we can get down to some serious training,' Shelly says triumphantly.

Fran's announcement that the lump was benign had come as a huge relief, as well as an excuse for a celebration – a bottle of champagne (Shelly had insisted Fran have at least one glass) and lunch at Gela's.

'Nothing fattening,' Fran had pleaded, 'this time it's for real. No more crap diets – just a healthy eating plan for the rest of my life! Or, at least until the Marathon.' Better not set unrealistic goals, she reminds herself.

Gela had bought a wild salmon and a variety of exotic salads from the local deli, Shelly had provided the champagne, and made a low calorie dessert with fromage frais and winter berries. She'd also bought Fran a voucher for an Aromatherapy body massage at the new Health and Beauty Centre, in town.

'Keep it for after the next distance run,' she'd warned. 'We start Monday, with a seven miler around Charlton Lake.'

'God, I can see there's no respite,' Fran had groaned. 'Still, I suppose I've no excuse now.' She feels as if she's been granted a new lease of life – a second shot.

'I knew it would turn out all right,' Gela says happily.

'No you didn't,' Shelly declares, high from having polished off most of the champagne. (Gela had barely touched her second glass). 'You were scared shitless!'

'Well she wasn't the only one,' Fran admits, taking a tentative sip and wincing at the curiously flat taste. 'Don't know how you drink this stuff,' she says, pushing her glass away. 'To be honest, I thought I'd already reached the finishing line! Christ, it really makes you think about your life, and not having done anything of note! A useless degree in home economics, endless charity work, three years on the

PTA! It's like my life never really took off. There were so many things I was going to do. I just kept missing the starting gun!' she sighs. 'I've only ever had sex with one man – apart from Brian!'

'Maybe it's still ahead of us,' Gela says hopefully. 'I mean not the sex with somebody else ... that's not worth it. Believe me, those things always backfire.'

Fran frowns, sensing some fascinating disclosure is about to follow, but Shelly cuts in with, 'Bruce is the best lover ever ...' She reaches for Fran's glass adding, 'there isn't a single place in the house we haven't done it. I could show that patronising cow and her ogre fiancé a thing or two! I've had it up to here with climbers, looking down their noses at me, just because I don't fancy dangling off some bloody ledge!' She knocks back the contents of her glass and stares wildly into the middle distance.

'You wait until you've run the Marathon,' Gela says in an effort to console her, curious about the "patronising cow and her ogre fiancé."

But Shelly is leaning forward, saying angrily, 'Bruce doesn't believe I can do it, none of them do.'

'Of course you can do it! If any of us can, it's you,' Fran states.

'Absolutely,' Gela echoes. 'Anyway, you're going to have to now!'

Shelly empties the dregs of the bottle into her glass, glancing at Marcus's wine rack hopefully before saying, 'we need to announce it ... get people to sponsor us.'

'Announce your intentions early,' Phil Dippides or Mr Dippy as she'd nicknamed him, advised, *'then there can be no going back.'*

'A bit soon isn't it?' Gela says. 'I'm not even sure which charity I'm running for, although I think it'll be the Meningitis Trust after what happened to Matthew.'

'I'm running in aid of breast cancer,' Fran states.

'MEMBERS, against male cancer,' Shelly says after a pause. 'My brother died at the age of twenty-five,' she adds briefly. She remembers how he'd said, 'make sure you grab life by the balls Shell, before it grabs you!'

'I didn't know. How awful for you...' Fran begins.

Shelly waves her hand dismissively. 'The family had already fallen apart by then. My father drank when things got really bad. He was in and out of rehab for years.'

The knowledge that there's a history of alcohol in the family hangs over her, but she can give it up at anytime, she tells herself.

'What about your mother?' Gela ventures.

'She, well, she passed away when I was a kid, but that's another story.'

'That must have been really tough,' Gela begins, aware of the shuttered look on Shelly's face. She has already cast Shelly as a woman with a troubled past (a grim family secret that will later be disclosed.)

'Yeah well, there you go. Shit! Is that the time, we've got to pick up the kids.'

'We've still got time for a quick coffee,' Gela points out, but Shelly is grabbing her fake fur jacket and making her way rather unsteadily towards the door.

Fran glances around Gela's chaotic kitchen for her car keys (she would do anything for her home to have that lived in look) although it takes her a while to locate her keys.

'Looks like I'm going to have to drive you two lushes,' she grins.

***

As they pull into the car park, Fran says, grimly, 'Oh God, the PTA is out in force today. Don't tell me they're already selling tickets for the New Year's Eve charity ball? I don't believe it!'

The pressure to raise money for the school's chosen charity was getting worse every year – so much so, tickets were being sold weeks in advance. Fran is aware of being slowly isolated from the decision making (no doubt because of her friendship with Shelly). Jasmine Fellows had recently sent her an e-mail saying, 'Re NSPCC BALL. (Fran had failed to convince her they should support terminally ill children this year for a change). **I've enrolled two extra helpers to sell tickets since you're so busy with your jogging.'**

Fran had e-mailed back saying, **'surely it's too early to sell tickets? We haven't even finalised the Christmas Craft Fair, which you also wanted to do in aid of NSPCC. I still think we should spread out our funds to support other worthwhile causes. And anyway, I'm not jogging – I'm running – big difference!'**

And maybe you should give it a go, rather than trying to run everyone else's affairs, she'd wanted to add.

'It's far too early to sell tickets!' she fumes now.

'Sodding Mothers from Hell,' Shelly murmurs from the back.

'You stay in the car,' Fran suggests, 'Gela and I will go and get the kids.'

But Shelly is pulling open the door, muttering, 'don't want Gary thinking I'm not coming.' She never wants him to go through the agony she went through that bleak winter afternoon, waiting for her mother to show up. She strides towards the gates, head high causing a hush to descend over the group of waiting mothers. She can almost feel the hostility emanating from the centre, where Jasmine is holding forth. Nobody even asks her if she wants to buy a ticket, even though she's given generously year after year. She has become an outcast, since the famous charity dinner – no longer even worthy of donating to the cause it seems. Something rises inside her, an urge to finish what she'd started that evening – punch Jasmine Fellows' smug face. She's not going to do it of course – she'll just say something cutting, then walk away.

She strides up to the group saying, 'I'm also trying to raise money for charity, as it happens. You probably know by now, that Fran, Gel, and me are running the Marathon. Fran's doing it in aid of breast cancer, Gela for the Meningitis Trust.'

There's a silence then a prim little woman called Cindy says, 'I'll sponsor Gela. I thought Becky had meningitis, too. It was awful, these huge purple bruises suddenly appeared right in front of my eyes.'

I'll give you purple bruises, thinks Shelly.

'And I'll sponsor Fran,' another adds.

Jasmine says nothing. Shelly notices she's put on weight and recalls rumours of marital problems. There was also speculation that she was having an affair with somebody in the village. Well she could damn well stay away from other people's husbands or partners, Shelly fumes, remembering how she'd sidled up to Bruce and quizzed him as to why he didn't want to get married again.

'That's really good of you two,' she says sweetly in the ensuing silence.

'Are you running for breast cancer too?' somebody inquires.

'No – bollocks actually,' Shelly replies, suddenly losing it.

There's a shocked silence.

'Take it easy Shell,' Fran warns, whilst Gela looks alarmed.

'Testicular, if you want to be more precise,' Fran fills in swiftly.

'The vulgarity,' Jasmine mutters whilst the other women exchange amused glances. 'Anyway what were we saying –

oh yes, we need to sell at least two hundred tickets if we're going to make our target.'

Shelly is beginning to wish she'd flattened the woman when she'd had the chance. She takes a deep breath feeling dangerously close to the edge. She hasn't been herself since that evening at The Cock and Bull – has the uneasy feeling that news of her drunken proposal has got around and now everyone is laughing about her behind her back. She hadn't even gone into the humiliating details of it, with Fran and Gela, fearing they too might laugh, or worse feel sorry for her.

'Clearly unhinged,' Jasmine says, incensing Shelly further. 'No wonder he doesn't want to marry the woman, completely crazy...'

Shelly steps forward, the word crazy igniting a red flash of light behind her eyes.

'What did you say?' she hisses.

'Nothing,' Jasmine mutters turning her back on Shelly as if there's nothing more to discuss.

'Right that's it,' Shelly fumes.

'Leave it Shell,' Fran whispers fiercely, 'don't let her wind you up.'

But Shelly is moving forward, jaw clenched, every muscle and tendon in her neck taut as wire. She pushes through the tight band of mothers, grabs Jasmine by the arm swinging her around, and deals her a stinging blow on the right cheek.

Jasmine lets out a shocked cry, and clutches her face dramatically.

There's an appalled silence, followed by a ripple of horrified exclamations.

Shelly is aware she's stepped over the line, will probably be ostracised by the whole village as well as the school. Cindy is now putting an arm around Jasmine, saying, 'are you all right Jas?'

'No I'm not,' Jasmine sobs, backing away and still

holding her cheek as if mortally wounded, 'she's completely deranged, no class! How dare you?' she splutters, 'you're going to pay for this!'

'Don't you threaten me,' Shelly hisses, 'unless you want everyone to know what you've been up to lately!'

Shelly, who has no idea if the rumours of the affair are true, is aware she's on the trail of something, notices the shocked look on Jasmine's face, the way she says guardedly, 'I don't know what the hell you're talking about.' A couple of mothers exchange knowing glances.

'Oh yes you do!' Shelly says, determined to find out more, but children are now flooding through the gates, like a tidal wave, breaking up the moment.

'Here comes Gary,' Fran warns.

Shelly takes a calming breath, anger and adrenaline still coursing through her.

Gary approaches uncertainly, sensing something is awry. He stiffens as Shelly tries to hug him, saying, 'yuck! You stink of wine. Can I go to Sam's house? He's got Final Destruction Two.'

Sam's mother (who Shelly has had over for tea and wine on numerous occasions) now hovers nervously in the background. 'I could bring him back later, if you like?' she suggests. 'I won't be able to stay because of my yoga class.'

Shelly nods, suddenly sick at heart, aware that Gary would inevitably be affected by this latest drama. Jasmine would label him accordingly, have him struck off birthday party lists, or manning a stall at the May fair. She feels horribly sober now, can taste the sour aftermath of champagne in her throat, and is already descending into that black void.

'Come on Shell,' Fran is saying, grabbing hold of Chloe, 'I'll drive you home.'

Jasmine strides past, with her immaculately dressed twins, Posy and Portia.

'Marathon, my arse!' Shelly hears her mutter scathingly.

Her gaze seems to take in Fran and Gela too.

'What a ghastly woman,' Gela breathes.

'That's it,' Fran fumes. 'I'm resigning from the PTA! I'm sick and tired of listening to a load of posing, control freaks pretending to do good works. You need to get yourself a life,' she adds, directing this at Jasmine. 'I'd like to see you training for a marathon – sweating for it for once, instead of telling everybody else to cough up the money.'

'I accept your resignation,' Jasmine says icily.

'Into the car everyone,' Fran orders. 'Let's get out of this viper's nest.'

***

'Christ the look on Jasmine's face when you hinted she was having an affair!' Fran exclaims, as they gather in Shelly's kitchen to discuss the drama in the car park. 'It must be true, although God knows who would want to shag her!'

'We're going to have to get to the bottom of it,' Gela says. 'You were amazing, Shelly,' she adds.

Shelly grins, suddenly at a loss. She's not used to anyone rallying around her, has never had any close female friends. She's always considered women a threat – manipulative, conniving, and self-obsessed – bound to let you down in the end, or desert you just like her mother had done. Besides she doesn't want anybody getting too close, breaking down the barriers she's carefully constructed.

'Thanks, you two,' she says finally, 'but you didn't need to resign Fran.'

'Oh yes I did. Charity work begins at home – not at the bequest of that vile woman. From now on I'm in charge of my own fund raising. Anyway, I've always loathed Jasmine Fellows.'

'She must have heard about the Karaoke evening,' Shelly says with a sigh.

Gela and Fran look at her blankly.

Shelly busies herself with the coffee, adding 'made a bit

of an arse of myself a few weeks back at The Cock and Bull. Drank too much. Decided to propose to Bruce on stage, after singing a Patsy Cline number! It was a bloody good performance mind you!' she adds with a grin.

'The anniversary?' Fran says astutely.

Shelly nods.

'I thought you didn't want to get married again,' Gela ventures. 'That things were well … already passionate enough?' She glances warily at the kitchen table, hoping Shelly and Bruce hadn't recently had sex on it.

'I didn't at first, but now, well things have changed. I have to think about Gary. I came out of my first marriage with nothing. I can't afford that to happen again. So I decided to propose on stage, and, well …' she looks sheepish, '…it didn't go down too well.'

'Maybe it wasn't the right moment?' Gela suggests.

'It never is! Commitment is not exactly Bruce's thing.'

'In some ways it must be nice, just living together – not being bound by all those old fashioned vows. I mean if you had an affair for instance or just a fling.' It wouldn't haunt you like it does me, she thinks.

'I don't want an affair,' Shelly cuts in, 'Bruce and I are perfect together! I just need to think about the future.'

'Maybe you should go and see a solicitor,' Fran suggests, 'get some kind of contract drawn up, just in case things don't work out.'

Shelly glances around the newly decorated kitchen. She'd spent months looking for the perfect oven range, choosing the colours, finding some original tiles. She has put everything she has into this family home of his. The last thing she wants is bitter wrangling and arguments as to who keeps the Patsy Cline collection.

'Bruce wouldn't go along with it,' she says at last. 'He hates solicitors. He's still paying The Mantis – that is his ex wife – alimony. We'll work something out between us,' she adds shortly. She's said enough, far too much in fact, 'anyway we're fine at the moment. Bruce would do anything for me,' (apart from this one thing) she thinks. 'Now, about Monday's distance run,' she digresses, 'don't forget to "carb up" over the weekend and bring some energy drinks.' She glances at them both challengingly. 'Did you know that if you can run seven miles, you're an athlete?'

— Chapter Thirteen —

'So let's get this straight,' Shelly says, as they gather in The Charlton Arms, after the seven 'miler', 'you shagged this Paolo guy in an off-licence and now Marcus is going into business with him?'

'Shussh keep your voice down,' Gela hisses, as an elderly couple at the next table glance towards them. 'I don't want the whole village to know!'

But Shelly, still high from the morning's achievement (they were athletes – even though Fran had walked the last mile) continues relentlessly. 'Fair marks to you girl, I would never have thought of an off-licence. It's the perfect place. All that booze!' She stares at her pint of orange and lemonade gloomily (she was never going to make it to the weekend). 'God and I thought you were a bit posh for that kind of thing!' She's finding Gela's unexpected revelation a welcome diversion from her own problems.

'I didn't intend having sex,' Gela emphasises, wishing she'd never blurted it out in the first place. Endorphins had that effect on her, brought things gushing to the surface – a sudden desperate need to confess. That and the fact she needed to confide in somebody. The burden of it all was becoming too much. She'd unloaded the whole story on mile two, when they were still together, but Fran had been too out of breath to comment apart from, 'Holy shit Gel...' Whilst Shelly's reaction had been one of incredulity, 'an affair ... you of all people?'

Now Fran's eyes are round with astonishment, whilst Shelly grins saying, 'sounds like this Paolo has got you over a barrel!'

'So, why, I mean, was it just the once?' Fran demands.

Gela nods. 'I had too much to drink, it was my thirtieth birthday. Marcus was away – he was always away at the key moments!'

It is after all a relief to talk about it, if only to make sense of it all.

'Turning thirty was a bit of a watershed for me,' she admits. 'I had big dreams of being a published author, not an editor in a second rate publishing house. Marcus was already a success – a real high flyer. He was travelling all over the place. Jamie was such a handful. I was drafting this novel at the time about a woman who risks her marriage for a one night stand ... and well,' she smiles wanly, 'seems like I took my research a bit far.'

'Research?' Shelly echoes, 'sounds more like lust to me!'

Gela shakes her head. 'He's not even my type – far too smooth – dark, Latin looking – although he's actually an East Ender, with a huge chip on his shoulder,' she shudders. 'I never meant it to go the whole way. I just wanted to imagine how it would feel so I could write about it. I must have put out the wrong signals, and he was really forceful!' She sighs, 'sometimes it only takes a word, or even a look, and before you know it you've crossed the line – and can never get back.'

'What was the word?' Fran inquires, with fascination.

'That's the odd thing. I just can't remember.'

Time and time she's been transported back to that evening, until she can almost smell the scent of his after-shave, warm and musty, like Sandalwood. She remembers him taking a bottle of vintage champagne from the glass-fronted fridge and opening it deftly with a celebratory pop. Had he locked the front door by then or did that happen earlier? It was only about a quarter to ten, which meant he must have closed the shop early. She remembers him teasing her about her lack of knowledge of wine, before going on to say that she was so 'incredibly beautiful, he couldn't think straight.' That she had 'gone to his head like vintage champagne', and if she were his wife he would never leave her alone on her thirtieth birthday ...

She doesn't remember him leading her into the back office, which means she must have been already drunk by then. She remembers him stroking her hair, trying futilely to smooth it. That was the moment she'd tried to break away, only his other hand was clamped around her wrist with an iron grip. It was all a blur after that – she must have blanked it out. But she can still recall him withdrawing from her numb body almost as swiftly as he'd entered it, looking down on her, a strange condescending smile playing around his lips. 'God, Marcus is a lucky bastard,' he'd said.

By then, she was beginning to sober up, had gone into shock, wondering what on earth she was doing half-naked, amongst the dusty bottles and bargain barrels of cheap wine.

'Could he have spiked your drink?' Fran demands, as Gela reaches the end of this extraordinary confession.

'More likely she was pissed,' Shelly says knowingly. 'Two glasses and you're anybody's! Sorry Gel, don't want to make you feel worse, but it doesn't take much!'

'I know I'm hopeless with alcohol,' she says irritably, 'but that's beside the point, the fact is, this could be the end of my marriage!'

Shelly frowns. 'Because you shagged somebody five years ago?'

'You don't know Marcus. He has this thing about fidelity. He was married before to a Dutch girl called Elspeth – blonde slippery hair,' (she would give anything for hair like that) 'blue eyes. He came back from a business trip and found her in bed with her ex. They'd decided to have a final fling before he went back to Holland. They'd only been married a fortnight! That was that! Marcus threw her out the same day.'

'I didn't know that,' Fran says.

Shelly raises her eyebrows. She could just imagine Marcus taking the moral high ground. 'Then you're going to have to deny it. It's Paolo's word against yours. If it comes up, say something like, 'in your dreams mate, I'd prefer to do it with a bottle of Blue Nun.'

Gela smiles in spite of herself. There is something enormously comforting about Shelly's reaction, turning the whole thing into a light-hearted romp.

'I don't know what Brian would do if I had an affair,' Fran muses, an image of Gerry Ryan instantly coming to mind. 'Fat chance come to think of it, unless he's into acres of a woman.' (The pig farmer's comment had gone deep) and in spite of losing almost a stone and a half, she still saw herself as acres of undulating flesh, rippling like fields of tall grass in the breeze. 'Anyway Shell's right, if this Paolo wants Marcus to go into business with him he's hardly likely to say, "by the way, your wife's a terrific lay." I mean he wants Marcus to invest in the business right?'

'That's the problem,' Gela says, desperately. 'I don't want Marcus putting money into it. I don't trust Paolo Conti. He's done the dirty on somebody before – ripped his partner off. It was in all the papers, Marcus didn't believe a word of it, said the other guy was a crook. In any case, Marcus had the idea of Fine Wines first.'

'Marcus is an intelligent man,' Fran points out, 'he's not likely to be conned, surely?'

'He's also completely blinded by successful people,' Gela says despondently. 'He would love to be in Paolo's shoes, running a business of his own – which reminds me Paolo is running the marathon too. God I hope he hits the wall!'

Shelly's eyes light up. 'You're going to have to whip his ass.'

'What an awful thought,' Gela says, taking it literally. 'What if he's planning to blackmail me, or something?' she wails.

'How?' Fran demands. 'There's no proof – unless you were caught on CCTV camera?'

'Oh my God,' Gela breathes.

'Unlikely,' Shelly states. 'The camera would be in the front of the shop guarding the expensive stuff. Calm down.'

Gela takes a sip of her cold coffee, wincing at the bitter taste. She could do with a bar of fruit and nut to go with it, but had vowed to cut out chocolate and crisps at least until after the marathon. 'I need to find a way of stopping the partnership going ahead. Maybe I should just tell Marcus – come clean.'

'No,' Shelly and Fran chorus. 'For Christ sake girl, don't start confessing now! It happened five years ago!' Shelly emphasises.

'Yeah, end of story,' Fran adds.

Yet somehow I have the feeling it's only just beginning, Gela thinks to herself.

— Chapter Fourteen —

Fran sets off alone that chill December morning in a bid to make up for all those lost miles. The village is deserted, it being a Sunday, the car park empty. Most normal people were still in bed it seemed, not setting off for a lonely seven mile run. She vows to complete the distance this time – no walking up the hill, or stopping for a breather half way. Last time she'd done that, her calves had seized and she'd ended up limping the whole way home.

'You're an athlete remember,' she tells herself. Fatlete more like it! All the same, since being given the all clear, anything seemed possible. She feels lighter of body as well as mind, has cut out fats and sugar again, fuelling herself with complex carbs – potatoes (without the butter), pasta, lentils and brown rice. She has started taking glucosomine sulphate for her joints, iron and vitamin C for strength, and her Rescue Remedy for courage.

She turns off the main road, slowing in preparation for the hill. As the road rises, she shortens her stride and focuses on the tarmac ahead. She knows better than to look up, but all the same without Shelly to cajole and bully her along, it takes every ounce of her will power to keep going.

You've had worse obstacles to climb, she thinks, forging on up the relentless incline of Charlton Hill. Her breathing has turned to agonising groans, as if she's on the cusp of an elusive orgasm, her lungs are on fire. With a final burst of effort, she propels herself towards the brow of the hill, letting out a climactic 'yessss!' before stumbling to a gasping halt. She can hear the roar of a four-wheel drive revving behind and pulls onto the verge so it can pass, but it stays behind her, engine throbbing, some freaky kerb crawler no doubt. She turns around, ready to curse the driver, then realises with a jolt it's him, Gerry Ryan, a look of wry amusement on his handsome face. God what must she have looked like – acres of wobbling flesh and brick red cheeks, not to mention those embarrassing groans? Her hair has broken free from its mooring and is hanging over her shoulders in long damp tendrils.

'On your own today then?' he inquires through the open window.

'Just putting in a few extra miles,' she breathes, praying her bladder will hold up.

'You're looking very strong and fit,' he comments, his eyes, travelling over her.

Strong and fit! Not elephantine – it has been years since anybody has dealt her a double compliment.

'So what are you doing out and about so early on a Sunday morning?' she inquires, trying to breathe normally.

'Had a bit of a night of it,' he grins. 'Started off at The Charlton Arms, and it went on from there!'

Yet he looks remarkably fresh and relaxed, she thinks, unlike her.

'Still planning to run the marathon then?' he inquires.

'That's the idea. Although God knows how … I might have to be airlifted out.'

He considers this for a minute then says, 'being a betting man I'd put my money on you any day.'

'In that case maybe you'd like to sponsor me,' she says provocatively. 'I'm running in aid of breast cancer.'

'I'll sponsor you all right,' he says, with meaning. 'Where do I sign up?'

'I'll be putting a form in the pub, or I could drop it in if I'm passing?' She's aware she's flirting outrageously, but can't seem to stop herself. In any case, unlike Gela's situation, she can always make a run for it.

His gaze is intense now as if he's weighing up his chances.

'I'd better get moving before I seize up,' she says. She

steps forward, and lets out a cry of pain.

'Are you all right?' he frowns, as she hops on one foot.

'Just a bit of cramp ... shouldn't have stopped, fatal.' She takes a tentative step, wincing as another jagged pain shoots up her calf. 'Be all right in a minute,' she breathes.

He is pulling into the side of the road now, and getting out of the Land Rover. 'Get in, I'll run you down to the cottage, we can put some ice on it.'

'Better keep going ... holy shit!' she moans.

'Here, lean against me,' he says, putting an arm around her waist and half lifting her (thank God she's lost some weight) into the Land Rover. He smells of the earth, she thinks headily, of wood smoke and bonfires.

'Maybe I'd better go straight home,' she begins.

'It's no trouble,' he says, turning down the lane towards the cluster of thatched cottages.

He pulls into the narrow driveway, jumps down, then comes around to her side to help her out.

'I'm actually fine now,' she says, glancing around nervously, aware that one of the PTA mothers lived further down the lane, but he's already unlocking the front door of the cottage and ushering her into a small cluttered living room. The walls are blistered and peeling and large rusting hooks hang like question marks from the ceiling.

'My grandfather was the village butcher,' he explains, following her gaze.

Fran has a fleeting vision of herself strung up by her heels to tenderise, like a side of beef.

'Do you live here alone?' she inquires, glancing at the mess in awe – empty beer cans, an overflowing ashtray, gardening catalogues, packets of seeds, on the floor a pile of clothing and muddy boots.

He nods – 'no woman would put up with me!'

What about the big woman called Rose, and the voluptuous blonde, Shelly had mentioned, Fran wonders?

'Had a relationship for a while, but it all got a bit heavy,' he says, pulling out a squashed pack of cigarettes. 'I'll get some ice – would you like some tea?'

Fran shakes her head. 'Tea gives me a stitch. Just a glass of water. At this rate I'll never get home.'

'What's the hurry?' he calls from the kitchen.

Brian, she thinks, who would be checking his watch, and wondering where she'd got to. She flicks through a gardening catalogue glancing at vivid photographs of spring shrubs – milky bellflowers, clematis, and purple foxglove.

'Keen on gardening then?' he inquires, appearing with a dishcloth full of ice and a glass of water.

'Yes, although if I had my way I'd let ours grow wild.'

Brian liked trimmed yew hedges and neat herbaceous borders. The pond, which he'd dug himself was a neat square with concrete edges. She had found him pulling up the lilies once, claiming they looked untidy.

'Sit back, relax,' he insists, guiding her towards a frayed looking sofa, which appears to have lost all its springs. He crouches down beside her and lifts up her leg, saying, 'where does it hurt?'

'Oh, just, well the whole thing feels stiff,' she answers, trying to remember when she'd last shaved her legs. (Brian made a fuss if she left bits of black hair in the bath). And what about her trainers – they must reek after all that pounding?

His fingers are manipulating the numb place where the ice had been as if kneading a lump of rather stiff dough.

God forbid he's now unlacing her trainer, peeling off her sock, and taking her bare foot in his hand. Her heart is pumping so frantically she's afraid it might go out of whack, that she'll die with her sweaty foot still clasped in his hands.

'Francesca, is it?' he says, lowering her leg and gazing into her eyes with such burning intensity, she has to look away.

'Yeah, but I'm more like a Fran, you know, solid!' She

needs to lighten the moment before she drowns in those green pools, and is lost forever.

'Frangipani?' he suggests.

Now he was likening her to a tropical flower when she must have smelt like a rancid onion.

'You know you have a beautiful face.'

It was a compliment that often came her way – one of Gwen's favourites with the unspoken condition, 'if only you could lose weight.'

'I noticed you straight away that day in the car park,' he is saying.

'Oh Gela's the beautiful one,' she says hastily. 'And she's got the figure.' She shifts her position, feeling something pressing into her back.

'Personally, I like a woman with a bit of flesh on her.'

'Well upholstered,' Fran jokes, thinking unlike this sofa.

He grins, his hands moving slowly up the length of her leg, sending the heat flooding to her cheeks.

'I should be getting home,' she says, weakly. She tries to heave herself forward, almost kicking him in the face.

'Here steady,' he says, taking both arms and pulling her gently to her feet. He holds her for a long moment, then says softly, 'when can I see you again?'

Time to say, 'I'm happily married, with a daughter, I can never see you again.' But her throat is completely dry, and she seems to be rooted to the spot, almost paralysed with desire.

Just once, a traitorous voice commands – the voice that reminds her nothing like this has ever happened before and probably never would again. OK so he was a serial shagger who jumped on any woman that passed his way. But it didn't stop her wanting to pass this way again.

"Sometimes, all it takes is one word or gesture then before you know it you've crossed that line and there's no way back." Gela had said.

Just one night of wild passion and romance and then I'll

go back to my old life insists the voice.

There had never been a passionate exchange with Brian – they'd met at a party in Brentwood, in the kitchen of course. She'd been ploughing into the sour cream dip, leaving a trail of broken crisps in her wake and the next moment he was standing beside her – trying to scoop up all the debris. She should have realised then he was a stickler for detail. But she'd liked his eyes and his rather clumsy jokes, the way he took care of her, had recognised that here was a man who would love, honour and never let her down. She'd even liked the way he instilled some order in her life, hadn't forced himself on her. On the other hand, perhaps if he'd swept her into his arms, tried to seduce her...

'The thing is,' she begins, but Gerry is pulling her towards him, and kissing her urgently, his tongue circling hers, his hands in the damp tangle of her hair. It is the kiss of life – and death – she thinks wildly. She can barely breathe, and when she finally comes up for air, she can still feel its burning imprint on her lips.

He releases her at last, saying, 'I've been longing to do that since the moment I first saw you.'

'I really should go,' she gasps. The cramp in her leg has gone, but it's all she can do to cross the room.

'All right,' he concedes, gently pushing a damp strand of hair from her face. 'But I'll be looking out for you – Frangipani.'

She had stumbled shakily down the path aware her knickers were slicing her cheeks into half moons. She'd turned at the end of the path, pulling in her stomach so he had the last view of her side on. Then set off for home (no time to do the distance now) her wayward heart swelling in her chest, the sense her life had taken a dramatic and inevitable turn.

— Chapter Fifteen —

At first glance it looks like a circular, Shelly thinks, wrapped in light cellophane, destined for the bin. Another competition perhaps, promising some elusive prize – only this one appears to be apologising for the fact she's not even in the running. When she examines it closely she sees the words, *We regret to advise you that your application to run the marathon has not been successful.* The letter is accompanied by a magazine called Marathon News which seems somewhat ironic.

She stares at it in disbelief wondering if it's some kind of sick joke. What the hell do they mean? It isn't a job application for which she's not qualified! This morning she'd run eight miles, for God's sake. She's been off the booze all week, and has started working out at the gym, building up serious muscle (with the help of some powerful bulking up supplements). She's so shocked she needs a drink even though it's Thursday and only mid-morning. She paces the kitchen debating whether to call Fran or Gela first. She doesn't want to tell Bruce yet, fearing he'd shrug, as if he'd known all along she'd never do it, had somehow willed them to turn her down. She stares at the letter again looking for a number to call; anger welling against a system that was not only random but totally uncaring.

Shelly had always believed that life was a lottery, but you chose the numbers. Now it occurs to her, you were simply the number whilst somebody else had the power to pick or discard you at will.

'Fuck,' she mouths, pulling the fridge open viciously and grabbing one of the bottles of Chardonnay she'd bought for the weekend.

She fills a glass to the brim and takes a hefty swig, before topping it up again. She could try and get a bonded place –

they were always advertising them in the running magazines with the added, unwritten condition you rake up a couple of thousand pounds first. Where the hell was she supposed to get that sort of money? Certainly not from the PTA, she concludes grimly.

She's half way through her second glass when the phone rings. It's Fran, her voice breathy with excitement.

'Shell? It's me, guess what...?'

'What?' Shelly inquires, knowing what's about to follow.

'I'm number sixteen thousand four hundred and forty three – can you believe it? I just had Gela on the phone. She's eight thousand nine hundred and something. I can't believe we're doing this!'

'I'm not,' Shelly states dully. 'I didn't get a place.' The fact she's the only one to be turned down, makes her feel even worse.

'What? How come?' Fran inquires.

'Who knows?' She glances at the letter again which says, 'once again demand for places has far exceeded supply.'

'How come Gela and I got in?'

'Luck of the draw,' Shelly states, unable to shake off the feeling it's something personal. She takes another slug of wine, adding, 'they must have had more than 30,000 applicants.'

'God there are a lot of lunatics out there,' Fran comments.

There's a silence then she says, 'we could apply for the following year. It would give us more time to prepare, get really fit? I'll be thin by then,' she adds.

'There's no guarantee you and Gela would get in again,' Shelly points out. 'Which means we'll be in the same situation.'

'Well we're not doing it without you,' Fran states firmly.

'I could apply for a bonded place, but that means I won't be able to run for MEMBERS. Plus most charities want at least a grand up front.'

'We could raise it,' Fran insists. 'Ask everybody we know. I've already been promised quite a bit from the school.'

'Those mothers wouldn't piss on me if I was on fire,' Shelly says gloomily.

'Oh, Shell, we'll find a way. We can't give up now! Look why don't you come over? I'll call Gela. We'll discuss it over lunch.'

'No, you come here,' Shelly says, glancing at the half empty bottle. 'I've plenty of food in the fridge.'

All those tantalising treats she'd bought for Bruce at the beginning of the week were still untouched. He was spending nearly every evening at the Climbing Centre now.

'Right,' Fran says, 'we'll find a way around this – I've told everybody I'm doing it. Not that they believe me!'

Shelly has an image of all those smug faces and knowing smiles she would have to face, once it became common knowledge.

I don't think anybody thought we'd ever actually go through with it, she thinks miserably.

***

Shelly is half way through the second bottle of wine by the time Fran and Gela arrive. She waves her hand at the fridge saying, 'help yourself – there's loads to eat – I'm not hungry.'

Fran takes control, pulling out tubs of hummus and taramasalata, olive bread, a wedge of camembert, sun blush tomatoes.

'There's a whole delicatessen in here,' she says in awe, glancing at tins of gourmet paté, bunches of asparagus, an M&S chocolate torte, a passion fruit pie. Food for lovers, she concludes, an image of her and Gerry naked and blindfolded (he'd need to be) feeding each other asparagus tips dripping with butter.

She hasn't told the others about that passionate encounter

yet (what with Gela's grim warnings of retribution) whilst Shelly would surely trample on all those romantic notions – kill them stone dead.

'Eat what you like,' Shelly says. 'It'll only go to waste.' She should have learnt by now the way to Bruce's heart was not through his stomach – that he was, and always would be a steak and chips man. 'Plates and mugs are in that cupboard. Have some wine,' she urges, sloshing some into a glass and handing it to Gela.

'If I drink wine, I'll want a cigarette,' Gela points out, 'and I'm only allowed to smoke in a crisis – oh what the hell?' she adds, taking a sip.

'Do you have any diet coke?' Fran inquires, pulling open a cupboard, stacked with sports drinks, glucose tablets, power bars and a large tin of something called BODY POWER sporting a man with hugely inflated pecks and a six pack.

'Are you taking this stuff?' Fran demands, studying the label, curiously.

'It's Bruce's,' Shelly says quickly, 'he's trying to build up for his climbing trip.' She doesn't want them knowing she's been swallowing hefty doses of the stuff. It was meant to be her secret weapon.

Fran frowns. 'I read up about sports products – a lot of them contain anabolic steroids which can damage your kidneys, and even your heart, and in the long term cause osteoporosis and a whole host of health problems.'

'Oh, that one is just creatine, which is found naturally in the body,' Shelly says dismissively. 'A lot of sports people take it.' She too has been reading up about Performance Enhancing Products or PEDS, has come to the conclusion there was no harm in taking them, at least in the short term.

'Anyway,' she says moving on, 'I'm out of the race, which means I can have a drink when I feel like it … cheers,' she adds bitterly, raising her glass.

'Gela and I have been discussing it,' Fran begins. 'We

thought we'd apply for one of those bonded places you mentioned, and find a way to raise the money.'

'I know Marcus will help,' Gela puts in. 'I'll get him to ask everyone at the office. We could pool the money and run for the same charity. I wouldn't mind – it's all for a good cause.'

'Why not?' Fran says, cutting herself a thin slice of olive bread and spreading it liberally with hummus.

'You wanted to run for breast cancer for your Aunt,' Shelly points out, knowing it was something close to Fran's heart. Fran had even announced her plan to have IN LOVING MEMORY OF LETTIE emblazoned on her t-shirt.

Now she shrugs. 'It doesn't matter – Lettie would understand.'

Shelly shakes her head. 'It was your mission,' she says re-filling her glass. The alcohol is not lifting her spirits, rather she seems to have drunk herself sober.

'My mission was to lose weight,' Fran states, looking longingly at the melting camembert. 'To be honest I had no intention of doing the bloody thing – I just went along with it to get you off my back. Then that boob scare made me think about things and I decided I'd have a go. Raise some money for breast cancer along the way. But I'd be more than happy to support some other worthy cause.'

'It was always for ourselves,' Gela admits. 'For me it was a way of getting out of the house, becoming inspired, write that novel.'

Shelly sighs. 'I could still train you both up.' She could then sit back and watch them run the race. She would be off the hook, free from all the doubts and fears. Yet the idea of Gela and Fran reaching the finishing post without her is unthinkable.

In any case Fran is having none of it. 'No way,' she declares. 'You said we were all in this together. Now how do we go about getting this bonded place?'

'The bigger charities tend to have more to give away.' Shelly picks up Marathon News adding, 'there are loads of them in here, but quite frankly I can't be arsed ringing around all of them.'

'I'll do it,' Fran says, grabbing the magazine.

'And I'll work on getting us sponsors,' Gela adds.

Shelly remains silent. I'm meant to be in charge of this mission, she thinks angrily.

'I'll make a list,' Fran says, giving in and cutting a wedge of camembert.

Shelly empties her glass, whilst Gela lights a cigarette saying guiltily, 'I know I shouldn't but this is a bit of a crisis.'

A boozer, a smoker, a fat cow and only two places between us, Fran thinks. It's not looking good.

Shelly gazes into her empty glass with a bleak look.

'Bruce predicted I'd never cross the starting line,' she says at last.

PART TWO

— Chapter Sixteen —

The following sixteen week schedule for Beginners and Intermediate runners will take you all the way to the finishing line! Mr Dippy writes. Remember success is a journey, not a destination!

Shelly stares at the programme gloomily – they were already way behind before they'd even begun it seemed. Since Christmas the training had fallen apart, and now as the New Year got underway, she was finding it impossible to get back on track. With no confirmed place, and the promise of only a couple of hundred pounds in sponsor money, it was hard to remain motivated.

Fran's announcement that MEMBERS Against Male Cancer had a bonded place with the added condition the runner pledge seventeen hundred pounds, had done nothing to spur her on.

'There's no way I can raise that kind of money,' she'd argued, 'forget it!'

Since returning from a week's break in the Lake District, she finds herself sinking into that dark place again, has been having those 'falling' dreams in which she's hurtling helplessly to the ground, only to wake with a violent jolt just before landing.

It was meant to be a romantic break, just her and Bruce – intimate evenings over a bottle of wine, plenty of sex (she'd bought a new outfit). More than anything, it was an attempt to bridge the ever increasing gap between them. She'd found a beautiful lodge on the edge of the lake, with a swimming pool for Gary; a place where Bruce could climb and she could run, where they could go for long walks together. Bruce had arranged for his daughter, Becky to join them, which meant she could keep an eye on Gary, so all in all it was perfect. Until the announcement that Ian and Marissa and another couple of climbing mates were staying close by, and keen to link up.

'I thought we were going to do things together for once,' she'd fumed.

'It's only a days climb and dinner,' he'd argued. Besides it would free her up to get on with her own training rather than hanging around the base of some rocky gorge waiting for him to descend.

An eight mile run through an alien landscape had done little to lighten her mood. All the same she'd gone to meet them at the descent, arriving at that bleak spot of outcrops known as Devil's Claw to find Bruce and Marissa still tethered together half way up, calling out to one another in the familiar tones of a couple lost in the thrill of a shared passion. Ian and the other two had apparently descended earlier and gone back to their hotel. It was the slippery slope, Shelly had concluded, anger and jealousy churning in her stomach. Bonds were formed in extreme conditions. *Besides, we're the ones who are meant to be tying the knot.*

Over dinner, the conversation had returned again and again to the days climb. Nobody inquired after her run – which route she'd taken, how far she'd gone. Even when Bruce mentioned she was trying to raise a couple of thousand pounds for a bonded place in the Marathon, Marissa had shifted the conversation back to a sponsored climb she'd done in aid of childhood leukaemia. Shelly had gritted her teeth and reached for the wine bottle.

Bruce had tried, in his clumsy way to include her, saying, 'Shell's starting to build some serious muscle from all the training.'

He didn't know she was taking supplements. Yet as soon

as they were alone, he was distant and monosyllabic, refusing to concede that Marissa had monopolised him all evening.

'I reckon she fancies your ass,' she'd said, 'I saw the way she was clinging onto your rope, trying to reel you in.'

'Don't be daft,' he'd hit back. 'She's engaged to Ian.'

'So how come she always attaches herself to you – literally?' Shelly suspected it was some kind of ploy to make Ian jealous.

'Ian's a more experienced climber,' he'd pointed out. 'Besides, it's better not to climb with your partner.' There was that cold little word again. Only Ian and Marissa were supposedly engaged.

'Funny they still haven't set a date for the wedding,' she'd stated.

'They're together aren't they?' Bruce had muttered, 'what is it with women and marriage? You're all obsessed!'

Shelly had turned away, thinking they were no further along the road. A bit like the training, she thinks gloomily. A freezing snap had turned the lanes to ice, which hadn't helped. This morning Fran had slipped and fallen, grazing both knees, whilst Gela who had complained bitterly and consistently about the cold, insisted they turn back before they broke their necks.

Shelly had finally given in. She simply didn't have the will or the energy to push the others on. It was all she could do to keep herself going. She can feel it slipping away – the dull anti-climax of a dream that's starting to fade.

Maybe it was out of reach all along, she concludes.

***

Gela was finding it hard to get back into the routine too, after returning from a week of glorious sunshine and snow in the French Alps. She had skied well, thanks to her new level of fitness, had even managed to join Marcus on some of the more difficult slopes.

The old closeness was back between them. On the last

night he'd presented her with a heavy gold bracelet; two bands cleverly linked together with a diamond clasp. When she'd asked what the occasion was, he'd shrugged, saying, 'just wanted you to know I'm always with you, even when I'm not.'

It was only when they were back at Manor Farm and he was preparing to leave for London, she'd steeled herself to say, 'so have you made any decisions about the partnership?'

He'd frowned, already mentally on his way. It wasn't the moment to talk about decisions – as usual her timing was wrong. Perhaps subconsciously, it was her way of not having to face the answer.

'Paolo has a different style of management to mine,' he'd answered, glancing around for his car keys.

Hope had flared for a moment only to be dashed the next.

'No doubt we'll find a way forward. In fact I've invited him and his girlfriend up for the weekend – give you a chance to get to know him better! Maybe you could go for a training run together!'

'When?' she'd demanded, dry mouthed.

'Oh, sometime in the next few weeks,' he'd answered, picking up his briefcase and kissing her on the forehead.

'Just stay cool,' Shelly had emphasised when Gela had announced this new twist in the tale. 'And for fucks sake don't go all confessional.'

'They say you should never admit to having had an affair,' Fran had added intently. She had recently become an avid reader of confessional magazines – articles such as "*SHOULD I TELL MY HUSBAND I'VE BEEN CHEATING ON HIM?*"

Gela wasn't so sure. Back and forth went the argument, until she was worn out from it all. It was a moral dilemma to which there was no answer, she'd concluded. It had started to eat away at her, leaving her mentally and physically drained.

All she wanted, was to climb into bed, switch her electric

blanket on and wake up preferably in the Spring to find this whole nightmare with the partnership had miraculously resolved itself.

**

It was Fran who was driving them forwards now – Fran who'd continued tramping the lanes over Christmas, asking everyone and anyone to sponsor them. She'd even approached a group of workmen digging up the road and been rewarded with a lecherous grin and two crumpled five pound notes. Yet in spite of her efforts the total amount raised so far remained disappointingly low.

Now as they gather in The Charlton Arms after the morning's aborted run, she says, 'we just need one generous sponsor to write us a fat cheque, and we're there.'

She'd urged Brian to ask everybody at work, but he'd claimed it was too soon after Christmas, nobody had any money left. He still hadn't added his own name to the list of sponsors – was clearly hoping the whole thing would fall apart now that Shelly had no place, which made Fran more determined than ever.

He'd gone on to lecture her about the dangers of running alone.

'You and Chloe could always follow me on your bikes,' she'd suggested. 'You could both do with the exercise!'

But neither of them had taken up the challenge, so she'd set off alone, along a now familiar route, up Charlton Hill towards Butcher's Cottage, but each time the lights had been off and there was no sign of the red Land Rover. She is beginning to feel she has dreamt him up – yet the memory of that encounter remains vividly alive, like a permanent ache inside her.

'I've been racking my brains thinking of ways to raise the money quickly,' she says now. 'We could announce we're running it naked! On the other hand, people would probably pay me to keep my clothes on!'

'And there would be nowhere to pin our numbers!' Gela points out.

Shelly breathes out impatiently. 'This business of raising money is worse than running the fucking thing.'

She's about to order herself a gin and tonic and to hell with it, when Fran says, 'the thing is we don't have a choice. We've got to find the money somehow … you see, I've made a pledge to MEMBERS. I signed the form, agreeing to raise the full amount. I sent it off the day before yesterday.'

'You what?' Shelly breathes.

'They were about to give away that bonded place. I didn't have a choice.'

'How much?' Shelly demands.

'As I said, they want one thousand seven,' Fran says quickly. 'It's a small charity, it needs all the funding it can get.'

'That's a lot of money,' Gela states.

'And where are we supposed to find it? Considering all your efforts have produced the sum total of two hundred quid?' Shelly says caustically.

'I've been promised a couple of hundred,' Gela says.

'Ah great, only another one thousand three to go,' Shelly snaps.

'Look no one's going to sue us if we don't raise the full amount. They're a charity for Christ sake,' Fran says hotly.

'Well that's something! I take their precious gold bonded place and hand in three hundred pounds saying, let's just call it quits. They've probably bought the place for more than we'll ever manage to raise between us! At this rate I'll be costing them! I mean no pressure or anything!' She turns towards the bar, calling, 'give us a gin and tonic would you Dave – in fact make it a double.'

The Fat Controller raises an eyebrow. 'Bit early in the week isn't it?'

'Yeah, well, the week never started as far as I'm concerned.'

'Look you wanted to run this bloody marathon,' Fran points out.

'I wanted to run a marathon, not a fund raising event,' Shelly says loudly, causing a hush to descend over the pub.

There's a strained silence, then Fran says, 'are you sure?'

Shelly leans forward, her eyes glittering. 'What exactly are you getting at?'

'I mean, how come having to raise the money is such an issue? Could it be something else? Like the long slog ahead of us? Having to give up the booze?' she adds, waving at Shelly's gin and tonic.

'Bullshit,' Shelly snaps taking a swig. 'I hardly drink these days – and anyway, you're the one who's always moaning about the long slog ahead!'

'Calm down both of you,' Gela urges. 'This isn't getting us anywhere.'

'You're right,' Fran snaps, grabbing her car keys. 'I've had enough. I'm going home. But one thing's for sure, I'm not ready to wimp out yet, even if you are!'

If I stop now, I'll never get going again, she thinks.

'I'll be in the car park on Monday morning ready to do the distance if either of you want to join me?'

'What is up with her?' Shelly mutters, as she heads for the door.

'I'm not sure,' Gela answers, with a frown.

'I reckon she's having an affair,' Shelly states, after a silence.

'The gardener?' Gela says. 'I did wonder, although she hasn't said anything to me. On the other hand, maybe she just wants to see it through. You know – reach the finishing post. Fran's not one to give up easily. We shouldn't either. Especially having got this far.'

Yet another unfinished story, Gela thinks.

When Shelly doesn't reply, she adds, 'Look we can't stop now – we've told everybody! Jasmine Fellows will have a field day! We're going to have to keep going …,' she hesitates, before adding carefully, 'but one thing's for sure, we can't do it without you.'

— Chapter Seventeen —

Speedwork or interval training helps to break up the monotony of a long training run, Mr Dippy writes. It can clear lactic acid from tired muscles, stave off cramp and refresh you. It's also handy if you're planning to pass somebody or make a quick get away! By pushing your body to the limit with controlled bursts of effort, your heart and lungs will become more efficient which will help if you hit a trough...

Gela feels her lungs are about to burst as she races along the rise as if pursued. There is a kind of release with each burst of speed, she thinks – a temporary respite from the calamitous jumble in her head.

'Fifteen seconds to go,' she hears Shelly shout from behind.

Since the row over the sponsor money, Shelly was back in force, appearing in the car park on Monday morning as if nothing had happened. 'We need to get a move on,' she'd said gruffly, 'we've a lot of miles to make up. Oh, and this is from Bruce and the gang at the peat farm,' she'd added, handing Fran a cheque for three hundred and fifty pounds.

'Great,' Fran had replied equally coolly, 'please say a big thank you from all of us.'

'I will,' Shelly had answered, before moving on to the new training schedule she'd drawn up over the weekend, an intense programme incorporating Mr Dippy's three key runs.

'Time's up,' she calls out now.

Time is up all right, Gela thinks grimly.

Marcus had announced that Paolo would be arriving this evening – alone (the girlfriend was not coming after all which was ominous). Marcus had asked her to book a table for three at Ashlington Falls, with the warning they might be late. He'd suggested she dig out a bottle of champagne from the cellar and put it on ice, no doubt to celebrate the partnership, which was to be signed and sealed the following week.

If only it was a novel, whereby she could control the sequence of events, a dilemma in which the heroine had to choose, in this case between ruining her husband's career, or her marriage. With fiction you could usually find a solution – bring in some hidden factor, surprise the reader with a revelation that comes as a bolt from the blue, yet deep down they had suspected it all along.

'For Christ sake woman, slow down,' Shelly gasps. 'You need to recover before the next burst. Get your heart rate down.'

'Sorry I was miles away,' Gela breathes, wishing that were the case.

'So is Fran by the look of things,' Shelly says, glancing around impatiently. 'We'll have to push on without her.' She glances at her watch, saying, 'right ten seconds … five ... four ... three ... two … one … go!'

It'll be all right, Gela says to herself as they storm into the car park. And if the worse should happen, and the truth came out, she would deal with it. After all she spent her life preparing for the worst.

Now as she drives home some two hours later, having been coerced by Shelly and Fran into The Charlton Arms for a drink followed by another, she feels almost calm. Perhaps it was a good thing she and Paolo would meet again. It might lead to some kind of resolution, and like a saga that has dragged on far too long – closure.

She turns up the driveway, her heart stopping at the sight of two cars parked side by side. Marcus's new Audi, which he'd bought for dashing back and forth to London in record time, and a glossy two seater convertible – a Jag by the look of it, black and squat with the crouched and predatory look of something about to pounce.

Her first thought is to reverse and drive away, but where to? She'll have to face them at some stage. 'Shit,' she breathes, tilting the mirror and shrinking from the sight of her fringe which has curled into two perfect ram's horns. The rest is waving around her face like some undulating underwater plant.

A vision of the kitchen flashes through her mind. She hadn't even cleared the breakfast away or taken the rubbish out.

She leans against the car for a moment, wondering if she could slip away through the back gate, across the fields claiming she had to put in some extra miles, but then what? She could run and run but where the hell would she hide?

She takes a deep breath, groaning. The air is foul today (at least eighteen in the gagging order) then makes her way slowly towards the front door. She steps into the kitchen, almost tripping over an expensive overnight bag; tan, leather, with a French designer label.

She can hear raised voices echoing from the sitting room, where they have retreated (no doubt from the mess). The dustbin bag is still there – fat and bulging, and none too fragrant beside the door. She tiptoes towards the stairs, planning to take them two at a time, before diving into the shower, but Marcus has his antennae out and has spotted her.

'Angel, there you are! I left a couple of messages on your mobile telling you we were on our way. We finished the meeting early so decided to get going – skip the traffic.'

'I would have come back earlier had I known,' she says, taking in the black-haired figure on the sofa.

'I told Paolo how busy you are writing sagas and running marathons,' Marcus states, loyally.

Paolo stands up and flashes her a dazzling smile. Were his teeth always that white she wonders?

'Angela,' he says, putting out both arms in a welcoming gesture as if he's the one on home turf.

She freezes, aware of her mad hair, and smudged eyes, not to mention her sweaty armpits and muddy trainers. He on the other hand looks smooth and glossy – expensive clothes, black hair, swept back artfully from his forehead, just the hint of a tan. His face looks sharper than she remembered – the nose slightly beaky – almost vulpine. Even at this crucial moment she finds herself taking notes, noticing the way his mouth has a slightly cruel twist, remembering how she had cast him as the handsome rogue.

His sleeves are rolled up, showing off a heavy gold Rolex. Even the hairs on his arms look glossy and conditioned.

'Hello Paolo,' she says at last.

He grins and steps forward, kissing her on the cheek, sending her hurtling back through time and space to that musty back office in Primrose Hill, when he'd loomed over her, naked and triumphant, breathing, 'God Marcus is a lucky bastard.'

'You're looking fit,' he states, 'how's the training going?'

'Fine,' she answers, trying to pull herself together. 'I gather you're running the marathon, too?'

'For my sins!' He raises one eyebrow, adding, 'I was kind of pushed into it. I haven't really got the time to train properly. Bought one of them fancy running machines, but it hasn't taken me very far!' He grins at his own joke.

He's the type of person who could probably pull it off with hardly any training, she thinks sourly.

'I'm hoping to join you on your run tomorrow morning, although you'll have to be gentle on me!'

'I don't run at the weekends,' she begins, but Marcus cuts in, saying 'you could do a short circuit. Show Paolo a bit of the countryside.'

He gazes at her intently, willing her to comply.

She shrugs, feeling as if events are already running out of control.

'How far do you want to go?' Marcus is asking him now.

'As far as she's willing to take me,' Paolo answers obscurely.

'I don't know how fit you are,' Gela says, sensing some kind of game is being played without understanding the rules.

'Why don't you take him around Charlton Lake?' Marcus suggests. 'It's about a five mile circuit.'

'Sounds perfect,' Paolo smiles. 'I shall look forward to it.'

The following morning he's waiting for her downstairs, dressed in acid green shorts, and a black t-shirt with HELP THE HOMELESS emblazoned on the back. On his feet, a pair of gleaming white trainers.

He's already helped himself to some grapefruit juice, and is standing by the dresser, gazing at a photo of her and Marcus on their wedding day.

'Well hello there,' he says, turning his dark gaze on her, 'sleep well?'

She nods, although she'd barely slept, had tossed and turned, glancing at the clock every hour, searching for a way forward.

Over dinner, Paolo had been polite and attentive, deftly steering the conversation away from business, with 'this must be deadly boring for Angela.'

'Not at all,' she'd answered. She'd been listening to every word, wanting to learn more about the proposed venture, if only to confirm what she'd suspected all along; that the idea behind FINE WINES had been Marcus's from the start. Paolo had simply bought into it and was now dictating how it should be run. Only he lacked Marcus's flair and polish, not to mention his knowledge of wines and ability to speak several languages. He also needed a hefty investment to get them up and running.

She sensed there was already a power-struggle, had noticed an undercurrent of tension between them over dinner.

They'd even argued over the wine, Marcus questioning Paolo's choice of a 1977 Bordeaux claiming it was a bad year. Paolo had snapped the menu closed, saying tightly, 'fine! You choose. Be my guest.'

Yet surely he was the guest? Gela thought.

Over dessert – a lemon sorbet that set her teeth on edge, he'd asked her about her training, wanting to know what time she was hoping to do on the day.

'I just want to finish,' she'd replied shortly.

'She'll finish all right, and do a good time,' Marcus had intervened.

Paolo had smiled oddly. 'I've no doubt. Who was it you said you were running for?'

'MEMBERS, the charity for male cancer,' (dicks like you) she felt like adding. She'd gone on to explain how they were trying to raise seventeen hundred pounds for Shelly's bonded place.

'I had no trouble getting in,' he'd stated, with the airy tone of someone who's never turned down. 'Decided to run for those poor sods who don't have a roof over their heads. I know what it's like to live rough.' He was always referring to his lowly beginnings in the East End of London, working behind a market stall – if only to emphasise the dizzying heights he'd now reached.

He'd insisted on finishing the meal with a bottle of vintage champagne to celebrate their reunion.

'Not for me,' she'd said, 'not if we're running tomorrow.'

'Ah come on,' he'd urged, filling her glass. 'I want to make a toast. To the partnership,' he'd said, raising his glass.

She'd taken a sip, wincing at the strange taste – remembering how it had gone straight to her head, sent her reeling out of control, until she no longer knew what she was doing, had somehow crossed the line, stepping into the shoes of the fictitious Donna – a woman who risks her marriage for a night of passion.

'Hard to believe it was only five years ago I met you guys – working in that shit hole for peanuts,' Paolo had commented.

He's come back to even the score, she'd concluded, queasily.

'Champagne all right for you?' he'd inquired, glancing at her full glass with a frown.

'Champagne has a weird effect on me,' she'd replied, meeting his gaze full on.

'Too much to drink and she changes personality,' Marcus had put in with a grin. 'On a couple of occasions I thought I'd climbed into bed with the wrong woman!' He'd reached for her hand fondly, 'luckily she doesn't do it too often!'

'Really?' Paolo had said with interest. His expression hadn't altered, yet she could almost feel the unspoken words hanging in the air between them.

It can't go on like this, she'd concluded. She was going to have to have it out with him – ask how he intended to work along side Marcus after what had happened.

Now in the cold light of morning he is handing her a blank envelope, smiling grandly, saying 'this is for you.'

'What is it?'

'Why don't you open it?'

He hadn't even bothered to seal it. She pulls out a cheque for seventeen hundred pounds and stares at it in confusion. Blackmail she thinks wildly.

'What's this for?'

'You were saying last night how hard it is to raise money. Couldn't remember the name of the charity so I made it out to you.'

'MEMBERS,' she says faintly. 'It's far too much ….'

'It's for a good cause,' he states.

She shakes her head. 'We've got enough … that is, more has been promised. Thanks but we really don't need this.' She doesn't want his money or anything to do with him, ever. She pushes it towards him but he folds his arms, a strange calculating expression on his face.

'It's for charity,' he emphasises. 'All charities need as much as they can get.'

'Well give it to the charity you're running for – the homeless,' she says, meeting his gaze full on.

'No, I want to sponsor you,' he says firmly. 'Let's just say, it's my way of ... well ... put it like this, starting afresh. Putting a line under the past.'

The line she'd crossed that evening she'd walked into THE WINE CELLAR she wonders? She stares at him coldly, her stomach churning, realisation dawning like a cold fog. She need have no worries, is what he's insinuating. He would never tell Marcus about that night – at least not until the partnership had been signed and sealed, not until he'd milked Marcus for what he was worth, then used his talent and expertise to turn the business into a success.

He is now gazing at a photograph taken soon after they'd moved into Manor Farm, the four of them standing against a backdrop of mauve wisteria, saying conversationally, 'how long have you guys been married?'

'Ten years,' she answers.

'Is it really that long?' he whistles through his teeth.

She nods, wondering where this is leading. The fact that somewhere around the half way mark, she'd veered off the track?

'That is something in this day and age.' He leans against the dresser, stretching out his calves.

'Shall we go?' she says, not wanting to be drawn into a conversation on the sanctity of marriage.

'You should always stretch your muscles before a run,' he comments. He lets go of the dresser and turns around, then lunges forwards one leg stretched out behind him, like a bronzed effigy of a runner poised on a plinth.

'It's better to do it afterwards, when you're warmed up,'

she answers, 'or you can injure yourself.'

'Is that a fact Angela?' He gives her a frank stare. 'I think it's time you and I had a little chat.'

***

Outside, the fields and hedgerows are blotted out by a thick white fog. She shivers under her therma-vest, nerves and the cold making her snap, 'so what is it you want to chat about?' She would let him do all the talking she decides, say nothing until she had all the information.

Only he is dictating when and where this conversation is going to take place. 'Let's warm up a bit shall we? Christ what's that foul smell?'

'Fertiliser,' she answers shortly. It was only about a number five in the gagging order this morning – either that or she must be getting used to it.

'Rural bliss,' he breathes, 'I couldn't do it.'

When she doesn't reply, he adds, 'must be tough with Marcus being away so much?'

'I'm used to it,' she states briefly.

'And to think I could be having a leisurely brunch at Sheldon House?' he jokes. 'Or the Forty Two club.'

She says nothing. She doesn't want to make small talk about the posh places he frequents. She doesn't want to belong to any of his clubs.

She increases the pace, hoping to exhaust him, but he matches her stride easily, inching ahead as they run through the deserted village towards the lake. He even keeps up a conversation, asking how the novel is going, before launching into a description of the book he's planning to write. 'My Grape Escape,' he says. 'How about that for a title?'

It would probably be a best seller, she thinks bitterly.

The way ahead is barely visible (but then it never was) she thinks. The road that leads to the lake has been swallowed up in the mist. But at last, she sees the vague outline of The Trout and Fly ahead, marking the turn off to a narrow farm track that winds around the lake. Tension grips her stomach, the suspense is too much suddenly.

'So what was it you wanted to talk about?' she says again.

He slows to an easy jog, as if they have finally reached their destination, his voice firm, business like.

'That what happened between us that night, is as far as I'm concerned our secret.'

So she was right. She feels sick suddenly. 'I don't have secrets from Marcus,' she answers stonily, 'I think he should know, since you're going to be working together.'

'What do you hope to achieve by that?' he inquires, his tone sharp.

Peace of mind, she thinks. An end to the partnership – the fear that Marcus might lose everything – a happy ending.

'I think if he knew, he would pull out,' she says icily.

She has, she realises with a jolt of satisfaction disarmed him. His face is tense now, his jaw set. 'So you want to fuck up this whole deal, because of some stupid guilt trip you're on?'

Deal...she thinks wildly, that's what it is to him. As for the guilt trip, surely he was part of it too?

'...I would have credited you with more intelligence.' Anger has changed his voice, brought out the nasal tone of his East End accent.

'That night,' she blurts, 'did you put something in the champagne?'

She registers the shock on his face and realises she's gone too far, crossed that line again, that the suggestion with all its implications has altered everything. For a moment he looks as if he's going to kill her – batter her to death on this lonely track and throw her body into the lake. Her teeth are chattering – all the heat seems to have left her body.

She takes a step back, hears him say nastily, 'give me a break – you were begging for it – gave me a whole sob story about being alone on your birthday ... you wanted it as much as I did!'

'That's not true,' she says wildly, trying to calm her jagged nerves – telling herself he was no murderer – just a wheeling dealing opportunist, who would grab at anything on offer. 'I never wanted drunken sex with you!'

'I didn't come knocking on your door at ten o'clock at night! There's no way you can point the finger at me. And if you try – I think it will reflect worse on you than on me! A woman who can't hold her drink, who undergoes a complete personality change – give me a break! You literally don't have a leg to stand on,' he grins, as if struck by the double irony.

She takes a step back, filled with anger and revulsion. He was right – none of her arguments would stand up to the overwhelming evidence that she had walked into his trap like the proverbial fly.

'I'm going home,' she says, turning away. The bad feeling has turned into the profound knowledge that the partnership must not go ahead.

She starts to jog along the track, but he's grabbing her arm, his voice low and confidential as if trying to reason with her now. 'Look, Angela, this is a unique opportunity for Marcus. You're talking big money. We're that close to finalising it – don't fucking screw it up for him now.'

For him or for you, She thinks?

She jerks away, saying 'I need to get back ...'

She's aware of his heavy tread behind her.

Keep calm, she breathes, accelerating, Coleridges tale of guilt and retribution suddenly coming to mind.

Like one that on a lonesome road,
Doth walk in fear and dread...

Like the Ancient Mariner, destined to tell his tortured tale to every third person he meets, she was going home to tell Marcus.

***

'You're back soon,' Marcus says, as she stumbles into the kitchen. He's tidied up and prepared breakfast. The smell of bacon wafts from the oven. He frowns. 'Everything all right?'

She nods, aware of Paolo coming in behind her.

'How did it go?' Marcus inquires, looking from one of them to the other.

'Good,' Paolo replies, 'she certainly gave me a run for my money!' He is all smiles and oozing charm again, Gela notes with disgust, thinking of that nightmarish run home. He'd remained closely behind her all the way, dogging her every step before accelerating, then surging past her up the hill as if demonstrating his power over her. He'd been waiting at the end of the driveway, gazing up at the old Manor House with a look that turned her to stone. 'Pity to ruin the family dream,' he'd said, as she drew level.

'Well done,' Marcus says now. He looks at her inquiringly as if trying to gauge her thoughts. 'How about some bacon and eggs?'

'I'll just have coffee,' Paolo says, 'Got a lunch meeting at The Savoy. Need to take a shower, then I'll be on my way.'

'So?' Marcus inquires, as soon as he's left the room, 'what is it?'

'I can't explain now – all I can say is, I don't want you going into business with him,' she begins.

'On what grounds? Another one of those bad feelings?'

'Look, he's got this other side, which you haven't seen, I … he …'

'Did he make a pass at you?' Marcus demands suddenly.

'No, but...,' she needs to start at the beginning, but how? Like the opening paragraph of a novel, the words simply won't come. Besides, if she blurts it out now, all hell will break loose.

She can hear Paolo moving about upstairs. He would be coming down soon, walking headlong into Marcus's rage. There would be a dreadful scene. The boys would hear it –

would come rushing downstairs demanding to know what was going on.

'We need to talk later,' she says at last.

Behind him the kettle boils madly, spitting water, which hisses against the hot plate of the Aga. 'Fuck! The bacon,' he says. 'I completely forgot about it.'

He bends down to take it out, muttering, 'can't cope with all this right now.'

***

Paolo leaves straight after breakfast, roaring away in his two seater. She pulls his crumpled sheets off the guest bed holding them away from her, and throws them into the washing machine, along with the used towels, but the house still seems impregnated with the warm Sandlewood smell of him.

Marcus has retreated to his study, saying he needed to go through a couple of reports before next week – no doubt preparing to sign the contract that would bind him and Paolo together for the unforseeable future.

She showers and blow dries her hair, then paces the kitchen unable to settle.

The boys immediately sense her mood. Jamie starts antagonising Matthew who bursts into hysterical tears. She manages to soothe them both, whilst Jamie demands, 'is that man Dad's new boss?'

'No, not really, they are going to be working together.'

'Do you like him, Mummy?' Matthew inquires intuitively.

'No,' she answers after a pause. 'I don't think he's a very nice person.'

It occurs to her Paolo had made no attempt to engage the boys, rather he'd seemed almost uncomfortable around them.

Marcus finally re-emerges from his study looking tense and distracted.

'I'm going to have to leave early,' he announces. 'I've

got a breakfast meeting at eight tomorrow and I've still got to go through some papers I left in the office.'

She takes a deep breath thinking time has run out. She can't tell him now. The boys are clambering all over him, as he prepares for the road.

She follows him outside into the darkening afternoon, rubbing her arms, against the wintry air.

'Look, I'll call you this evening,' he says, putting his laptop carefully into the boot. 'We'll have a proper chat then.' It strikes her that nearly all their worst arguments had been resolved over the phone rather than face to face.

'Do you have to dash off so quickly?' she begins, as he kisses her goodbye.

'I need a quiet evening alone,' he emphasises, 'just to run over a few things.'

And then haltingly at first, struggling to find the right words, before plunging in clumsily, she tells him the whole sordid tale.

***

The following morning, she waits for Fran and Shelly in the safety of her car.

Fran pulls open the door, saying 'Jesus Gel – you look awful! What's happened?'

Shelly is hovering behind her. 'You look like shit,' she emphasises.

'I told him,' she sobs, 'it just came out. I couldn't go on the way it was … it was terrible … Paolo was ... it was like he was blackmailing me…he gave me this cheque for the Marathon ... the whole amount … called it our little secret, it was a nightmare – so I told him,' she repeats wildly.

'And he took it really badly?' Fran sighs.

Gela nods, the tears pouring down her face. 'Worse. He's left me.'

— Chapter Eighteen —

Fran immediately takes control, ushering Gela out of the car, grabbing her handbag off the seat, making sure she's got her keys.

'Let's get out of here! Too many Mother's from Hell about. 'We'll go back to my house. Brian's working from home today but we'll ignore him.'

'We'll do our twelve miler tomorrow,' Shelly agrees.

'Twelve miles?' Gela says dazedly. This morning she'd automatically pulled on her running clothes and trainers but right now she can barely walk, let alone run. She feels drained from emotion and lack of sleep, with that sense of unreality that comes from changing time zones. She'd asked Jamie to take Matthew to his classroom this morning, saying she wasn't feeling well.

'Will Dad come back from London to make you better?' Matthew had inquired astutely.

'I don't think so,' Gela had mumbled. 'I'll get better on my own,' she'd added, keeping her face averted so he wouldn't see her tears.

What a fool she'd been to blurt it out like that, especially in the light of what had followed.

Fran is now bundling her into the passenger seat, whilst Shelly climbs in behind. The interior smells of some sickly air freshener, making Gela's stomach heave. Not that there's anything in it. She hadn't eaten since breakfast the day before and even then she'd only picked at Marcus's burnt bacon.

To her relief neither of them asks her any questions. Instead Fran says soothingly, 'he'll be back, mark my words,' whilst Shelly mutters, 'total over-reaction. You've damaged his ego, that's all.'

They are pulling into the cul de sac now, towards the neat, half-circle of semi-detached houses, where Fran lives.

Fran leads them into the kitchen and bustles around producing tea and some low calorie biscuits. 'I've green tea if you prefer or how about some flapjack? 'Fraid it's low cal too.'

'Can't face anything,' Gela states.

Fran puts out a selection anyway, and helps herself to one. After all, this is an emergency, she thinks.

Brian appears from the other room, frowning at the sight of the three of them gathered silently around the kitchen table.

'Gela's not feeling too good, Brian,' Fran states, in warning tones.

'Too much pounding the road, if you ask me,' he mutters.

'It's nothing to do with the training,' Fran snaps. 'It's personal.'

'Ah,' Brian nods, withdrawing immediately.

'Marcus will be back,' Fran repeats, 'he loves you to bits – he just needs time to cool down.'

Deep down, Fran is shocked by Marcus's reaction which raises a number of disturbing questions about the wisdom of having even a brief fling.

'You don't know Marcus,' Gela sobs. 'I told you about his first wife, he threw her out that same afternoon.'

'He still took the plunge again and married you,' Shelly points out. 'That's pretty rare,' she adds, with a trace of bitterness. 'You've got two sons together.'

'So what happened?' Fran asks at last.

Gela sips her tea, saying, 'I just couldn't go on the way it was, the whole business was haunting me.'

She tells them everything – from Paolo presenting her with the cheque, and the bizarre feeling he was trying to buy her silence. 'He knew if I told Marcus, it would be the end of the partnership ... look!' she says, producing the crumpled cheque from the inner pocket of her bag where she'd quickly stuffed it, after finding it lying on the dresser. 'Look, he's even made it out to me – the bastard, I'm going to rip it up.'

'Wait a minute,' Fran says, snatching it from her. 'We might as well send it to the charity. After all, everything is in the open now.'

'Absolutely – let him pay for all the grief he's caused,' Shelly agrees.

Gela shrugs, too weak to argue. She moves on to that almost surreal run around the lake, when she'd finally confronted him. 'I asked if he'd put something in the champagne, that night.'

'Oh my God,' Fran breathes.

'Of course he denied it – said I was the one who'd made all the advances, that I was "begging for it",' she quotes with a shudder. She moves on to how she'd finally blurted it all out on the driveway, Marcus's reaction which had gone from incredulity to anger and finally disgust. How he'd suddenly put his head in his hands, in what seemed like a parody of despair, breathing, 'I don't believe this!'

Then the questioning had begun. 'Did he or did he not force himself on you?'

Her blundering replies, struggling to find the right words, 'well yes and no – he plied me with this weird champagne. It could have been spiked.'

'Spiked!' Marcus had echoed, cynically. 'More to do with your taste buds and the fact you can't hold your drink. Did he or did he not force himself on you?' he'd repeated.

'If you're asking did he rape me then no, not in that sense' (although that's what it felt like) 'but he was really forceful – took advantage of the situation. It was sex without consent, because I wasn't in any position to stop him.'

'Ah,' he'd said, sounding like a lawyer preparing for the next line of questioning. 'So what were you doing going in there so late?'

'I went in to buy a bottle of wine.'

'There was plenty of wine at home,' he'd pointed out.

'Yes, but I wasn't going to open your precious Chablis,

just for myself – as you're always saying, I don't have the taste buds to appreciate it. You would have considered it a waste! Anyway I wanted some crisps, those sea salt and cracked pepper ones they sold in there.' Had she hoped to convince him by going into the finer details?

'So you drank a bottle of champagne with him and then what?'

'I don't know exactly ... all I know is I never planned to have sex with him. I was writing AN INNOCENT AFFAIR at the time – remember? About the woman who risks everything for a night of passion...'

He'd looked at her blankly.

'I was trying to get into the character's head, imagine how it would feel. I wasn't planning on doing it.'

'A night of passion,' he'd repeated cynically.

'For God's sake Marcus, this has been a complete nightmare for me, knowing you were planning to go into business with him, knowing he's a liar, and a cheat.'

'Yeah right,' he said in his icy voice. 'And what does that make you?'

She'd flinched as if he'd struck her. Frustration had caused her to shout, 'you were always away Marcus! There was always some bloody meeting! Like when Matthew was ill ... you weren't there! It was my thirtieth birthday. We were meant to be going to Venice, but work always came first!'

'Yeah right, blame me for the whole thing. You're right, I was too busy trying to build the family dream!'

She'd shivered, thinking how Paolo had used the same expression.

'A home in the country so you could write your novel, working my ass off whilst you went out and got yourself a lover.'

'Paolo was never my lover,' she'd cried, 'he's a manipulative bastard, who wants everything you've got and more! You're so blinded by his success you can't see it! It's like he wants to own you, Marcus.'

It was the most eloquent speech she'd made in years, but he'd shaken his head, saying flatly, 'if Paolo had really forced himself on you, had sex with you without your consent, as you call it, you would have told me straight away. It's as simple as that.'

'I didn't think our marriage would survive. Especially after what happened with Elspeth.'

He'd closed his eyes for a moment as if he didn't want to look at her anymore. 'I can't take this on board,' he'd said, making her freeze. 'Not a second time.'

'So you want to ruin everything because of something that happened five years ago? For God's sake Marcus think about Jamie and Matthew!'

But he'd looked away as if he was no longer hearing her.

'Please Marcus, at least let's talk about it…'

'I need to get on the road,' he'd said stonily.

'When will you be back?'

'Don't know. Might look into renting a bigger flat so the boys can come up.'

'This is madness! Now you see why I couldn't tell you. I should have just kept it to myself. I only did it because I didn't want you putting money into the venture.'

And then the final irony of all. 'I wasn't going to sign. I'd made up my mind to pull out – sever ties from Paolo. I was going to tell you after tomorrow's meeting with a solicitor who's been going through the terms of the contract for me.'

'Fuck me,' Shelly breathes, as Gela reaches the end of this story.

Fran simply shakes her head as if too stunned to speak.

'I should have listened to you both,' she sobs, 'I should never have told him – God knows, I managed to keep it quiet for five years!'

'So why the sudden turn around with the business?' Fran inquires, after a silence.

Gela shrugs. 'I don't know. He did say that Paolo's style of management was different to his, but I was sure it was going ahead. The fact he invited him down for the weekend…' She recalls their raised voices in the living room, the tension between them over dinner. How Marcus was still going over the contract at the last minute. She'd been far too caught up in her own fears to register anything, it seemed.

'He must have seen the light,' Shelly says, wondering if there is any wine at all in Fran's house, (she could do with a stiff drink) 'which means he'll come round once his ego recovers.'

'Shell's right,' Fran agrees.

'He talked about finding a bigger flat in London so the boys could come up,' Gela tells them, her voice breaking. 'God I could do with a cigarette ....'

'No you don't,' Shelly says.

'Have some flapjack,' Fran suggests.

Gela shakes her head.

'Now listen to me girl, you're going to have to pull yourself together, you need to be strong for the training,' Shelly says.

'I couldn't possibly,' Gela says, 'not now.'

'You've got to keep going,' Fran insists, 'it'll keep your mind off it – you can't sit around moping all day,' she adds.

'Everything's changed,' Gela says hopelessly. 'I'm not strong enough for this. I'll never be able to cope. Nothing like this has ever happened to me. I've had such a sheltered life,' she adds.

Both her parents loved her to bits, had always been there for her, even though she hadn't seen much of them lately. Right now they were away travelling across New Zealand, visiting some long lost relatives. There was no way she could tell them about this over the phone. With no brothers or sisters, she had always had their un-divided love and attention – and apart from a couple of unhappy years in a posh boarding school, it had been a trouble free life.

'Of course you'll cope,' Shelly says, 'you're going to have to be strong – and don't you dare start begging him to come back! Don't tell me he hasn't had the odd shag on one of those business trips?'

'I don't think so,' Gela says miserably. 'He's always going on about fidelity.'

'It's not a crime,' Fran points out. 'You just chose the wrong person. I mean a lot of people have affairs,' she adds lamely.

'I'm so worried about Jamie and Matthew,' Gela continues, 'Jamie will go off the rails ... Matthew's so sensitive. This will rock their world!'

'You're going to have to be strong for them,' Shelly says, putting her arm around Gela's shoulders, struck by how bony they are. 'Which means keeping fit, carrying on with the training. We've got that marathon to run.'

— Chapter Nineteen—

'If you can't manage fifteen miles comfortably, then forget about running a marathon,' Mr Dippy warns.

It's becoming a race against time, Shelly concludes desperately. They should be running at least fifty miles a week by now with a distance run of fifteen.

Almost a fortnight had been lost, getting Gela back on track. She and Fran had taken to dropping in every day, in an effort to coax her out. They'd arrived that first morning to find her slumped on the sofa, surrounded by magazines, and discarded chocolate wrappers, gazing unseeingly at the television. Her eyes were red-rimmed from crying, and she'd made no attempt to blow dry her hair. Fran had immediately set about tidying up (apparently the cleaning lady had walked out too, unable to cope with the mess). The dustbin was overflowing with take away pizza cartons and there was hardly any food in the fridge.

'When did you last eat properly?' Fran had demanded.

'Can't face food,' Gela mumbled.

'You need to eat,' Fran stated. God, if only she went off her food in a crisis – she would have lost a ton of weight by now, she'd concluded enviously.

'He hasn't even called to see if we're all right,' Gela wept.

'You've got to pick yourself up, and get back to the training,' Shelly urged, alarmed by how white and drawn Gela looked. 'We need you on board.'

'We can't do it without you,' Fran echoed, but Gela had shaken her head. 'I'm just not up to it.'

After that, they'd taken it in turns to drop in, armed with gifts – the latest best seller (which just happened to be about a marriage in crisis with a happy ending) a bottle of sparkling wine from Shelly (the joke about it being non-vintage champagne had fallen a bit flat) Rescue Remedy from Fran – Ignatia for shock, and apple and walnut for healing. And finally a t-shirt from MEMBERS – they each had one emblazoned with, *Most charities want you to examine your conscience. We want you to examine your testicles. Members Against Male Cancer.* That at least had produced a ghost of a smile.

'We'll give you until Thursday, then we're coming over to drag you out,' Shelly threatened.

'Otherwise we're going to have to send all the money back, which means Shelly will have to give up her place, and I can't do it alone ...,' Fran had added.

Gela had finally given in, defeated, had even managed to run a couple of loops – pushing up Charlton Hill with angry strides, pouring forth her fury over Marcus's announcement he was taking the boys to Ashlington Falls for the weekend.

'It's as if he's trying to punish me and win them over at the same time,' she'd fumed, 'I just don't know him anymore! '

Shelly had listened patiently, as Gela went over the same ground again and again.

Now, as they stand in the car park cooling down, Shelly says meaningfully, 'we need to move on.'

The double entendre is lost on Gela who mutters, 'we might not be there when he comes.'

'You're going to have to park this for now,' Shelly states firmly. 'We've got work to do.'

Gela had turned away with a stricken look.

'Sorry Gel – but you're getting obsessed, and believe me it only makes things worse. As I was saying, we need to get some serious miles under our belts. Do fifteen. I know it's a big step but time's moving on and we're way behind schedule. I need to find a flat route, with no cut off point,' she adds, directing this at Fran. 'We'll stick together – run it slowly. It doesn't matter how long we take, as long as we do the distance.'

'Ashlington Falls must be about fifteen miles away,' Gela says suddenly. 'I don't see why we shouldn't go there too! We could run there, have a sauna afterwards, and a massage, followed by lunch.'

'Bit posh isn't it?' Shelly puts in, 'they won't want three sweaty women arriving for lunch.'

'Or dinner,' Fran comments dryly.

'We could drive over in the morning with a change of clothes,' Gela suggests, 'and measure the route. We'd have to take two cars.'

It's the first time she has shown any enthusiasm for days, Shelly thinks.

'The food is fantastic, they've got this French chef.'

'That's it, you're on,' Fran grins.

***

Distance, Fran thinks, is not simply the space between two places as defined in the dictionary, but something elastic, distorted, and now, as they wind their way through the open countryside, towards Ashlington Falls, apparently without end. She feels as if she's been running forever, that the sight of the tarmac beneath her feet is all she's ever known. When all this was over, she would treat herself to a weekend at a health farm, laze around in fluffy towelling robes and have someone tend to her aching limbs. She can feel herself slowing again – luckily Shelly and Gela appear to be struggling too, Shelly's MEMBER'S t-shirt is dark with sweat. Fran can hear her cursing under her breath as the road ahead rises through another bleak stretch of countryside.

'Can't be much further,' Gela mutters. 'Should be just beyond those fields.'

Fran has grown suspicious of comments such as 'not far', 'just beyond' and 'nearly there.' The truth was distance was horribly deceptive – what seemed like a few centimetres on the map could stretch for eternity.

She groans, knowing there is no short cut home, allowing her thoughts to drift down a familiar avenue – in which Gerry Ryan is leaning over her, massaging her body with essential oils, seeking out those points of pleasure and pain.

He was back – at least she'd seen his Land Rover parked outside The Garden of Eden Centre in West Charlton. She'd pulled in, with a thumping heart, thinking she would buy some more water-lilies, since Brian had pulled out most of them. She'd wandered up and down the potted plant area for a while, then past avenues of saplings, but there was no sign of him. When she returned to her car, the Land Rover had gone making her wonder again, if she'd dreamt him up. Perhaps it was just as well – certainly in the light of Gela's drama, that it remain a fantasy. Yet some things it seemed were out of our control, Fran thinks. Beneath the rationale and reason, more powerful forces were at work. Her heart seems to be permanently accelerated, which couldn't be good, and her chest ached from all that suppressed longing and suspense.

Only yesterday she had driven past the empty Butcher's Cottage again, desperate for a glimpse of him, if only to fuel the fantasy – somehow keep the dream alive.

***

Shelly is flagging too. It always seemed to happen around the ten mile mark – this sudden leaden exhaustion, coupled with a dull ache in her side (she must have strained a muscle during a particularly strenuous session at the gym.) She takes a gulp of her sports drink (this one has added minerals and electrolytes, to replace the sodium, chloride and potassium, lost in sweat) then reaches for her bottle of water. She seems to be permanently dehydrated these days, even though she's cut down on her alcohol consumption dramatically, at least during the week. The weekends however were a different matter. She'd spent the previous one at a wedding of an old school friend (everyone seemed to be getting married suddenly.) Bruce had cried off, saying he'd planned to climb Eden Gorge, but then weddings were clearly not his thing. Shelly had managed to get through two bottles of champagne, which had done nothing to blank out the thought of him and Marissa tethered together half way up the Gorge. Rather she'd ended the night being violently sick. She appears to have become less resilient to alcohol now even though she's so much fitter - which is somewhat ironic. She alters her stride, in an attempt to ease the ache, which has crept into her lower back, cursing her flagging body after all she's done for it. The iron supplements which Fran insisted she take with a glass of orange juice for absorption, the creatine powder for muscle strength, plus she has been working out at the gym most evenings, doing squats and lunges, leg presses and deadlifts, pushing herself to the limit. Perhaps she should try to get hold of some performance enhancing supplements – there was a website where you could order them easily enough. She would only take them for a short time.

'I can see the railway bridge,' Gela announces, 'which means we're not far – it's just beyond the next bend.'

'I've heard that one before,' Fran mutters.

'For fuck's sake pull it back,' Shelly snaps, as Gela surges forward in a burst of optimism. 'We need to finish comfortably.'

Gela feels her heart lifting now they are nearing Ashlington Falls, a sense of detachment from the pain and misery of the last few days. Either that or the pain in her heart has shifted into her legs. She has gone through the gamut of shock, anger, burning injustice, and even the irrational need for revenge. Now she feels strangely calm, ready for the long solitary battle ahead. She still hasn't mentioned the break up to her parents, reluctant to go into the details over a long distance phone call. Besides if it was the end of the marriage, which she fears it might be (looking at the bleak side) then they would know soon enough.

Over the first few days, she'd called Marcus's mobile numerous times starting on a calm note, asking what his plans were, explaining that Matthew was becoming increasingly anxious, and Jamie was getting into trouble at school.

Each time he'd repeated in this terrible flat voice that he didn't have a plan, that right now he needed time, space.

He had plenty of that, she'd concluded cynically, thinking about the spacious company flat he'd moved into, since returning to work full time.

It struck her he was the one who had got her over a barrel now, stringing her along like a high court judge withdrawing from the house to make his final verdict.

The announcement he was taking the boys to Ashlington Falls for the night had tipped her over the edge.

'Don't you think they might wonder why I'm not included in this plan?' she'd stormed.

'I'll tell them you needed a break,' he'd answered calmly. 'Which I'm sure you do from the sounds of it. You were always complaining about being a single mother, even when I was around.'

'You are a complete and utter bastard,' she'd shouted, slamming the phone down, thinking she wasn't going to reason with him anymore. If he wanted out, he could stay out. But she was damned if she was going to make it easy for him to see the boys when he felt like it.

She feels a surge of adrenaline as they reach the bridge – the knowledge she is strong enough to cope after all. After all she's run almost fifteen miles. Surely nothing more can hurt her now. She's ravenous suddenly, could eat a three course meal, plans to order an expensive bottle of wine and put the whole lunch on his bill.

Ahead the road narrows and bends splitting off into a narrow track across some ploughed fields. There is a vile smell in the air suddenly – way over twenty in the gagging order. She clamps her hand over her mouth, muttering, 'oh my God!'

As she rounds the next bend, she sees the source of it – a massive slurry tractor bumping along the mud track towards them. It's pulling out in front of them now, a monstrous thing, oozing slime from its backend – great glutinous trails that swing like elastic snot before spewing onto the ground.

'OHMYGOD,' she shouts again, 'it's going the same way as us!'

'It's just pig shit,' Shelly breathes.

'Jesus,' Fran echoes, 'what do they feed those pigs on?'

'Human shit?' Shelly suggests.

Gela heaves, acid bile rising in her throat. 'We're going to have to pass it,' she shouts desperately.

'Wait 'til the road widens,' Shelly warns, but Gela is accelerating, head down, trying to dodge along its side, ignoring the brambles tearing at her arms. There's an ominous clunk and the next moment the sky is full of black rain. Gela sees it arc into the air, and closes her eyes in horror as it lands on her hair, her face, her shoulders, thudding onto the crown of her head, before sliding down her cheeks.

She dives into the verge, aiming at a gap in the hedgerow, where a thin stream of black water is draining into a slime-encrusted ditch. 'Shit,' she shouts after the driver, 'I'm covered in it.'

'I told you to slow down,' Shelly states, stalling to a halt and looking down at Gela with a mixture of horror and amusement.

'Jesus, Gel, are you all right?' Fran inquires.

'Oh, just great,' Gela snaps. 'I mean, how much more shitty can things get? My life has literally gone down the drain.'

'Oh Gel,' Fran says, biting her lip, trying not to laugh. She and Shelly are pulling her out now, attempting to wipe the sludge off her hair and face.

'Everything is just shit!' Gela moans, glancing at her bare legs, where a trail of the stuff is snaking downwards. 'Looks like I've.... oh God,' she gulps, suddenly seeing the funny side. They are all laughing now, Fran bending over groaning in agony. 'Stop, I'm going to pee on myself.'

'We can't go to Ashlington like this,' Gela wails, as the laughter dies down. 'I need to wash it off. There was a stream a few miles back.'

'I'm not backtracking now,' Fran states firmly, whilst Shelly says, 'they're not going to turn you away. You're a member for fucks sake. Come on. Let's get going before we seize up.'

Gela hesitates. Six months ago she wouldn't have gone to the village shop without blow drying her hair – the thought of arriving at Ashlington Falls in this state is inconceivable. But Shelly and Fran are setting off again, shouting at her to follow. She takes a deep breath, gagging from the smell thinking with irony that Marcus would have cheered her up – joked it was probably the best hair conditioner ever, that he might even be able to market it.

She can see the sign for Ashlington Falls ahead now, with its long tree-lined avenue, hears Fran mutter, 'thank God,' whilst Shelly takes the lead saying, 'well done everybody – fifteen point two miles. We're back on target!'

Thank God, she breathes.

She tries not to think about the eleven remaining miles, still stretching in front of them like some cruel joke. Right now it seems unattainable, forever out of reach.

'Let's go and celebrate. I need a stiff drink.'

****

In the Health Club, languid women lounge around in snow-white robes, and turbans. A couple of them glance up in disbelief as Gela leads Shelly and Fran towards the desk. The sleek blonde receptionist blinks and takes a step back, before muttering something to the older woman beside her.

'Can I help you?' demands the older woman who looks stretched and shiny, plumped up with so many chemicals, she might have been made of wax.

'Yes, we would like a swim and a sauna. After we've had a shower of course.'

'Are you a member?' she inquires, the tip of her nose twitching delicately, her eyes as cold as flint.

God the woman didn't even recognise her. 'Yes, Gela Harvey-Wood. I came by this morning, explained to the other receptionist we were running all the way here from Charlton Haven. We left our clothes in the lockers.'

Surely she wasn't going to turn them away?

'I do need to see your card,' she is saying briskly. All the white robed women are watching this exchange now, with horrified fascination.

'I left it with the receptionist this morning,' Gela says desperately.

The younger woman has found it now. 'Angela Harvey-Wood,' she frowns. 'Don't you have a room booked for the weekend? Yes here it is, Mr Marcus Harvey-Wood and two children.'

Gela feels as if she's been struck in the face.

Shelly moves forward immediately. 'Well that's the weekend isn't it? And today is today! And right now Mrs Harvey-Wood has run fifteen fucking miles to get here. She is a member, in fact we are all members,' she adds pointing to her MEMBERS t-shirt with its reminder to EXAMINE YOUR TESTICLES. 'We are training to run the Marathon in aid of cancer. Now can we have three towels please and the keys to our lockers?'

The waxen-faced woman hands them over wordlessly.

'And if anybody would like to sponsor us,' Fran adds to the silent slanty-eyed onlookers, 'please make your cheques out to MEMBERS against Male cancer.'

— Chapter Twenty —

It hadn't been part of the plan, at least Fran hadn't planned it this time. She'd just dropped into The Charlton Arms on her way back from the supermarket to check if any more sponsors had signed up, and there was Gerry Ryan, large as life and twice as handsome, propped up at the bar chatting to the Fat Controller.

'Well hello!' he'd said, greeting her with that slow smile, sending her pulses racing. 'I've been looking out for you. Where've you been?'

'We've been running different routes – must have covered the whole country by now,' she'd answered, taking in the uncombed hair, and slightly uneven mouth, the moist lips that had left their burning imprint on hers. 'How are you?'

'Better now I know I didn't just dream you up,' he'd grinned.

You're not the only one, she thought dazedly.

'You've lost weight,' he commented, his eyes travelling up and down the length of her body. 'You're not going to disappear altogether, I hope?'

God she loved him for that. 'Fat chance,' she smiled, 'if you'll pardon the pun.'

'Sit down, have a drink!'

She hesitated. 'I'd better get back. I just dropped in to see if any one else had sponsored us.'

Ironically the money was flooding in now – cheques from old school friends and relations, as well as people she'd only briefly met. There was an anonymous donation of thirty pounds, plus a stack of coins after she'd put a collecting box on the hall table asking anybody who dropped in to donate their loose change. Even the Fat Controller had had a whip-round, before handing over forty pounds. It occurred to her that she could now run in aid of breast cancer after all.

'You managed to raise enough then?' Gerry is saying, as she glances at the list, noticing three more names have been added.

'More than enough. Everyone's been so generous,' she turns to the landlord, adding 'thanks again for your support.'

'Barking bloody mad, the three of you,' the Fat Controller replies curtly. 'Not stopping for an Irish coffee then?'

'Irish coffee?' Gerry repeats, with amusement.

'It's the only way I can drink alcohol! Shouldn't really, well all right, just go easy on the cream. I don't want to turn into acres of a woman again!'

'I think you're a beautiful woman,' Gerry had said softly.

And so it had begun – those lunch-time rendezvous, meeting in out of the way pubs, one of which was conveniently called The Hideaway.

'Don't want people getting the wrong idea,' he'd joked, as he led her to a hidden snug at the back. There they would sit over an Irish coffee for her, a pint (or two) of local ale for him, a plate of potato skin dippers between them. For the first time ever she couldn't manage a full portion – her appetite seemed to have deserted her. He was remarkably easy to talk to, although she seemed to do most of it – telling him about Gwen (who called every other day now, with some new ailment) describing how she'd left when Fran was a baby to follow the hippy trail to Katmandu.

'Now she lives on benefits and complains nobody gives a damn about her!' she'd added. 'I suppose it's not her fault. She has no maternal instinct. She was only nineteen when she had me. I was the result of a one-night stand – a celebration of all that free love, only she must have been so high on dope, she forgot to take the pill! I don't know anything about my father except he was another hippy who looked like John the Baptist!'

'Sometimes better not to know,' he'd remarked, adding

his father was a drunken bully, who hadn't spoken to him for years. 'I've learnt to keep away from people who do my head in,' he'd concluded.

He'd moved back to the village in search of a stress free life, he told her, gardening in the summer, lying low in the winter, until the money ran out. Then if he didn't get lucky on the horses, he would pick up work on one of the building sites. He was the proverbial free-spirit, Fran thought, the kind of man she'd always imagined she would end up with – whilst being aware she would never be able to pin him down. But that was fine – it was just a brief interlude, she tells herself, a taste of forbidden fruits, then she would return to her normal life.

He laughed at her jokes, and teased her about her obsession with her weight, telling her she was a magnificent looking woman. Not long ago she would have misconstrued that as large, but coming from him, it sounded wonderful. Even when she'd mourned her flat chest (thinking she'd better warn him) he'd said, 'well you wouldn't want them bouncing around when you run that marathon.'

In any case, he would be the judge of that he'd added, sending a shiver of anticipation and slight fear running through her. For here, it seemed lay the first obstacle. Butcher's Cottage with its peeling walls and rusting hooks, was a far cry from the cosy love nest of her imaginings. Besides, it was far too risky. So instead they would climb into his battered Land Rover and drive through the hidden country lanes to secluded places he knew. He would park out of sight, switch off the engine, and reach for her, but each time he attempted to remove her clothes, she would pull back, unable to cross that line (or the gear stick, come to think of it).

'Not here,' she breathed. 'I want to spend the whole night with you.'

I want the candlelit dinner, a four-poster bed, with linen sheets (Brian insisted on the synthetic ones since they didn't crease) not sex in the back of a Land Rover – with all the gardening tools.

He'd taken it remarkably well considering – teasing her about being a load of hot air. Thank God she hadn't worn her pump-up bra.

'We could go away for a weekend,' she'd suggested, 'find a hotel, where nobody knows us.'

'When?' he'd breathed, kissing her urgently.

'As soon as the training tapers off,' she'd promised.

She'd already laid the groundwork, announcing to Brian that a visit to Gwen was long overdue. She'd even found the perfect hotel in Brian's Michelin Guide, with a superb sounding restaurant and luxurious suites with four poster beds. It was only fifteen miles from Dulcote Marsh where Gwen lived. It was just a question of making the reservation. Yet somehow she couldn't bring herself to pick up the phone.

'You could do with a break,' Brian had agreed, 'a proper rest. Why don't you spend a few days away, treat yourself?'

She wished he hadn't been so accommodating, had put some obstacle in her way. Rather there was something in his manner that alerted her. Lately she'd noticed him watching her from time to time and he'd starting coming back from work early, saying he'd decided to work from home.

Now, as she limps into the hallway, after a gruelling hill session (Shelly had insisted they run up Charlton Hill ten times) planning to shower and lie down for an hour before going to meet Gerry at The Hideaway, she finds Brian is already home, clearing out the broom cupboard. The tidying up had got worse she'd noticed, this desperate need to instil order, as if perhaps he could no longer control what was going on beyond the neat square boundaries of home.

'How was it?' he inquires, his gaze searching.

'Fine, but I'm absolutely knackered. I need to lie down,' she states, her spirits sinking. Now she was going to have to send Gerry a text saying she wasn't able to come. Which reminded her, she also needed to delete all the sent messages just in case.

'How many miles is it this week?' he'd suddenly demanded.

'I don't know – we're doing our distance run on Friday.'

'How far?'

'Oh, about eighteen.'

He was also closely monitoring her training, clocking the miles in his head, calculating the time she was spending on her feet, which was unnerving since some of those miles had been spent in Gerry's Land Rover.

'Do you realise you'll have run over a thousand miles in preparation for twenty six point two?' he says now.

'So what? You spend thousands of hours on the computer, creating databases or some program you'll never even use,' she hits back.

'Oh, Francesca, all I'm trying to say, is you look exhausted, you've lost so much weight!'

'That was the idea,' she answers tersely. 'I need to have a shower.'

'I'll bring you a cup of tea,' he says, with a sigh.

She had flung herself onto the bed for a moment, and promptly fallen asleep, only to be woken by the phone ringing.

'Frannie? It's Gwen! Did you get my messages? I called three times this morning – been having them stomach pains again. Had to go see the doctor.' A list of ailments had followed, including an in-growing toenail, making Fran snap, 'maybe you should take up long distance running, and with a bit of luck it'll fall off!'

There was a silence then Gwen said, 'the doc says I have to have a hysterectomy, means I've got to go to hospital in three weeks time, stay overnight. He's made the appointment. But I need someone to drive me there and take me home afterwards. That's why I called. I been waiting for you to get back to me. You never return my calls.'

'I was out running,' Fran says tightly, feeling a sudden welling anger, wanting to say that what goes around comes around, only her heart has started to accelerate and it's all she can do to murmur, '...call you back a bit later.'

She can hear Brian's footsteps on the stairs, no doubt bringing up a cup of tea and a low calorie biscuit, sees him frown at the sight of her lying on the bed like a beached whale trying to regulate her breathing.

'Right that's it! I want you to pull out of the marathon,' he says heaving her up and jamming a pillow behind her head. 'Long deep breaths, as if you're blowing into a balloon!'

'I'm not pulling out,' she gasps as soon as she can breathe. She fumbles in her bed-side drawer for her Rescue Remedy, adding, 'I can't let Shelly and Gela down. Anyway it's not the training, it's Gwen who's stressing me out, always trying to make me feel guilty.'

'Your mother is one issue, but the fact of the matter is you've got a heart condition.'

'My heart's fine,' she'd snapped. (Even if it's in the wrong place she'd thought). 'I haven't got this far only to pull out! If I feel bad, I'll walk it! Jesus, Brian, try to support me for once!'

'I've always supported you,' he says sounding aggrieved.

'You have not! You haven't even sponsored me, for Christ sake!'

'I was going to talk to you about that, only you're never here!'

'Forget it. We've got enough money now anyway,' she says, moving on. 'You've always put some obstacle in the way .... like when I wanted to do that nutrition course you said it was too far to travel, every time I try to lose weight, you lecture me on my health. I'm starting to feel trapped.'

'Trapped?' he repeats, with a hurt look. 'Can't you see that I'm just concerned about you?'

'I know, but you're beginning to stifle me.'

Whereas, Gerry makes me feel free.

'I'm sorry, but I just can't sit back and watch my wife…'

'Stop watching me then, for Christ sake,' she cuts in. 'Asking me what time I'm coming back, I'm not an invalid, I'm running the marathon, Brian,' (even if it kills me) she'd almost added, 'anyway I hate these synthetic sheets,' she adds, 'they make me itch, and why does everything have to be so bloody…neat…?'

He'd shaken his head as if bemused by this sudden outburst.

As soon as he'd left the room she'd picked up the phone and dialled Gwen's number.

'Look, I could come up in three weeks as it happens,' (the training would have eased off by then). 'What date did the doctor give you? Fine. Tell him I'll drive you to the hospital and stay somewhere close by.'

'I wouldn't want you to go out your way!'

'I'm offering to help.'

'Well it would be a help. I've been ever so worried about the bleeding…'

'Call me back when you've made your appointment,' Fran interrupts.

She'd hung up then dialled Woodstock Manor House in Fernhampton. 'I'd like to book a room with a four-poster bed,' she'd said quickly, pulling out her credit card. Thank God she'd insisted on her own bank account. 'Yes, er, Mrs Fellows, (what had possessed her to use Jasmine's name?).

'Yes, we'll be there in time for dinner.'

— Chapter Twenty-One —

'You should be reaching the peak of your training now running 19-21 miles for your distance run, getting used to time on your feet. Psychologically this is tough as there will be no cheering crowds, or medals at the end – just you and your mental resources. So dig deep !'
writes Mr Dippy.

Shelly has measured out a twenty-one mile route, starting from The Old Foundry, and winding around the edge of the moors where Bruce ran his peat business. From there they would wend their way back towards the village along familiar lanes, finishing at Shelly's house with a celebratory lunch, which she'd prepared in advance.

She has donned her luminous vest and stopwatch, brought extra supplies of water, sports drink and energy bars, and taken one of the performance enhancing supplements she'd ordered off the internet to get her through the ten mile trough.

They had set off almost three hours ago, in the teeming rain, but now as they make their way back to the village, the clouds have disappeared and the sky is a watery blue – as if they have finally emerged from the depths of winter and into the spring.

Fran had kept up most of the way – striding out easily, as if, Gela thought, noticing the spring in her step, she was in another world.

Shelly had managed to prise it out of her as they struck off the miles and the conversation opened up like the long road ahead.

'I know what you're both going to say,' Fran had breathed, 'especially after what you've been through Gel. I know it's not going anywhere, but I don't care – he makes me feel free.'

'As long as Brian doesn't find out,' Gela had said with concern.

'Just go easy on the shagging – remember you've got a marathon to run,' Shelly had put in.

Shelly too, had opened up briefly, disclosing her fears that she and Bruce might have reached the end of the road. But when Fran had suggested there had to be a way forward, that they needed to sit down and thrash it out – preferably not over a bottle of wine, Shelly had clammed up again, shifting the conversation to Gela.

Gela had immediately poured out her worries over Jamie, who was behaving badly again, how he'd announced he didn't want to go to school anymore, had refused to get into the car that morning unless she promised to call Marcus and ask him to come home. And now there was the added and shocking news (she was still in a state of disbelief) that Marcus was already seeing somebody else.

On the evening he'd brought the boys back from Ashlington Falls, she'd been almost beside herself with fury and resentment, had waited until Jamie and Matthew were upstairs, before turning on him and saying, 'look it can't go on like this – splitting up the family over something so ... unbelievably ... trivial!'

He'd remained stiff and silent, his face devoid of expression.

'Trivial,' he'd repeated finally, his pale blue eyes like ice. 'Is that what you think?'

As usual he was baiting her, forcing her to answer her own questions.

'Look, Marcus ... I know I've hurt you ... '

'Do you?'

'For God's sake can't we sit down and discuss it like normal people?'

'What's there to discuss? Frankly I'd rather not know the gruesome details.'

Which meant there was no way forward, she thought, incensed by his hidebound expression. 'Then maybe you should just go!'

'You're right, why don't I?'

She'd pursued him to the door, and flung the dustbin sack out after him.

'You were never there when I needed you, anyway,' she'd shouted.

She'd watched him drive away then burst into floods of hysterical tears causing Jamie to fling himself at her, shouting, 'tell Dad to come back quick! Call his mobile.'

'He doesn't want to come back right now,' she'd sobbed, aware of a white faced Matthew hovering in the background.

It had taken the whole evening to calm them both down, and then she'd lain awake all night terrified they would be traumatised for life thanks to her foolish admission, not to mention Marcus's ridiculous pride.

The news that the weekend at Ashlington Falls had not been a success had initially brought some comfort.

'He was talking on the phone all the time,' Jamie had stated crossly, 'and he was really stressy, and they didn't have any *Nutella*.'

'And we couldn't even go to the pool because Dad was with that lady,' Matthew put in.

'What lady?' Gela had inquired, with a beating heart.

'I don't know,' Jamie had answered. 'She had these really pointy shoes and long black hair.'

'Young or old?' Gela had persisted. Surely he couldn't have met somebody already?

'About twenty five,' Matthew had said to her further alarm, 'but you're prettier Mummy. Anyway I'm never going there again without you,' he'd added, winding his arms around her legs, bringing more tears welling to the surface.

Since then Marcus hadn't attempted to see the boys or lure them to London for the weekend, which was something, yet somehow his silence was even more threatening.

Well he could do a running jump as far as she was concerned. She could manage without him. There was hardly anything she couldn't do – apart from checking the air in her tyres (she'd soon learn) emptying the mousetrap (she'd buy the humane ones and let Matthew release them into the garden). Carving the Sunday roast had never been her forte, but she hadn't bothered with roasts since he'd left. She'd even managed to overcome her fear of being alone at night, and, as if finally released from a straight jacket, she'd started to write - the words flowing onto the computer screen – a gritty account about a sexual encounter told through a single narrative voice. Donna had finally come alive. She would sit at her computer, long into the night, whilst the house creaked and settled around her, pausing every so often to gaze into the black space beyond the window pane, wondering what she had been so afraid of. It struck her there was nothing left to fear now – there was after all life after Marcus, although at times the future seemed as black as the view through the mullioned windows. She couldn't see herself staying in this grand old house alone – not now that the family dream was over.

She can see the village ahead and turns around to check on Shelly. Fran had fallen back some time ago, shouting to them to go on without her. 'Just leave me some lunch for Christ sake!' she'd called. Whilst Shelly seemed to be running on automatic, her face set, rivulets of sweat running down her cheeks like rain water.

Gela has noticed a change in Shelly recently, a kind of nervous energy – a bit like Jamie before one of his hyper fits. This morning she'd seemed pale and edgy, desperate to get going as if perhaps all that new found energy might suddenly desert her. Her body was changing too, becoming visibly more muscular, and she didn't seem to tire so easily, although she complained about a persistent pain in her side. She pushes past Gela now, taking the lead for the final stretch, as they inch their way towards The Old Foundry.

'Twenty one miles,' she breathes, as they stagger into the house. 'We've cracked it! That's it, we can do it....'

'We still have to run another five,' Gela groans. 'Right now, I couldn't manage another step.'

Nor could I, Shelly thinks to herself.

It was as if the finishing post was as distant and illusory, as the rainbows end.

'The crowds will keep us going,' she says, with an assurance she doesn't feel.

Gela flops down onto Shelly's newly covered sofa, and grabs her bag, which she'd brought over earlier with a change of clothes. She attempts to comb her hair, then checks her mobile just in case. There are four answer phone messages. Marcus, she thinks, glancing at the number on the screen. Now what? Was he calling to announce he was moving in with the raven haired woman with the pointy shoes?

His voice sounds gruff and strained, and as cold as ever. 'Call me back, when you get in,' he says.

The second message is from Jamie's teacher, Miss Baine. 'Mrs Harvey-Wood, I would be grateful if you would call the school straight away, on my direct line.'

'Jamie,' she breathes, the sweat on her body turning to ice.

The third message is from Marcus again, saying 'have you heard anything?'

And finally a brief message from the headmistress telling her not to panic and that everything was being done to find Jamie.

'Oh my God,' she cries, dragging herself to her feet, pain piercing her calves and hamstrings, like knives.

She's aware of Shelly hovering beside her, saying, 'what is it? What's happened?'

'It's Jamie,' she cries. 'He's run away from school!'

Shelly is now taking over, picking up the landline and

dialling the school.

'When, what time?' Gela hears her demand. 'So you last saw him after lunch, in the playground? Yes, but what time was that? Hold on a sec, there's someone at the door.'

She limps towards the front door, before reappearing with a dishevelled looking Fran.

Gela hears Shelly mutter, 'Jamie's run away from school.'

Fran staggers across the room and puts a consoling arm around Gela. 'Oh Gel, he'll turn up, try not to worry – I ran away from school when I was that age. I remember hiding in the neighbour's shed.'

Shelly is on the phone again saying, 'did you call the police straight away?'

'I need to get back,' Gela sobs, 'he could be locked out of the house.'

'Apparently somebody has already gone up there,' Shelly says calmly. 'They're searching the school grounds, and the lanes.'

'Oh God.' It's too much, suddenly. She sags against Fran, with a sob, feeling as if she's breaking into hundreds of pieces – will never be whole again.

'Come on, I'll drive you home,' Fran says, 'I walked the last couple of miles, I've still got a bit in the tank.'

'We'll all go,' Shelly says, supporting Gela under one arm and helping her to the door, and into Fran's car. 'They'll find him,' she soothes. 'Jamie's a smart kid, he won't have gone far.'

'This is all Marcus's fault,' Gela says wildly. 'I'll never forgive him if something's happened to Jamie.'

A police car is parked on the driveway. Gela starts to shiver uncontrollably as a young officer appears from one of the outhouses, and walks towards them.

'Mrs Harvey-Wood?' he begins, his eyes instinctively seeking out Gela.

'You haven't found him have you ... oh, my God,' she sobs.

He shakes his head. 'Kids do this all the time. Try not to panic. Was he in trouble at school by any chance, or being bullied as far as you know?'

'He's always in trouble. I don't think he was being bullied. More to do with the fact his father decided to do a runner.'

'I see,' the officer says, absorbing this.

'And where is your husband right now?'

'In London,' Gela replies through chattering teeth.

'I'd like to have another look around,' the officer says. 'Does he have any secret hiding places?'

'Only inside the house. Unless he's managed to climb through a window or something,' she says hope flaring. 'For God sake somebody do something,' she cries.

'She needs to sit down,' Shelly says, leading her towards the front door. 'We've just run twenty-one miles.'

'Good God,' says the officer. 'Are you training for something special?'

'We're doing a marathon,' Fran says, resisting the urge to ask him to sponsor her.

Inside, Fran somehow finds the energy to make a pot of tea, while Shelly picks up the phone again. Gela hears her say, 'they need to comb the whole area straight away – no time to waste – I want to know what's being done.'

Gela sits in a state of frozen shock, trying to push aside the image of Jamie's battered and bloodied body, lying in some shallow ditch. The phone rings again – it's Miss Baine wanting to know if there is any news. 'He did have a bit of a run in with Posy Fellows,' she begins, 'I told him I would be calling you about it. He has been very unsettled lately.'

Jasmine's twin daughters were almost as vile as the woman herself, Gela had discovered.

'Yes well he's been through a hard time – his father's

walked out on us!' Gela flares.

'Ah, I did wonder if something was bothering him.'

Then why the hell didn't you call me? Gela is about to say, before recalling there had been two messages from the school on the answer phone, asking her to call back, only she'd kept putting it off.

Some time later, she hears Fran say gently, 'Gel, Marcus is here. You two need to talk.'

Everybody seems to melt away as Marcus comes into the room. That was how it had been once. Right now, she feels only a burning resentment towards this distant stranger who is her husband. She notices him pause as if he too is unable to cross the great chasm that has opened up between them, hears him say, 'I'm going out to look for him,' and before she can answer, he has turned away again and is making his way towards the door.

Hysteria is rising making her want to scream out loud, only her throat seems to have closed up, and she can't catch her breath. This has always been her worst fear, yet no amount of imagination could have prepared her for the terrifying reality of it all. She is dimly aware of Fran trying to put a mug of hot tea in her hand, whilst Shelly searches the wine rack saying, 'she needs a stiff drink – a brandy.' Shelly pours one for both of them saying, 'listen to me Gel, it's going to be all right. Trust me, they'll find him.'

Some time later – it might have been minutes or even hours – she's lost track, Marcus is back, standing in the kitchen, and she hears a sweet high-pitched voice saying 'Hi Mum.' For a moment she thinks she's hallucinating and then she's staggering to her feet, faint with relief. 'Jamie,' she sobs, pulling him into her arms weeping hot tears all down his neck.

'He was up at Amy's hanging around the stables – waiting for you to come back from your run. I had a feeling he wasn't far away,' Marcus is saying.

Not for him, visions of bloody corpses.

'Sorry Mum, I didn't want to sit at the front of the class anymore – and Posy Fellows called me a lamebrain because I'm dyslexic so I pushed her into the sandpit, and she went mental! I knew they'd call you so I decided to run all the way home and tell you first. You said it was only two and a half miles but it's way longer, I reckon. Then the house was locked so I went to Amy's. Can I stay at home now?'

She nods and pulls him closer.

'Jamie and I have had a chat,' Marcus says, 'I've told him I'll always be here for him.'

Gela stares at him wildly. Do you call this being here? she wants to say.

'I think we should have a word with the headmistress about the fact he's been segregated from the class. It's not the way to handle behavioural problems.'

Once again he was trying to control things from the sidelines. She wants to say all this and more but the constant dialogue that has parried back and forth in her head, has vanished, replaced by the overwhelming relief Jamie was safe. She's aware of Fran and Shelly withdrawing again, Fran taking Jamie's hand saying, 'why don't you show Shelly and me your bedroom and all your toys?'

'Are you all right?' Marcus inquires, as soon as they are alone.

'Fine,' she replies coldly. The fact that some basic instinct had led him to Jamie (whilst she'd been too blinded by fear to think straight) doesn't mean anything right now. For the moment he is the cause of all this – he is the one who has ripped the family apart.

'Well I'll be getting back now,' he says at last, without moving.

'Fine, you go,' she says, finding her voice at last. '...wouldn't want to hold you up. I'm sure you've got meetings...a busy agenda,' or perhaps a dinner date with the woman with pointy shoes.

He takes a step back – his face set, aware that now the crisis is over they are back on hostile turf again.

'You've got my number if you need me,' he says all business like again. He stands there jangling his keys, as if waiting for a further signal from her.

'Are you sure you're all right?' he says again.

She nods. 'I just want you to go,' she says at last.

'Right,' he mutters coldly, 'I'll go and say goodbye to Jamie then.'

She hears his car drive away, is aware of Shelly and Fran coming back into the room wanting to know what happened – hoping for a happy ending.

Gela shakes her head. 'He's gone – we barely talked,' her voice breaks from emotion. 'I don't care anymore.'

'That's not true,' Fran says.

'It's over,' Gela insists. 'Maybe it was over before this happened. We were always on different schedules – we've grown apart.'

And now there's so much distance between us, we can't find our way back, she thinks.

— Chapter Twenty-Two —

You don't need to run a marathon to be able to run a marathon, Mr Dippy declares. That would be counter productive since you will be using up precious energy reserves, as well as risking an injury. Relax – the excitement of the race and the cheering crowds will pull you forward on the day!

Yet Shelly knows instinctively it's going to take more than a crowd of cheering spectators to get her to the finishing line.

'We need to do another long run,' she says, as they gather in The Charlton Arms at the end of the week. 'A proper rehearsal, which will give us confidence on the day.'

'Do you mean run the whole twenty six, point two?' Fran demands incredulously.

'I thought we were meant to be winding down now?' Gela adds.

'We need to know if we can do the distance…' I need to know, she thinks.

'We can do it,' Fran insists, 'even if we have to walk the last bit.'

'Well if you're so confident!'

'I'm not! I just don't want to overdo it – I'm still recovering from the last long run! Anyway all the manuals warn you not to over-train, (Brian had done his research, pulling out pages of information from various running websites) 'at this rate we'll be too bloody knackered to run the thing.'

'I agree,' Gela says, 'I'm exhausted – what with that drama with Jamie. I never knew being a single mother was so hard!'

I'm just going to have to get used to it, she thinks

hopelessly – coping with teenage angst and tantrums, prepare the boys for a fractured life, being sent from one parent to the other....

'Also I've got to pay a visit to Gwen next week,' Fran announces. 'I'll need all my strength for that.'

'I thought you said you weren't going again after the last time?' Shelly says, frowning suspiciously.

'She's got to go into hospital,' Fran says quickly. She doesn't want Shelly knowing she's planned a romantic weekend away with Gerry. 'She's having a hysterectomy – you'd think it was a heart transplant the way she goes on,' she adds raising her eyebrows. 'In any case, Brian will have a fit if I do another long run.'

'Fine,' Shelly says tightly – 'I'll do it on my own – maybe over the weekend in Wales whilst Bruce is climbing Helter Skelter.'

I might even attempt the whole distance, she thinks.

***

She has been dreading the climbing expedition – had even considered staying back, claiming she needed to do a last long run close to home. Bruce probably wouldn't have minded, she'd concluded gloomily. Their relationship seemed to have reached rock bottom - so to speak. Perhaps a weekend away from one another would give them a chance to take stock. But then he'd let slip that Ian and Marissa had split up, which hadn't come as a surprise. It also meant (somewhat conveniently) that they would now be two couples – Bruce and Marissa and Bruce's weird buddy Phil "the Phoenix" who'd leapt off a balcony high on heroin some years ago, and survived. He would be bringing his girlfriend, Sam. Shelly was damned if she was going to let Marissa turn it into a cosy little foursome.

Things had reached a head when she'd finally put her cards on the table late one evening, after he'd returned from the Climbing Centre, announcing that she'd spoken to a solicitor friend of hers in Manchester. 'Nothing heavy,' she'd begun, 'I just need to know where I stand if you decide to throw me out!' The answer was as she had suspected all along. She had no claim on The Trout and Fly unless he agreed to put the pub in her name, nor on any of his other assets. Cohabitees (God that was even worse than partner) were not entitled to a share of the finances after a split, or to their partners' pension after they died. They didn't even count as legal 'next of kin', although there was talk of a change in the law. But even if a contract was drawn up between them, it was often impossible to enforce.

Bruce had again stalled for time, claiming The Mantis was still on his back demanding more maintenance. His hands were tied – which meant he couldn't do anything for the moment.

'You never will Bruce! You just keep stringing me along and now time's running out.'

'Is this some kind of ultimatum?' He'd inquired at last.

'I didn't realise I had any bargaining power!' she'd answered, adding that after the marathon something had to change, otherwise she would be making some plans of her own.

'You're becoming a tough woman,' he'd said with irony.

She'd turned away, thinking she may have sounded tough, but she was crumbling inside, was going to need a huge reserve of inner strength to leave him.

***

Now she sets off for the ultimate distance run, through a damp Welsh landscape of jagged peaks and mountains looming ominously against a bruised sky.

It had taken her a while to measure out a route but eventually she'd mapped a circuit through the mountain pass, towards a small mining village with an unpronounceable name, before winding back past slate grey houses and slag heaps towards the lodge where they were staying. It was a bit bleak but at least it was flat. The meter showed six point three miles which meant she was going to have to run it at least four times. She would do it at her own pace - after all there was nobody to compete with, just her and her stopwatch.

She tries to visualise the end goal, following Mr Dippy's three step process – of mental imagery.

Firstly, set the goal, secondly relax, and finally imagine yourself succeeding! But somehow she can't find her rhythm. She feels heavy and disoriented, out of tune with the landscape, which is slightly menacing now – massive boulders poised precariously along the sweep of the mountain, like a frozen landslide. A few lone sheep munch mournfully on tufts of grass adding to her sense of isolation. She misses Fran's laboured breaths, and Gela's angst ridden confessions. Whilst vivid images of Bruce and Marissa inching their way up Helter Skelter play tortuously on her mind. She grits her teeth, thinking of how Marissa had once again monopolised him the evening before as they gathered in The Mountain Goat to plan the day's climb.

'We'll approach from the west face,' she'd said producing a map, 'there are a lot more over-hangs. Best if I belay you.'

Over my dead body, Shelly had thought.

When Shelly had inquired after the 'Ogre' (knowing perfectly well the engagement was off) Marissa had said with a strange little smile, 'oh, he's out of my life, thank God. Now I can start having some fun.'

Not with Bruce, you don't, Shelly had almost blurted. She'd spent the rest of the evening listening to climbing anecdotes and being lectured to by Phil the Phoenix about 'facing her fears.' 'I was shit scared of heights after the accident,' he told her. 'So I decided to get over it, by learning to climb – you just got to look the devil in the eye!'

Shelly had considered this, before concluding that some fears were best left buried – beneath the rocks where they belonged.

She shivers, thinking she should have brought her *Ipod*, listened to Patsy Cline, anything to distract her from the negative thoughts.

'Crazy...' she sings to herself, her mind travelling back to that humiliating evening at The Cock and Bull. Was that when her problems had begun, she wonders? Or had it started way back, one freezing November afternoon, when her mother hadn't appeared in the school car park to collect her. Had instead driven to Cravenhead Quarry, and plunged thousands of feet to her death. Leaving just a note saying *'I can't go on – love you always, Mum'* From then on life seemed to have been a series of compromises – leaving school early with no qualifications, finding herself adrift – marrying Nick, because it felt better than being alone. When getting hammered out of her skull somehow numbed the ache in her heart.

It has started to rain now – a sleety slanting rain, tunnelling down the side of the mountain in stinging gusts. She pushes on grimly, setting her face against it, trying to distance herself from the memories.

She's on the second loop now, running back along the mountain pass. The Loneliness of the Long Distance Runner, she thinks to herself wryly. It strikes her she would never be free of that sense of aloneness, whether she married Bruce or not. That she'd been pursuing something illusory. You only had to look at Gela – held to ransom over a shag she'd never even wanted, Fran desperate for a fling. Whereas she and Bruce had once been as solid as the great boulders in front of her – until she'd tried to pin him down.

Yet what else could she have done – jogged along indefinitely, risked being dispossessed for the second time? She needs to carve out a life for herself, as well as provide for Gary, give up the demon booze completely, (she's never been keen on half measures). Maybe she'd move back to Manchester, get a job in one of the Health Centres, as a fitness instructor.

She is reaching the end of the second loop now, has

managed to run through the ten-mile trough. The Performance Enhancers (she didn't want to think of them as drugs) must be working. It strikes her, that in spite of all the miles, she's run full circle – has arrived back at the start, to find nothing has changed. She can see the dark copse of pine trees where the lodge is situated and fights against the temptation to skip the last loop and go back to bed for a long nap.

'...just do it,' she murmurs, mentally preparing herself to turn around.

Ahead, the mountain ridge has turned black with rain. She glances towards Penryth Peak, beyond which lies the gorge, and Helter Skelter, and sees something circling above. She strains her eyes but it has disappeared. She can hear a faint rumble, a low vibrating thud rippling through the valley and then she registers the helicopter hovering like a vulture, over the far peaks where Bruce and the others had gone.

— Chapter Twenty-Three —

What on earth do you pack for a weekend of passion, Fran wonders, gazing at the growing mound of clothes on the bed? Her wardrobe has shrunk substantially, since losing all that weight – she'd decided to get rid of her fat clothes for good, since there would be no going back this time. All those elastic waisted trousers, shapeless tops and voluminous skirts (in various shades of greys and charcoals) had been replaced with floaty blouses in pinks and pastels, a short denim skirt, a pair of low waisted jeans. She had bought new underwear too (with the weekend in mind) a glossy push up bra, silky camisole and lacy French knickers. It had been a whole new shopping experience.

Now she stands in front of the mirror in her new underwear struck by her shapely contours – her slimmer hips and thighs. Her bum is half its former size, the rolls of fat around her stomach have all but disappeared, unfortunately so have her boobs, setting her off on that familiar train of thought.

For a while she'd thought she could put up with her 'meagre offerings' – at least they were healthy. But now, in the light of the huge improvement of the rest of her body, they were an insult. Like little buds, only unlike buds, these would never bloom – rather they seemed to be withering away, disintegrating into the bony underworld of her chest. She'd been fooling herself, imagining she would ever look sexy or seductive in a slinky black dress.

Without telling a soul, she'd returned to the Health Centre with its glassy blue windows, and spoken to a consultant on the fourth floor. Explained how she'd tried to come to terms with her flat chest, but now she'd lost so much weight, she felt cheated. Pump up bras were all very well when you were walking along the high street, but hardly seductive when it came down to it (especially if you were planning a weekend away with your lover) she'd thought. She was seriously considering implants.

The consultant (a handsome Indian in his early forties) had been sympathetic and encouraging, claiming the scarring was virtually undetectable these days. There were risks of course. Fran had read one unfortunate story of an implant bursting, causing toxic shock and near death. The woman likened the smell, once it was removed, to rancid fish oil.

'But a lot of women are very happy with the results,' he'd concluded. What did her husband think?

'I haven't told him,' Fran admitted after a pause.

It had been hard enough to persuade Brian she'd needed liposuction – there was no way he would support her having breast implants.

'I think you're fine the way you are,' he would say. He had already predicted that once the training was over, her boobs would return to their original size (like the rest of her, if she wasn't careful.) In other words she couldn't have her cake and eat it. The idea is preposterous. Having sweated for a slimmer body, put her heart at risk and lost two toe-nails, she's damned if she's going to sacrifice all that for an added inch of bosom.

The consultant had seemed to understand this, whilst pointing out that she needed to ask herself why she was doing it, and for whom.

Fran had thought long and hard about this. Clearly not for Brian who loved her unconditionally, nor if she really examined her feelings, for Gerry Ryan. Whilst nervous of exposing her whole body to him (he'd had a pretty good feel of it already) it wasn't just the size of her breasts that worried her – it was more to do with some complex emotion deep down, the fear that Gela might be right, the fantasy was better than the reality. No, the longing for a pair of decent breasts had begun before she'd met Gerry, had its roots buried way back in her teens when the desire to wear plunging necklines and halter necked dresses, (thereby shifting the focus from her bum) was all consuming. Besides, if she was going to be big, she might as well be voluptuous all over.

'I'd be doing it for myself,' she'd said finally, 'to feel more like a woman.'

He'd asked about her medical history, dismissed her heart condition as having any bearing on the procedure, although she would need to consult the surgeon about that. He was clearly impressed with her plan to run the marathon and had showed her photographs of some successful implants done at the clinic.

Fran had pounced on an image of a pair of 36 Cs – full, upright, but not grotesquely swollen like some of the photos she'd seen. 'I want those,' she'd said firmly.

The next obstacle was cost. She could hardly take it out of the joint account without Brian noticing, which meant she was going to have to come up with the money herself. And here was the uncomfortable part. There was almost enough (and more trickling in) with her savings, to cover the operation. Only the money didn't belong to her. Rather it was destined for the breast cancer charity. She'd hidden the bulk of it in her underwear drawer telling herself she would send it off after the marathon – only now things had changed. Of course it was unethical, but she would find a way of replacing it, she tells herself – would organise a big charity ball at some later date.

'I'd like to go ahead with the surgery,' she'd told the surgeon, who'd examined her next. 'As soon as I've recovered from the marathon.'

Now she twists and turns in front of the mirror, envisaging those glorious breasts transposed on her. The glossy new bra only seemed to reinforce the depressing fact that there was nothing underneath it. Perhaps she should stick to her old faithful, she thinks, a simple cotton bra, medium size knickers with a bit of lace, girlish but true.

She eventually settles on three different outfits – her new jeans, plus a pair of smarter trousers for the evening, the denim skirt, with a floaty blouse and some looser trousers in case she has a fat day. She throws in some jewellery - moonstone ear-rings and a matching necklace, some silver bangles. She has drawer-fulls of accessories, since they were constant and forgiving as her weight fluctuated. She adds a satin negligee, which is not really her, but she can hardly sleep in her old cotton pyjamas, she packs scented candles in case the lighting is too harsh, frangipani oil, Rescue Remedy, and a box of hand made chocolates to eat in bed. Lastly, she adds mouth-wash and a spray in case she has morning breath. An hour and a half later, she is showered and ready to go and meet Gerry at the back entrance of the Garden of Eden Centre, only her mobile is vibrating with a text message saying *'Can't gt away b4 noon – G.*

Shit, she breathes, Brian could come back from work at any moment to find her dressed to the nines. She was going to have to get out of the house. She dithers for a moment wondering what to do, but it's too late – she can hear the front door opening (he must have come back to check on her.)

She hurriedly pulls an old cord jacket over her new blouse, as he steps into the room.

'Thought I'd better check your tyres before you leave,' he says, a shadow passing across his face at the sight of her made up face and bulging weekend bag.

She says nothing. They both know he's already checked the tyres at the beginning of the week.

He carries her bag downstairs, then pulls out an envelope from his pocket, saying 'I have this for you. It's towards the marathon. I was waiting until I had a lump sum from the guys at work. I told them I'd be doubling it. There's over two thousand pounds of sponsorship,' he adds.

'Oh Brian, that's amazing,' she says, feeling almost limp

with guilt, but unable to backtrack now.

'It's for a good cause,' he states.

She nods, unable to speak, aware she now has more than enough for the breast implants.

'Well have a good weekend. Put your feet up – treat yourself to a massage. You deserve it.'

'Thanks,' she mutters, an uncomfortable image of Gerry massaging her calves with frangipani oil making her say, 'I'll call you.'

He hadn't even asked where she was staying, had said, 'I presume you'll have your mobile switched on, if I need to get in touch with you?'

She makes her way to the door, glancing around to give him a reassuring smile, but he's busy sorting through a pile of mail, putting all the circulars in one pile, envelopes in order of size and importance.

'Take care of yourself,' he says, without looking up.

— Chapter Twenty-Four —

It doesn't mean anything, Shelly tells herself, as she drives through the swirling mist and rain towards Penryth Peak. The helicopter could be searching for a lost hiker. It could be something as trivial as a broken ankle– whilst all her instincts tell her something has happened to Bruce. There's still no signal on her mobile, and nobody at the lodge has heard anything – only the warning on the radio that the weather was closing in. She'd returned to her room, unable to shake off a growing sense of unease, changed out of her damp running clothes, and without bothering to shower, found the car keys and a map and set off along the mountain pass, desperate to put her mind at rest.

She has been driving for some time now, must have missed the sign for Penryth Peak. She pulls into the side of the road to study the map, trying to work out where she is. An hour later, she's still driving through a bleak mountain pass, through misty vales and looming rocks, when she sees a battered sign, saying – Pathway to Penryth Gorge. According to the map you could walk all the way to the top which would give her a bird's eye view of the peaks, weather permitting and hopefully Helter Skelter.

She hesitates, thinking of the climb and the inevitable drop on the other side, then turns up the narrow rutted track, until she can drive no further and gets out of the car. The path is steeper than she'd feared – stones and rubble slide beneath her feet as she goes – but she forges on, her calves and hamstrings screaming from the added effort. The path is finally levelling out now, before winding away around the lip of the Gorge. She can just make out the peaks, and the phallic tip of Helter Skelter, but needs to get closer to the edge to get a view of the whole rock. Gusts of wind and slanting rain buffet her from all directions – she imagines being lifted into the air and tossed into the abyss like a piece of debris. She hesitates, her heart thumping, thinking of Phil the Phoenix telling her to face her fears – look the devil in the eye. She takes a tentative step forward, trying to get a better view of the base of the rock, but it's been blotted out by the fog. There is no sign of life, yet some strange compulsion impels her closer to the edge until she's looking over the great white void beyond. She stands there swaying slightly, a terrible vision of her mother's body hurtling helplessly through the air, wondering what dark thoughts had caused her to make that fateful leap into the unknown rather than face another day. A drunken husband? A failing marriage? Lack of money? Was that enough to push you over the edge? Had she seen it as an escape from all the pain and compromises, from the inevitable slide into old age? Or had she some kind of premonition of what lay ahead – a son who would die of cancer, a daughter who would make a complete mess of her life?

We are all running away from our problems, Shelly thinks.

She feels a terrible aching sadness, where the anger had been – a dry welling of emotion (she's not one for tears). She turns away, longing to be back at The Old Foundry with Gary and Bruce, to feel Bruce's calm and solid presence, to go back to the way it was before the rift.

She drives back to the lodge in a heightened state, willing him to be safely ensconced in the pub, but there's no sign of him or the rest of the party.

Just when the waiting becomes unbearable, the news filters through to the main lodge, that there has been an accident. One of the climbers has been injured and lifted by helicopter to Abergavenny General.

Shelly arrives at the hospital some forty minutes later. She sees the wheelchair first and is struck by the fact Bruce is far too big for it. She registers his bandaged foot, before seeing Marissa lean forward and put her hand on his shoulder, before whispering something in his ear.

Shelly is flying along the corridor towards them now, the pain in her legs forgotten, feeling as if her heart is exploding in her chest.

'Fuck what's happened?' she demands, kneeling in front of the wheelchair, and examining his familiar rugged face.

'Shell?' Bruce says, sheepishly.

'Shit…' she groans – 'I knew it would happen one day – I'll look after you – I'll never leave you … forget about all that marriage shit I was laying on you, I don't care about any of it.'

'Hey take it easy,' he interrupts. 'I'm all right – just some cuts and bruises. Scraped a load of skin off my foot. I don't need this bloody contraption, being treated like a bloody invalid!'

'I saw the helicopter,' Shelly says faintly. 'I was on the second loop. I climbed to the top of the gorge trying to spot you. I've been worried sick!'

'Phil!' Bruce states. 'Picked a fine time to lose his nerve! He's going to be all right – although it was a close one this time. He's dislocated his shoulder and broken his collar-bone and a few ribs, but he'll rise again! Sam's with him now. I'm just waiting to be discharged.'

'Here's the doctor now,' Marissa says, 'could you move out the way, Shelly?

Shelly straightens up, her eyes blazing. 'No, you move out the fucking way – I'm quite capable of pushing a wheelchair.'

Marissa shrugs. 'Go ahead then,' she replies coolly. She leans towards Bruce and murmurs, 'better go, I'll be in touch.'

Bruce nods without replying.

On the way back to the lodge, he fills her in, explaining how when the weather had suddenly deteriorated, he'd suggested they abort the climb. Only Marissa had been keen to push on it seemed, and in the middle of this debate, Phil had suddenly frozen on a narrow ledge, unable to descend. Bruce had elected to stay with him, trying to coerce him down, but he'd panicked, lost his footing and fallen several feet (almost taking Bruce with him). After a few terrifying minutes, in which they'd lost half their ropes and equipment, Bruce had managed to hoist him up to the ledge again, where they'd waited in the wind and rain for the rescue team to arrive.

'What if they hadn't come in time and it got dark? You would have been there all night!' Shelly had said, absorbing the horror and closeness of it all.

He'd shrugged, confirming what she already knew. He might not be able to put it into words, or commit anything to paper, but he would have stayed there, clinging onto that narrow ledge, until the bitter end.

— Chapter Twenty-Five —

Fran waits in the car for Gerry at the side entrance of The Garden of Eden Centre in a state of nervous anticipation. It has gone noon and there's still no sign of him. She's just debating whether to drive away and keep her marriage intact (if it weren't for Gwen she could just go home) when she sees him standing by the surplus bags of Wainwright's Peat Moss. Her heart does its usual somersault – she's caught between desire and fear – that and the knowledge no good can come of this. But he's ambling towards her now, smiling his lazy smile and suddenly there is no way back.

'Where the hell were you?' she demands, tension making her short.

'It's only ten past,' he replies.

'Get in before somebody sees us – where's your bag?'

He pats his breast pocket saying, 'got my toothbrush in here somewhere.'

Christ, she'd bought three changes of clothes – not to mention all the accessories.

She's about to pull out onto the road when she notices a bottle green four-wheel drive coming towards them, the driver slowing to get a better look.

'Oh, my God,' she breathes, 'Jasmine Fellows – one of the PTA mother's from hell – a real cow.'

He glances back with a frown. 'Do you think she saw us?'

'She could hardly miss us,' Fran states. He seemed to take up most of the car whilst she was all dolled up – big hair and lipstick, not to mention the vibrant pink top.

'Now it'll be around the whole school! I'll have to say your Land Rover broke down and I just happened to be passing, and gave you a lift home. If only you'd been on time!'

'It was your idea to meet here,' he comments, pulling out

his cigarette papers. 'You should have picked me up at The Hideaway.'

'It's in the wrong direction. God, Gerry the car is going to stink.'

'It already does – that air freshener is bloody horrible! Lavender – my arse,' he adds. 'I can't believe anybody buys this stuff.'

'It's better than cigarette smoke,' she answers tersely.

He immediately opens the window, letting in a blast of cold air, causing her hair to whip across her face, and stick to her lip gloss.

'Forget it, I'll put up with the smoke,' she snaps.

Once they were out of the village she'd started to feel better. He'd stroked her thigh, and told her she looked dead sexy. She put on her favourite CD and hummed along – *and our hearts that beat as one...no more love on the run.*

By the time they reached the M3 she was starving – her body needed its carb fix. She'd pulled off the motorway at the next exit, and stopped at a pub called The Green Man, with a sign outside saying GOOD FOOD. It didn't look too promising but she decided it would have to do.

'I'll have the pasta and vegetable bake,' she'd told the waitress, thinking it was the most healthy sounding thing on the menu. He'd announced he wasn't hungry – would just have a pint of local ale.

'Have something to eat,' she'd urged, 'we've still a long way to go.'

'This will fill me up,' he'd grinned, taking a hefty slug.

The pasta bake had clearly been micro-waved judging by the cheese which had turned to elastic, but she was so hungry, she didn't care.

'Bloody hell you sure can put it away,' he'd commented as she battled with long washing lines of cheese.

'I've got to carb up for the Marathon,' she'd replied defensively. 'It's only ten days away.'

'You really going to run it then?' he'd said, raising an eyebrow.

'No actually, the last six months was just for a laugh! We thought we'd run over a thousand miles to see how it felt!'

'Hey, take it easy, relax,' he says, putting his hands up in a gesture of surrender. 'You're really uptight – I'll have to give you a good rub down.'

'Sorry,' she mutters, thinking a 'rub down' didn't sound that appealing all of a sudden. 'It's just the thought of seeing my mother tomorrow' (not to mention the evening ahead) 'doing the dutiful daughter act when I feel like wringing her scrawny neck.'

'Don't know why you bother, if she's such a pain,' he comments.

She sighs. 'I suppose I'm doing it for myself as well as her – that old guilt thing.' She's going to feel twice as bad by the end of the weekend, but that's another matter – she feels permanently guilty these days (she's been given a date for the breast operation) and asked for a deposit. She pushes the thought to the back of her mind – into her underwear drawer with the rest of her bad conscience.

The rest of the journey had gone from bad to worse. She'd had to stop twice so he could pee, then she'd been caught in a long tail back of cars; they were digging up the motorway yet again. He'd then announced he was hungry and needed a sandwich, after which he'd fallen fast asleep and she'd missed the exit to Fernhampton.

'I thought you knew where you were going,' he'd yawned as she cursed and swore that now they were going to have to do a huge detour.

'Well I don't...' she'd replied. 'I'm not in the habit of staying in remote hotels.'

By the time she'd finally pulled into the driveway of Woodstock Manor House, she was exhausted.

The receptionist had greeted them warmly saying, 'ah Mr

and Mrs Fellows?'

It had taken a minute for Fran to remember she'd booked the room under Jasmine's name, by which time Gerry was saying, aggressively, 'no, Ryan's the name.'

'So you're not Mrs Fellows?' the woman had asked a flustered Fran.

'Yes, no I mean, it is the name I booked under. I still use it – I'm only recently divorced.' She could feel the heat scalding her cheeks. Now the woman would think she was a real tart.

'You're in the Crimson Suite,' she'd stated, as if that said it all.

'What was all that about?' Gerry muttered as they were being led up a flight of stairs.

'I couldn't book it under my own name, for Christ sake.'

'But why Fellows?'

'I don't know – probably because Jasmine Fellows is the last person I would ever spend a weekend with!'

He'd frowned as if she was quite mad.

At least the bedroom had lived up to her expectations – a beautiful four poster with crimson drapes, dark oak furniture, and thick tapestries on the walls. The lighting was perfect, so was the adjoining bathroom with its cast iron bath, standing on crabby feet.

She'd planned to freshen up, have an Irish coffee to calm her nerves, but he was already pulling her towards him, stroking her hair, and cheek, massaging her shoulders, each kiss becoming more urgent. He wasn't taking no for an answer anymore. She could feel his rough hands under her blouse searching for her breasts – lingering briefly before moving downwards, over her hips and stomach – tugging urgently at the button on her new trousers. He was lifting her onto the bed now – and falling on top of her, almost bringing the curtain down with him, causing her to bump her head on one of the posts.

'Jesus, Gerry, slow down!' It was a far cry from the romantic scene she'd envisaged – the long lingering kisses, followed by a slow sensuous massage.

'You're just so…ripe,' he'd breathed, his hands returning briefly to her breasts before moving downwards towards more promising territory.

Afterwards, she'd lain there in a state of numb shock, thinking, well that's it, I've done it, crossed the line – have become a statistic, joined the ranks of adulterous women all over the world. Not that it had been bad. It just hadn't lived up to her expectations. How could it? A fantasy that had been played out in almost cinematic images had turned into a physical reality. And although he'd paid attention to her needs (once she'd got him to slow down) it had felt all wrong. Brian may have been a bit mechanical but he was dear and familiar to her – with his clean smell of soap and aftershave.

Brian would have loved the evening she thought with a pang, would have lingered over dinner, ordered a pudding, tucked into the chocolates that came with the coffee. Gerry had just picked at his food, claiming it was too rich, then ordered another beer. He'd complained bitterly that the restaurant was non smoking.

'Can't you wait until we go to the bar,' she'd said, tucking into her Crème Brulee – with raspberry coulis – she was damned if she was going to stint on dessert just so he could have a cigarette.

After dinner and another drink at the bar, in which she'd downed two Irish coffees, they'd headed for the bedroom, by which time she was too full to make love straight away.

He'd discovered the T.V which was hidden in a mahogany cabinet and watched the horse racing whilst she'd futilely tried to sleep. She was still awake at dawn, listening to him snoring, wondering what the hell she was doing in this romantic setting with this handsome man, with whom she had nothing in common – no past to giggle over, no future to plan.

Just the here and now – and right now he'd made a horrible mess in the bathroom.

***

The following morning she'd left him fast asleep and driven to Dulcote Marsh, to the line of terraced council houses where her mother lived. Gwen had opened the door, still in her dressing gown, the ubiquitous cigarette clamped between her lips. She looked awful Fran thought, taking in the bleached straggling hair, black at the roots, the ashen complexion.

'Frannie love, good God, you've lost weight, you look really well! Didn't recognise you!'

'Thanks,' Fran had said sourly.

'Come in love. I'm a bit behind – couldn't get out of bed this morning. Put the kettle on would you?'

Fran had stepped into the small front room, bracing herself against the stale smell of more smoke and patchouli oil - which Gwen had started wearing again. The room hadn't changed since her last visit or the one before. The shabby furniture was shrouded in beaded throws, the walls covered in framed posters from the sixties. There was a card table in one corner with a candle and incense, where Gwen told her fortunes. She'd attempted to read Fran's palm once, but Fran had snatched her hand away, saying, 'I don't want to know what's ahead of me – (lest it becomes a self-fulfilling prophesy, she'd thought). The mantelpiece was crowded with souvenirs from Gwen's travels in India and black and white photos of Gwen looking gauntly beautiful at some rock concert, Gwen and Lettie as children, Lettie frowning darkly as if she already knew the cards were stacked against her. A photo of Fran as a baby, another as a toddler, then as a surprisingly slim teenager – fragmented mementos charting a life they'd never shared.

Fran makes her way into the kitchen which is a mess – chipped mugs all higgledy piggledy – God she was getting as bad as Brian, she thinks, fighting an urge to straighten them. In the cupboard, the boxes of herb teas and jars of vitamins she'd brought the last time, still unopened. Gwen only drank PG tips now. 'Do you want some?' she calls wearily.

'Yeah – weak, with plenty of milk and no sugar. You know how I like it.'

Fran grits her teeth. Yeah, but you don't know how I like it, she thinks – would ever guess that right now I could do with an Irish coffee.

'So how did you manage to lose all that weight?'

'I told you we've been training to run the Marathon – it's a week on Sunday.'

'Will I see you on the tele?'

'I doubt it Mum, there are about 30,000 runners.'

'Well you look bloody good, I'll give you that,' Gwen says, appearing in the kitchen, still in her dressing gown. 'You haven't got a lover by any chance?' she adds suspiciously.

Christ, maybe there was something in this fortune telling lark, Fran thinks.

Fat chance she's about to answer but says instead, 'of course not.'

'You're a very attractive girl,' Gwen states, 'especially now you've slimmed down – mind you don't go piling it on again.'

'I won't. I've decided I'm going to become a nutritionist. I've been talking about it for years,' Fran states. 'Once the marathon is over.' The idea had come to her as she was driving down the motorway with Gerry asleep beside her. Only this time she would do it.

'You always liked your food,' Gwen says archly, lighting a cigarette.

'Shouldn't you give those up?' Fran snaps. 'It can't be helping your blood pressure.'

Gwen shrugs – 'going to snuff it one day anyway – probably sooner than later. Haven't been feeling right for months now.' This was accompanied by a violent coughing fit.

Fran, who could sense a catalogue of ailments about to follow, says, 'maybe if you ate properly, and did some exercise, you'd feel better! Why aren't you taking any of those vitamins I brought you?'

'Them fishy ones kept repeating on me,' Gwen states, 'we never bothered with vitamins when I was growing up.'

You never grew up, Fran thinks irritably, as Gwen embarks on her second favourite subject, her youth, when everybody was making love and not war – of all the weird and wonderful people she'd met on the Ashram – how everybody rallied around in those days. Whereas, now nobody gave a damn.

Fran can feel a violent anger rising from deep inside. Guilt, exhaustion, and disappointment causes her to say, 'Rubbish! That whole hippy thing was just a way of running away from reality and responsibility! I mean where did I come into all this – whilst you were going off to find yourself! It was all about you wasn't it? It always has been?'

'That's not fair, Frannie. I always cared about you.'

'So much so that you decided to do a runner the moment things got a bit tough!' Fran is trembling from emotion – from years of anger and resentment.

'I wasn't well enough to bring up a child.'

'There is nothing wrong with you Mum, there never was, it's all in your head. Lettie was the sick one.'

Fran's heart has started to accelerate alarmingly. She takes a deep breath, her voice breaking, 'Lettie was the one who needed healing.'

Gwen stares at her with a stricken look. 'What can I say, I never pretended to be a proper mother. I never planned to be a mother. Your father ... he forced himself on me ... he raped me Frannie!'

John the Baptist, with his flowing locks and Jesus sandals – surely not?

'I thought it was all about peace and love...?' Fran says incredulously.

'The damage was so bad they had to cut you out – that's why I've got to have a hysterectomy. You were bright blue ... thought you were going to die on me ... couldn't have coped with that.'

That part was true at least. She remembered Lettie saying that after Gwen had given birth, both mother and baby had the blues. So the rest could be true – which would go some way to explaining some of it.

'So I was just a bad memory?' Fran says, after a long silence.

'No, I loved you, very much. But I was only nineteen – just a child – Lettie was the mature one. She wanted so badly to take you on, couldn't have children of her own as you know. I wasn't well enough physically or mentally, Frannie. A friend suggested I went to the Ashram to be healed.'

Fran shakes her head in despair. 'You could have come back once you were better – given it a chance, at least kept in touch with me over the years. But you couldn't even do that. It's like you couldn't do the distance!' she says brokenly. Her heart is now racing away without her – she grabs her handbag and searches for her Rescue Remedy.

'You all right?' Gwen says, looking at her in alarm.

'I'm fine,' Fran mutters, breathing deeply, and putting the liquid drops under her tongue. 'It only happens when I get stressed,' when I see you, she thinks.

'Never forget when the doctor told me you had a heart defect! I was in bits, I was. I didn't know what to do, love – I'm sorry.'

It is the first time Gwen has ever attempted to apologise. Fran thinks again how tired and haggard she looks – as if the full weight of the past has finally caught up with her.

'We'd better get going,' she says, or you'll miss your appointment.'

Gwen looks away, sheepish now. 'Thing is, they cancelled it. Shortage of beds – you know the NHS!'

'What – why the hell didn't you tell me?'

'I only found out this morning – I did ring but Brian said you'd left. I was going to ring your mobile, but I reckoned you'd be driving, so…'

'So I came all this way for nothing?' Fran finishes. If I'd known I mightn't of come – which means I wouldn't have slept with Gerry she thinks bitterly.

'So have they given you a new date?' she demands, trying to control the rising anger.

Gwen shakes her head.

Fran frowns. 'Are you sure they cancelled it, or did you chicken out – because you couldn't go through with it?'

Gwen says nothing.

Fran can feel some of the anger drain away. 'Look, I know how you feel – God knows if anyone should know it's me! I was only twenty nine when they took out my ovaries. I would have loved more children. Thing is you can't keep running away from things, Mum!'

'I don't want to die in some filthy hospital ward,' Gwen states stubbornly.

'You're not going to die, it's just a routine operation. Look why don't you go private? I'll pay for it. I know you think all doctors are after your money, but at least you won't have another long wait. I'll come with you – and hold your hand, but I can't do it until after the marathon.'

'All right,' Gwen says finally, as if she's doing Fran a huge favour. 'Where's that cup of tea you offered me?' she adds.

Fran hands her a mug saying, 'I'm going to have to get back' (before I ring your neck she thinks) 'I've things to sort out at home. Let me know when you've made the appointment.'

Gwen nods. 'You're a good girl Frannie,' she says

suddenly. 'I did one thing right in my life,' she adds, with a sigh. 'I made a good daughter.'

***

Fran drives back to the hotel in a state of exhaustion, sharp points of pain pressing her temples. She pushes open the door to the Crimson Suite to find Gerry lying on the bed, with his shoes on watching another horse race.

'My Frangipani ... how did it go?'

I'm not your Frangipani any more she thinks crossly. 'Not well – I shouldn't have come. I need to go home.'

'That bad, eh?' He picks up his mobile, muttering, 'need to put a bet on Big Mo – he's only ten to one, but he's performing well this season – I've got a strong hunch.'

'I shouldn't have come,' she says again. 'It wasn't the right thing to do.' Her head has started pounding – she needs her feverfew and ignatia for headaches, plus pine and white chestnut for guilt and despair.

'I told you to keep away from people who do your head in,' he grins. 'Come here…'

She shakes her head. 'I want to go home,' she says.

'Ah,' he replies, as if the knowledge is finally sinking in. 'You really don't know what you want do you?'

I do actually she thinks. I want my little family back before it's too late.

Hardly a word passes between them on the long drive home. She has nothing to say to him anymore. She racks her brains for a way of ending it, without hurting his feelings. But when she glances sideways, he's asleep again, his feet propped up on the dashboard.

She reaches the village at last and turns up Charlton Hill, towards the thatched cottages. She should have taken the back route, but is desperate to get home now. He straightens up and yawns widely then pulls out his mobile, muttering, 'Damn, Big Mo fell at the last post.'

'Look Gerry, I really think …,' she begins.

But he's straining forwards suddenly, his eyes focussed on a car parked directly outside Butcher's Cottage.

'Keep driving,' he says, attempting to sink down into his seat.

'Why... who?' Fran begins, registering the bottle green four wheel drive and the equally astounded face of Jasmine Fellows at the wheel.

'Oh my God,' she says, suddenly understanding. 'Jasmine – you're shagging her aren't you? That's why you were so upset when the receptionist called you Mr Fellows... oh, this is just great!' She remembers the rumours that Jasmine was having an affair with somebody from the village, how she'd said blithely, 'who the hell would want to sleep with her?' Gerry Ryan apparently. Fran feels sick, with misery and shame – and the humiliation of it all.

'I've only seen her a couple of times,' he says at last.

'Oh Jesus,' she breathes, thinking it would be around the whole school by Monday. It wasn't as if Shelly hadn't warned her – he was a serial shagger – with a penchant for big women with flowery names – Rose, Jasmine, Frangipani – women who were easy to flatter because of their size and lack of confidence. He would never have gone for Gela or Shelly, knowing they would see right through him. He'd put his money on her from day one, knowing she was the favourite, the odds were good. She was the one he'd chosen to sponsor – yet all she'd ended up with was a crumpled ten pound note and a terrible conscience. And maybe some awful disease. She'd never even thought about asking him to use a condom since she couldn't conceive, but what about all those sexually transmitted diseases? Fran shudders, saying, 'please go Gerry, it's over.'

'Fine,' he says, as if it was all the same to him. There were always other bets – he'd had a good run for his money – she may have fallen at the last post like Big Mo, but he'd had a free night away, and a bit of sex.

She drives home blinded by tears, cursing herself for the pain and misery she would cause, once it was all out in the open.

***

Brian appears in the hallway, as she opens the door. He looks tired and drawn, she thinks with a pang, and not altogether thrilled to see her back so soon.

'I ... we didn't expect you back,' he says, blocking her entrance to the sitting room.

'Gwen cancelled the operation. She was doing my head in,' (she hesitates, catching herself using Gerry's expression) 'so I decided to come home.'

'Oh,' he says without moving. 'It's just that... well, I thought you were going to have a bit of a rest?'

She is suddenly alerted by his tone, can hear alarm bells ringing. 'Where's Chloe?' she demands.

'I've just driven her over to Clare's house – she insisted on a sleepover.'

'I didn't expect you back,' he says again. 'I was, well in the middle of something.'

'You've got someone here, haven't you?' she says. That was why he'd been so insistent she went away for the weekend, so he could have his own passionate affair.

Fran feels an overwhelming misery, as if she's drowning. The awful irony of the situation is lost on her, so great is the shock.

Yet was it so shocking? Over the last few months she'd paid little attention to his needs – had turned away from him night after night, too weary for sex, treated his concern over her well being, with resentment and anger.

He still doesn't answer, whilst she can bear it no longer. She pushes past him, wanting to know what kind of woman he's turned to in his hour of need – a big breasted woman with small round buttocks, who laughed at his jokes perhaps?

'I'd rather you didn't,' he says hopelessly.

'I don't care,' she almost sobs.

She pushes open the living room door and stops in

- 210 -

amazement at the scene in front of her. The room is strewn with bits of coloured paper and tape, the floor covered in a large sheet, with the words, *GOOD LUCK FRAN, YOU CAN DO IT LOVE BRIAN AND CHLO* – he hadn't put the E in yet.

'A banner... meant to be a surprise,' he says sheepishly. 'You were supposed to see it at mile ten, then fifteen, and twenty. I've replaced the sheets with some Egyptian cotton ones,' he adds. 'I know you hate the non iron ones.'

'Oh Brian,' she says, her insides melting, tears flooding her eyes.

'Also I bought some more water lilies for the pond and some wild flower and lawn grass seeds – you just scatter them on the lawn, and, well theoretically you end up with cowslips, daisies, all the flowers you like.' He suddenly pulls her into his arms as if he senses the turmoil raging inside her. It strikes her he has become more in tune with her moods than ever lately.

'Why don't you go and have a nice soak in the bath, and I'll bring you up a cup of tea?' he suggests. 'Chloe made you a special energy cake – says she and I have got to lose weight, and get fit now so we can keep up with you!'

'Thanks,' she murmurs, making her way towards the stairs.

Later he brings her up a tray of tea and a generous slice of Chloe's date and walnut cake.

'I've put your car in the garage. I had to change the air freshener – there's a terrible smell of cigarettes,' he tells her.

'Gwen,' Fran says too quickly. 'She chain smokes, as you know. I took her out for a short drive.'

She can sense him analysing the information in his head, working out there had been no trip with Gwen to the hospital, and that it was unlikely they would have gone for a short drive together.

'Best to leave the windows open overnight,' she puts in.

He nods. 'It can take a while for the smell to fade away,' he says at last.

— Chapter Twenty-Six —

With only days to go, you need to fuel yourself with complex carbs, for example Breakfast: muesli, with skimmed milk, or porridge and fruit – banana is the best bet – or wholemeal toast and honey plus a glass of fruit juice.
Midday: a snack of dried fruit – and an apple.
Lunch: a baked potato with a lentil salad.
Dinner: chicken or fish – with rice or potatoes. Avoid red meat towards the end of the week as it's hard to digest. Dried fruit, especially raisins are good for snacking on.
Remember to get plenty of rest. Prepare your mind and body – and your feet by rubbing on a layer of Vaseline before you go to bed every night. This will help prevent blisters.

Gela digs out the last raisin from a bar of fruit and nut chocolate, resisting the urge to devour the crumbling remains after Shelly's strict instructions to follow the pre-race menu. She turns her attention back to the computer screen, and reads over the last paragraph. Writing about sex was never easy – especially when it came to exploring the more unpleasant aspects of the act itself. She had sat up most of the previous night whilst the boys were asleep, pouring her story onto the screen - an explicit account of a sexual fantasy that turns into a nightmare. The first draft of CROSSING THE LINE was almost completed now – the story had finally taken flight, as her own life had plummeted. It was only the ending that was still unresolved.

She is interrupted by the sound of a car crunching across the gravel, and pulling up on the driveway. She listens, wondering who on earth could be calling at this time of night.

Had someone finally come to murder her? The Growler's snores turn to vibrating growls, as a car door slams and the sound of footsteps hurrying along the paved path grow louder. She's just wondering if she should call the local police station when she sees Fran's white face framed at the window, hears her say, 'it's only me!'

'I thought you were away?' Gela says, unbolting the door and ushering her inside. 'What happened?' she adds, sensing what's about to follow.

She has already written off that particular affair – made Fran's character, 'Jen' see the light and return to her husband (who is the forgiving sort). Now she waits to hear the real version.

'Are you ready for this?' Fran blurts, 'the bastard has been shagging Jasmine Fellows all along!'

'Oh my God, you're kidding! I'd heard she was seeing someone, but it was him! Oh, Fran... ' Gela breathes, unable to disguise her relief. 'I thought you were going to tell me Brian had found out, and thrown you out or something!'

'I think he suspects,' Fran says miserably. 'Anyway it'll be all around the school by Monday morning.' She relates the story, explaining how she'd left Brian asleep and crept out of the house leaving a note saying she couldn't sleep, so had driven over here, to make sure Gela was all right. 'I figured you'd still be up writing ... Oh, Gel I've done the most awful thing!'

'Sit down! Let me get you a drink. I've no diet coke only those dreaded energy drinks. We're meant to be off alcohol – I suppose we could have a hot chocolate?'

'To hell with that! Have you got any whisky and cream?' Fran inquires.

Gela grins. 'There's plenty of whisky,' she says, pulling out a dusty bottle of ten year old malt. 'Marcus would have a fit if he saw me pouring it into a cup of coffee – but then he's not here,' she adds, with a bitter little laugh.

There has been no word from him for over a week now, and then it had only been a brief phone call informing her he would be away for a while, this time in Bordeaux on a wine tasting trip. No doubt languishing in some chateaux with the dark haired woman with pointy shoes, she'd concluded miserably. He was now head of a new department, with a new company car and a generous expense account, just like the old days.

'I haven't got any cream,' she tells Fran, 'it's not on our list. I could froth up some semi skimmed milk, make a whisky latte!'

Fran nods. 'That will do.'

'So?' Gela inquires, as she sets about preparing the coffee and opening a bottle of *Chateaux neuf du Pape – Premier Cru* for herself. She'd acquired quite a taste for expensive wine since Marcus had left. 'What happened?'

'Oh, it was disaster! He's a slob Gel – he didn't even bring a change of clothes! Jasmine is welcome to him. I should never have gone, it was a total anti-climax,' she adds, with irony. 'You were right. God knows, you and Shell tried to warn me.'

'Maybe you had to do it,' Gela suggests, 'just to know.'

'The weird thing is I didn't really want to have sex with him. It was the lead up that was so intoxicating – the thrill of knowing somebody fancies you! That first kiss! A bit like having a delicious starter – you don't really need the main course.'

Gela smiles at the analogy.

'I had this vision of a romantic evening with a candlelit dinner, only I picked the wrong man. He's just not my type.'

'They never are – the ones you think you fancy,' Gela says dryly. The thought of Paolo still sends a shiver of revulsion down her spine.

She hands Fran her whisky latte and looks around for something to munch on, thinking banana chips would have to do.

Fran takes a sip, saying, 'woah, that's strong! Never thought I'd end up hitting the bottle. I don't even drink! As for having an affair – that was never on the cards. Everything's changed ... I've changed. Maybe it's losing all that weight!' She gazes into her glass with a stricken look. 'I'm not sure the thin me is a very nice person,' she adds hollowly.

'Oh that's daft,' Gela says. 'You're a really good person. You look fabulous whatever weight you are – you're a fantastic Mum – and look at all your good works for charity.'

Fran's face immediately clouds over. 'I've done an awful thing,' she begins.

'No you haven't,' Gela cuts in ... 'you've had sex with another man – like half the population – including me! Now you're going to have to move on. We've just got to make sure Brian never finds out.'

'He's bound to. Jasmine will announce it to the whole school! She's had it in for me since I resigned from the PTA. God, will you ever forget the look on her face when Shelly laid into her! This is a perfect chance for her to get back at us ... at me.'

Gela considers this. 'I'm not sure – remember, Gerry was her lover first. She's got her pride. Besides I heard she and her husband were trying to make another go of it. They've put the house on the market and are planning to move back to London. Maybe she was about to tell Gerry it was over when she saw you with him?'

Gela has recently become attuned to all the break ups and divorces around her - forever measuring them with her own situation. Only to conclude hers was unique, that she had married a man who could neither forgive nor forget.

But Fran's no longer listening. 'It's not just Gerry,' she says, 'the thing is, well you know I'd raised quite a lot of money for breast cancer ... almost two grand ... which Brian has since doubled ...'

'That's fantastic,' Gela states.

'It would be, only, well the thing is, I never actually sent it off.'

'So? It's not too late?'

Fran hesitates. 'I could do with another latte – except I won't be able to drive home.'

'You could stay the night, only won't Brian be worried?'

'He'll sleep in tomorrow – he was wiped out. But I'll send him a text, just in case. He always checks his mobile the moment he wakes up.

...as I was saying, about the money,' she continues, as Gela refills her glass. 'I actually had no intention of sending it off. I was planning to use it for ... well for something for myself.'

'All of it...?' Gela inquires curiously. 'What exactly?' she adds, unable to take the suspense.

'Breast implants,' Fran states, after a pause.

Gela stares at her in astonishment.

'I know what you must be thinking, and you're right – all those women out there dying of breast cancer, and here she is planning to pump herself up with silicone. I was planning to raise it again somehow. Organise a summer ball or something …' She frowns, 'not very ethical, I know.'

'Wouldn't Brian have paid for the implants?' Gela inquires, after a silence.

'No way! He'd worry about my heart, say he loves me the way I am! Although not anymore,' Fran adds miserably. 'Now he'll think I'm doing it for Gerry. God the whisky has gone to my head, Gel. I'm shattered, feel so awful…,' she closes her eyes, muttering, 'who was it who said, charity begins at home – I'll be punished for this – probably disfigured for life.'

Gela smiles. 'Rubbish, you haven't done anything that awful,' she begins, but Fran is fast asleep.

Gela goes upstairs to find a spare duvet and pillow, and

returns to the room to find the phone is ringing.

'Who the hell?' Fran mutters drowsily.

Marcus, Gela thinks, hope and dread flaring at the same time.

It's Brian, his voice sounding strained, as he says, 'Ah Gela – er, sorry to call you so late, Brian Taylor here.'

'Oh Brian, she's here,' Gela begins, keeping her voice low so as not to wake Fran. He doesn't seem to hear her.

'It's Francesca – you probably know she went up to see her mother last night – came back very upset.'

'Gwen always has that effect on her,' Gela says immediately.

'You're right there, only the thing is I think she's seeing somebody else. A few times I've come back from the office early and she wasn't home. Her mobile has been switched off every day between twelve and two, and there are other signs. I didn't mean to pry. I was just tidying up, she leaves her clothes everywhere, and well she's bought some new underwear. I found quite a bit of cash in her drawer. Do you think she's planning to run off with this guy whoever he is?'

Gela tries to gather her scattered thoughts. This was not the time to flounder. She takes a deep breath. 'She's not seeing anybody else Brian. I know that for a fact.' (It was true inasmuch as the Gerry interlude was over). 'Fran and I have become really close since we've started the training,' Gela continues. 'She would have told me – anyway she wouldn't have any energy left for an affair, believe me! No, you've got it wrong Brian – Fran loves you to bits.'

'I love her too,' Brian says, after a pause. 'She means everything to me. I haven't given her much support over the last few months. I was worried about her running the marathon, what with her heart problem. To be honest, I hoped she'd pull out. When I realised she was determined to do it, I rallied around, getting sponsors, but I fear it's too late.'

'No it's not,' Gela says with conviction.

Brian sighs, 'For all I know she could be with him now.'

'I told you she's here – asleep on the sofa. She sent you a text to say she was staying the night.'

'I didn't check my phone,' he answers.

'She's actually drunk rather a lot of whisky – she was very stressed after seeing Gwen, so we decided to have a couple of drinks. You know how it is?'

There's a silence, as if he doesn't believe her.

'I think she's woken up,' Gela adds. 'Shall I put her on?'

'Would you?'

Gela's heart constricts at the joyful relief in his voice. He would look no further, turn the page, she thinks with a pang.

'It's Brian,' she says, handing Fran the phone. She grins. 'I warned him you'd hit the bottle!'

***

Gela hears Fran say, 'of course I do – why did you think that? You know what Gwen's like? Finally driven me to drink … just a couple of whisky lattes! Fell asleep on the sofa. Of course I'll be back first thing in the morning. I know, I'm sorry if I've been a bitch lately. It's like the training has taken over everything ... I know, I don't blame you! Oh that ... it's for the breast cancer fund – yeah I know I should have lodged it in the bank but you're always on about having to pay bank charges so I thought I'd just stash it away then hand it over in one lot. What did you think I was going to do with it – have a boob job?! On the other hand I wouldn't mind ... I have looked into it as a matter of fact ... but you wouldn't approve would you? You what? You devil! No, 36C is my limit – well, I'll take you up on that.'

She puts down the phone and turns to Gela – her eyes brimming with tears.

'He says he's more than happy for me to have the operation. It could be my birthday present from him. Oh Gel, I heard what you said. You were amazing! I know Brian, if he wants to believe something, he'll find a way to put a line under it. I just pray you're right about Jasmine keeping her big mouth closed.'

'We'll tell her Shelly will be round to finish her off if she doesn't,' Gela grins.

They're hugging one another now, while Fran says, 'I've been so selfish keeping you up all night with my dramas when you're the one who needs taking care of.'

'I would have stayed up anyway,' Gela says. 'The novel has been keeping me up – I'm just so relieved you and Brian are going to be all right.' She smiles. 'It would have ruined my plot!'

There were such things as happy endings, she thinks to herself – but not for her and Marcus, for whom there had always been that invisible line – a line which he had drawn, and which she had dared to cross.

***

Over a breakfast of organic muesli and sliced bananas, Fran who feels surprisingly clear headed in spite of the double whiskies, says, 'now I want to hear all about the novel. Would you let me read some of it?'

'It's a bit personal, at least parts of it,' Gela admits, thinking of that graphic scene when the fictitious Paolo (renamed Paul) had "hovered over me" (Donna), "his erect penis poised like a weapon – a quivering arrow, ready to plunge into the core of me." God had she really written that?

'I wrote the famous episode through a single narrative voice, which made it easier, but it doesn't make very comfortable reading,' she warns. 'I'm going to have to censor it,' she adds, as Jamie hurtles into the room, demanding his morning fix – a banana smoothie, with honey. Gela had finally weaned him off chocolate milk, *Nutella* and anything with E-additives. 'I hardly dare print it out.'

'Ah come on Gel,' Fran urges, 'I'm dying to read it.'

Some time later, she leaves Fran with the printed text and goes upstairs to shower and check on Matthew.

When she comes down Fran is still lost in the script. She looks up at last, her expression one of disbelief. 'Jesus Gel – this is harrowing stuff. I don't know how accurate it is, but if this is what happened then that creep should be locked up. This isn't passionate sex between two consenting adults – this is a description of a drunken woman being taken advantage of!'

Gela feels the hairs rising on the back of her neck. 'That's how it felt,' she says at last.

'Marcus should know about this.'

She shakes her head. 'He doesn't want to know the gruesome details – he said. Anyway I'd never be able to convince him I didn't have a part in it! The damage has been done – it's too late now.'

Fran sits up. 'I want you to e-mail this to him.'

'He doesn't reply to my e-mails. For all I know he's met someone else.' She'd told Fran about the woman with pointy shoes, but Fran had immediately dismissed her fears saying, 'probably some work colleague.'

'I told you already, it's been over for a while. We never wanted sex at the same time, were always arguing about stupid things, like whose turn it was to put the rubbish out! Marcus was a great one for controlling things from the sidelines.'

'Sounds like normal marriage to me!' Fran comments dryly. 'Anyway it must be great to be allowed to be messy when you feel like it! Why is it I have this gut feeling you're still in love with him?'

Gela shrugs. 'A part of me hates him for the way he's acted over this – but yes, I do still love him. I love his intellect and his optimism, his philosophy on life – he made me feel safe.'

'Does he pick up his e-mails when he's away?' Fran inquires suddenly.

Gela nods. 'He takes his lap-top everywhere.'

'What's his address?'

'I don't have e-mail on my computer, only on his, and anyway there's no point.'

'Have you backed it up on a disk?' Fran continues.

Gela nods.

'Right, all I need is the disc and access to Marcus's computer. Twelve years with Brian must have taught me something!'

Fran gazes around Marcus's cluttered study curiously. There are photos of him and Gela on their wedding day, another of them caught in a passionate embrace, Gela emerging, lithe and beautiful from the sea, Gela with her hair wet and slicked back like a seal, Gela and the boys on the ski slopes. This was not a man who was running away from his wife, Fran thinks, more likely from himself. She inserts the disk, then tries to bring it up on the screen.

Some time later, she picks up the phone and calls Brian, hears him saying sleepily, 'Brian Taylor.'

'I just called to say I'll be home soon, and I love you,' she says.

'That's a coincidence, because I love you too, Mrs Taylor.'

'Also I need your help.'

'Fire away.'

'How do I send an e-mail from a floppy disk?'

— Chapter Twenty-Seven —

The night before the race, pack your kitbag with the following items,' Mr Dippy advises.
Your running number and chip, which will record your time all the way to the finishing line. Without them you're out of the race!
Energy drinks, the one you're now accustomed to.
Energy bars, again nothing you haven't tried before.
Snacks, banana chips are great as they don't bruise, or a packet of jelly babies if you've got a sweet tooth.
Plasters.
Vaseline, to prevent chaffing in all those hidden places!
An old jumper you're prepared to fling into the crowd once you've warmed up.
A bin liner to keep you dry at the start. Cut out a hole for your head and two for your arms – and don't let anybody tell you you're rubbish!
Money, in case you need a taxi at the other end to drive you to the nearest pub.
A towel, to mop up the sweat.
A change of clothes, something loose and warm.
A good book to help you relax....

'We need to relax,' Shelly says agitatedly, as they stand on the platform waiting for the London train. 'There's nothing more we can do now.'

I should have done the distance, she thinks – if only to know...

'You're the one who needs to relax,' Fran states, as Shelly checks her sports watch for the umpteenth time. 'No point timing the train for God's sake! It's bound to be late.'

Shelly sighs impatiently. She's been on edge all week, wildly hopeful one moment, filled with nervous despair the next.

She had decided they should travel up together on the train the day before, so they could register early, pick up their numbers and chips. Bruce, whose injured foot was almost healed now, would be driving up on the morning of the race to wait for her at the finishing line.

'Most of the roads will be closed,' she'd warned, 'you'd be better off taking the train.' He was bound to leave too late, she thought, might miss her altogether. On the other hand, she didn't want him getting there too early.

'I'll be there,' he'd answered as if used to dealing with far greater obstacles than a few road closures. 'Be careful,' he'd added oddly. He seemed about to say something else, then changed his mind, muttering, 'best of luck!'

'Here comes the train,' Gela announces. 'No turning back now.'

'I need to pee again!' Fran wails. She's been sipping water all morning following Mr Dippy's instructions to "drink until your pee is the colour of pale straw."

'I don't think my bladder can take much more,' she groans. 'At this rate I'm going to have to run with a catheter!'

Gela smiles, whilst Shelly thinks there are worse things. A period (she'd taken a pill to avoid one) an upset stomach (she'd added *Immodium* to her list) and had planned to get up half an hour early and get to the bathroom first and take a couple of Performance Enhancers. Now she finds herself wondering about the wisdom of sharing a room – Gela's idea, so they could be nervous together.

'Come on,' she urges impatiently, as the train thunders in. We've got a marathon to run.'

***

At Paddington, they argue about whether to take the tube or get a taxi.

'Taxi,' says Gela immediately. 'We need to conserve our energy. Anyway I hate the tube – it's so claustrophobic. I got stuck in the tunnel for an hour once!'

Shelly raises her eyebrows. 'Maybe this time there'll be a fire, or a terrorist bomb!'

Gela sighs, 'Fine, we'll take the underground. You win!'

'Maybe we'll get stuck in the tunnel all night and miss the race,' Fran puts in hopefully.

On the tube everybody seems to be munching bananas. A group of women wearing track-suits and trainers get in, shouting to one another. One of them is wearing a t-shirt emblazoned with 26.2 MILES AND STILL STANDING, and all of them carry bottles of mineral water.

Hope I'm still standing by tomorrow night, Shelly thinks.

'They look fit,' Fran says miserably.

'So are we!' Shelly is tempted to ask them what time they're hoping to do.

'As long as we get to the finishing line,' Gela states.

'Preferably before nightfall,' Fran adds, thinking everything has taken on a feeling of unreality – as if she's embarked on a journey that has no end. Brian and the three kids (he was bringing Jamie and Matthew up) would be waiting for her at various points along the way, which was comforting. They might have to pick up the pieces, she thinks fearfully.

This morning he'd fussed around her, packing and re-packing her kit bag, cracking jokes, as if trying to steer away from any darker issues lurking beneath the surface.

She hadn't told him she'd had a flutter in the night, nor had she mentioned it to Shelly and Gela. She had thrown in some Rescue Remedy just in case, trying to blank out visions of herself gasping for air by the side of the road like a proverbial fish out of water.

***

London had brought it all back, Gela thinks. The teeming crowds and traffic, the noise, and diesel smell of city life. Jumping into a black cab to meet up with Marcus at Bellini's Bar for a snatched lunch, the designer boutiques and shoe shops, her favourite hair salon - now all seemed part of that other life. As they crawl along the Marylebone Road, towards the hotel (she'd insisted on a cab, after they'd spent almost three hours registering for the race and wandering around the huge exhibition hall picking up free samples) she can see the white pillared building of Marcus's office on the right. She glances up at the window where his desk used to be, remembering how she'd stormed into the building that afternoon, interrupting a board meeting to announce she was pregnant with Matthew.

'Sorry guys, you'll have to go on without me,' he'd grinned to the grey suits around him, 'I need to honour my beautiful wife.'

She pushes aside the memories – no point going down that road, as Shelly would say. Marcus hadn't even called to wish her luck. She had phoned his mobile during the week, demanding to know if he was planning to come up for Jamie's birthday the weekend after the marathon. She was also keen to find out if he had read Chapter Eight of CROSSING THE LINE, which Fran had e-mailed.

If he had, he made no reference to it. He sounded miles away – for all she knew he was still in Bordeaux. She heard him say something about being back in the office at the beginning of that week and away again at the end, but he would try to come down for a day and a night in between.

'I'm taking a few kids from his class to Ashlington Falls for a swim and a birthday tea,' she'd filled in. 'You could always stay there like the last time,' she'd added caustically.

There had been a silence, then he'd said, 'tell Jamie I'll be there.'

She had put down the phone thinking well that's it – perhaps she should change the title of the novel to *THE END OF THE ROAD*.

***

A large screen had been set up in the hotel lobby,

showing clips of last years marathon, with two Kenyan runners streaming along on legs that might have been carved from ebony. Groups of ultra-fit looking men stand around talking about tomorrow's race.

'Oh my God,' Fran wails – 'I can't cope.'

'You're not going to be competing with them,' Shelly soothes, before marching up to the desk, and saying, 'I booked a triple room under Wainwright.' She had used Bruce's surname out of habit – all those climbing weekends away in damp lodges. Soon she'd have to get used to Preston again.

'Breakfast will be served from five a.m. onwards,' the receptionist replies, handing over a key. 'There will be a coach outside at seven to take you to the start of the race.'

'Hardly any point going to bed,' Gela groans.

An athletic looking man standing with the group behind her mutters, 'you could always join us in the bar for a carb fix?'

The owner of the voice is tall and powerfully built with eyes the colour of amber, which are now trained on Gela.

'We've got the pasta-do remember?' Fran puts in.

MEMBERS had invited them to a pre-race pasta supper in Putney to thank them for their fund raising efforts. Shelly had insisted they all go, since they were all in it together, but would only stay for a couple of hours. 'We need all the rest we can get,' she'd stated.

Gela meets that amber gaze full on, then to Fran and Shelly's surprise says, 'why not, a carb drink would be great! That is if we're back in time.'

After all there is life after Marcus, she thinks to herself.

— Chapter Twenty-Eight —

'Don't worry if you don't sleep the night before the big day,' Mr Dippy writes. *'As long as you rest your body, and if possible your mind. Remember you have been preparing yourself for this for months. Nothing is going to stop you now.'*

At four a.m. Fran is still wide awake listening to the traffic thundering along the Marylebone Road.

What if they have to cart me off in an ambulance she thinks? On the other hand that might be less humiliating than getting to the end only to find they've taken down the finishing post. Her heart is beating ominously fast. Maybe she should pull out, call Brian and tell him she's decided not to go through with it. She could stand on the sidelines with all the other spectators cheering Shelly and Gela on. Nobody would blame her, Brian would be quietly relieved, Chloe would be disappointed, but life would go on. On the other hand she could set off and see how it goes. She remembers Gerry saying, 'I'd put my money on you any day.' Better to fall at the last post like Big Mo than not be in the race perhaps? She cringes at the memory of that disastrous affair, of hitting her head on the bedpost – not to mention the humiliation of colliding with Jasmine Fellows.

So far Gela's theory had been right. Jasmine had kept her mouth shut – no doubt desperate to save her own reputation as well as her marriage. And now her house was on the market she would be moving away from Charlton Haven and hopefully out of their lives.

It's four forty – they would be getting up in less than an hour. She concentrates on her breathing, feeling her heart steady, then reaches for her mobile, thinking she would send Brian a text, telling him, what exactly? That she was afraid to go through with it? He was bound to check his phone as soon as he woke up, would pile the kids into a taxi and come straight over. There is already a message from him, saying *'I'll be with you all the way ... and forever after love B xxxxx.'*

She stares at the ceiling, taking deep calming breaths, then empties the screen and writes, *'see you at the finishing line.'*

Moments later, she hears Gela whisper, 'what time is it?'

'Quarter to five,' Fran murmurs.

'For fuck sake, it can't be,' Shelly states, sitting up. 'I haven't been to sleep yet!'

'Nor have I,' Gela groans. 'We'll be exhausted before we start.'

'We're going to be fine,' Shelly states with a confidence she doesn't feel. She had finally drifted off around three thirty only to have one of her plunging dreams, which had made her bolt up in bed, convinced they'd missed the race. She hadn't slept again after that. She stretches her legs, aware of that familiar ache in her side - and her hamstrings come to think of it. Phantom pains no doubt, flitting through her body with ghostly warnings of what lay ahead.

'Look, we're super fit – we can do this,' she emphasises, climbing out of bed and placing one foot tentatively on the floor. 'We need to do some stretches, and then start carbing up. I'll mix up some energy drink,' she adds, causing the others to groan. 'First, I need the bathroom.'

She locks the door behind her, and grabs her wash-bag, searching for her 'secret weapon.' She wouldn't be needing the Performance Enhancers, after today, she thinks, popping one into her mouth and taking a gulp of tap water. She checks herself in the mirror, struck by the still unfamiliar blonde hair, which looks a nasty yellow in the harsh light. She would go back to her natural colour (whatever that was) after this, she thinks. Get rid of the barmaid look since she was not going to be running The Trout and Fly now. Time to walk away from that dream, she thinks resolutely. Next, she sets about the laboured business of emptying herself, sensing even before she sits down on the cold toilet seat it's going to be a long old struggle.

***

Make sure you eat a powerful breakfast at least three hours before the race. Even if you can't face food you need to top up the glycogen stores in your liver (otherwise you risk hitting the wall). Keep to your usual menu. If you're staying away, bring supplies with you rather than alter your routine.

P.S. If you're too nervous to eat, don't panic – a meal replacement drink might be the answer, and some energy bars for the road. As long as you drink loads of fluid on rising (not too much tea or coffee as they are diuretics). However, a shot of caffeine can give you a boost.

'I can't eat a thing,' Fran states, glancing at the breakfast table, which is laden with bowls of cereal, yoghurts, fruit, rolls and croissants. It is one of life's bitter ironies, she thinks, that just when you're liberated from counting calories – could probably devour a whole banquet – you lose your appetite. She still has the burning aftertaste of the energy drink in her throat.

'Nor can I,' Gela says faintly. 'In fact I feel really queasy.' There is a distinct smell of body odour (not to mention sweaty trainers) in the air. She must be the only runner to have applied an extra layer of deodorant this morning, as well as a thick layer of vaseline, before spraying on loads of perfume to mask the smell of petroleum jelly. She cringes as a man with hairy armpits wearing only a singlet and shorts, stretches across her for a bread roll.

'Well you're going to have to try,' Shelly states, loading a tray with bananas and rolls. (She's brought some supplies from home – banana chips, jelly babies and a bar of Bruce's favoured Kendal mint cake). 'We need fuel.'

Gela is still dithering beside the breakfast table, when she sees the runner with the amber eyes coming towards her. She attempts to smooth her hair, which is all over the place. Shelly had teased her mercilessly when she'd tried to straighten it earlier.

'I waited in the bar for you last night,' he says, sounding aggrieved.

She glances at the logo on his t-shirt, which reads FEEL SUICIDAL? DON'T SUFFER ALONE – CALL ABYSS

'We went straight to bed after the supper,' she tells him. They'd actually stopped for dessert on the way home after Fran complained that the meagre bowl of spaghetti bolognaise MEMBERS had provided was not going to sustain her for twenty-six miles.

'Didn't sleep a wink mind you,' she adds.

'First marathon?' he inquires.

She nods. 'Never dreamt I'd do anything like this!'

He grins. 'I'll be looking out for you. What's your number?'

'I think it's twelve thousand nine hundred and something,' Gela says. She had pinned it onto her MEMBERS t-shirt this morning then pulled one of Marcus's old cricket sweaters over it. She planned to fling it off as soon as she was warm enough (a symbolic gesture, to show she'd moved on). Now she peers down her front, saying, twelve thousand nine hundred and eleven!'

'I'm six one nine one.' His gaze is intense now. 'Or maybe I'll see you back here after the race for a proper drink in the bar? What are your plans afterwards? It's going to be a hell of an anti-climax.'

She hesitates. She doesn't have a plan as such, has tried not to think too much about afterwards. As to the immediate arrangements, they'd made a vague plan to return to the hotel to shower and pick up their bags, before going out to eat somewhere. (No more pasta, Fran had begged). Fran and Brian were staying on an extra night in a luxurious hotel Brian had found in his Good Hotel Guide. He had already booked her a full body massage in the Health Suite. For them, at least life would return to normal. Whereas Shelly had a number of issues to resolve – but at least she had a 'fall back' plan. She and Bruce were driving straight home after dinner since Bruce had to be back at work the next morning. Gela had decided she and the boys would go back with them.

'I don't really have a plan,' she says at last.

'Great! Here's my mobile number,' he says scribbling it on a paper napkin. 'I'll be in the hotel bar later.'

'What was all that about?' Fran demands, as Gela sits down with her tray.

'Oh, he just asked me to have a drink at the bar afterwards, gave me his mobile number, but I'll probably be too exhausted. He's very good looking, and all that... but I don't know – the thought of starting all over again. I don't even know his name – he's running for the suicidal! I haven't quite got to that stage yet,' she adds, with a wry grin.

Shelly says oddly, 'I thought about running for that charity.'

The others exchange glances.

'My mother, she committed suicide when I was twelve years old. Never turned up at the school gates to pick me up. Jumped off Craighead Quarry instead.'

'Oh Shell, how awful,' Fran says, after a shocked silence.

'Funny thing is, she was scared of heights, too.'

So that was the dark secret, Gela thinks, which explained so many things. 'How terrible for you,' she says.

Shelly glances away, muttering, '...for years I was full of anger... hated her for what she did; only recently, well, I've sort of come to accept it. She must have been desperate to have done what she did. I know what it's like,' she adds, wondering why she is suddenly baring her soul. Must be the fear of the twenty-six mile journey ahead and what lay at the other end. 'I suffer from depression, which probably explains why I'm such a pain in the arse,' she grins, lightening the moment. 'Come on you two, get some carbs into you, we've got a marathon to run.'

***

Outside the coach is waiting in the misty dawn to drive them to the start of the race.

'How about you just drive us straight to the finishing post,' Fran says to the driver causing a murmur of laughter around the bus, followed by silence as they crawl along the traffic clogged roads towards the start.

'Everyone all right?' Shelly inquires.

Gela nods, 'Just about.' She's still reeling from Shelly's admission, wondering if she can weave something similar into the novel.

'Why are we doing this?' Fran demands wretchedly.

'Because our lives weren't going anywhere, remember,' Gela answers, 'and you said you kept missing the starting gun ... and I've never seen the finishing post.'

And I never managed to do the distance, Shelly thinks.

— Chapter Twenty-Nine —

At first glance it looks like a circus with large marquees set up in a semi-circle, and smaller make-shift tents selling sports equipment, tea, coffee, and hot-dogs. People are walking around in fancy dress; a clown on stilts holding a bunch of coloured balloons, a group of men in matching tutus and tights, a giant bear with a bucket collecting for Great Ormond Street, a woman dressed as a skeleton running for osteoporosis. A helicopter hovers overhead, and loud-speaker announcements boom across the heath welcoming everyone to the event. Runners are warming up, jogging on the spot or doing acrobatic stretches beneath the trees, and the air smells of camphor oil, and frying food.

'It's like a carnival,' Fran says, gazing in awe at people of all shapes and sizes, honed looking athletes in indecently short shorts, older men with white, veiny legs, women with wobbly bits just like her.

'Let's get a cup of tea?' Gela suggests, visibly cheered.

Fran shakes her head. 'It'll go straight through me. I already need the loo again!'

'We also need to find the baggage tent, then do some stretches,' Shelly says taking charge. 'Follow me.'

***

The sun is finally breaking through, burning away the mist, and a loudspeaker announcement is now telling everybody to move towards the start.

'Need to pee again,' Fran mutters, as runners stream past.

'It's just nerves,' Shelly tries to assure her.

Marshals in luminous coats are corralling people into numbered pens like sheep, according to age and estimated time.

'We start together,' Shelly says firmly, grabbing hold of Fran's arm and ducking under the tape.

'But I'm meant to be way back with the 'fun runners' – the plodders,' Fran points out.

'Just follow me,' Shelly insists, shielding Fran from a marshal who shouts, 'four and a half to five hour runners only.'

Shelly is inching forwards now towards the front of the pen saying, 'we're starting together, whatever happens.'

They are wedged in all sides, in a miasma of body heat, sweat and anticipation.

Shelly turns to Gela and Fran her eyes blazing. 'Good luck you two! We can do this. We're athletes remember! I'll be waiting at meeting point F for Fran,' she adds, 'we'll have the biggest celebration ever!'

'Thanks,' Gela mutters, shivering from nerves. 'You too – and take care.'

Shelly nods grimly. 'I will. Remember to pace yourself.'

'Best of luck Frannie,' Gela says, squeezing her hand, 'see you at the end.'

Fran nods, aware of a distinct flutter against her rib cage.

Nerves – she says to herself, taking a slow deep breath and counting to ten.

Fran doesn't hear the starting gun, only a booming voice echoing from the loudspeaker, as the countdown begins.

'Nine, eight, seven…' she joins in '…three, two, one...' then silence. Nobody moves.

'Is this it?' she inquires, as everybody finally inches forward a couple of centimetres.

'Suits me,' mutters a hefty looking man beside her.

'At this rate I'll never make it to the first Portaloo in time,' says another voice.

Fran grins. Her heart seems to have steadied – she just wishes her nerves would subside.

There is movement again as the great centipede lurches forward, then heaves to a halt, repeating the pattern until it seems to Fran her segment is too dense to move, she's destined to be part of this giant human causeway for ever. She has already become separated from Shelly and Gela, as she's propelled forwards - now part of the sea of moving bodies all running for a different cause. A woman with, LOVE YOU SAL printed on her back, people running for the blind, the handicapped, and the terminally ill. Fran feels a great lump form in her throat. 'Miss you Lettie,' she breathes as she plods along, part of this snaking human tide, carrying their messages of hope.

She is crossing the starting line at last – is aware the journey has finally begun – all the months of pain and sweat, the hours spent pounding the lanes have been leading to this moment.

'Holy shit, girl, you're running a bloody marathon!' she exclaims, in disbelief.

***

Shelly glances at her sports-watch as she crosses the line, registering it has taken her nine minutes to get there. The clock has started ticking now, recording her time all the way to the finishing line. She sets the timer, knowing the first mile was bound to be slow, trying to break through the wall of runners. She feels uncoordinated, unable to find her rhythm, in this massive stampede. Gela is still with her, weaving her way through the gaps of flaying elbows, a dizzying blur of bobbing heads. Crowds of spectators stand on the kerb, shouting and cheering, some singing or chanting as the great flood of bodies surge past.

'We need to settle down' Shelly says nervously, 'find a comfortable pace.'

'Just have to go with the flow,' Gela replies, thinking it's a relief not to have to think about the pace – to be swept along with the tide, in the hopes it would eventually bring you safely to the shore.

'You're feeling good,' Shelly tells herself, setting her sights on a woman with a wobbling behind and puckered thighs ahead. No need for Fran to have worried, she thinks. She sets about passing her, checking Gela is still with her, before choosing her next target – a tiny Asiatic woman with bow legs who is running extraordinarily fast for somebody with such a short stride. Next, a man dressed as a toilet. How the hell did he manage to get so far up the field with a seat around his waist? Now an elderly woman with straggling grey hair – for somebody so ancient she was flying along. On she goes, striking them off one by one – all that locked up energy flowing into her muscles. Her body feels highly tuned after all the weeks of training – more than capable of delivering her to the finishing line. She weaves past a woman dressed in lycra 'cut offs', and a G string for heaven sake! She'd probably be sliced in half by the end, a man in skimpy shorts, exposing a pair of hairy buttocks. He is chatting away on his mobile. Shelly hears him say, 'I'm on mile two, only twenty four to go.' When she looks around Gela has gone.

She slows, feeling oddly vulnerable, then takes a deep breath and looks around for her next target. Somehow she'd known they would become separated, but not quite so soon. She had envisaged cheering Gela, and after a long wait, Fran on, watching them cross the finishing line. It is vital she gets there first – as team leader, and coach and well … because she needs to lead by example, she tells herself, praying that her secret weapon will sustain her to the bitter end.

She takes a sip of energy drink (which she'd made extra strong) deciding to skip the water station – no point wasting precious time – and pushes on, dodging past discarded bottles, towards the next mile marker.

***

Gela feels a sense of relief now Shelly has gone – she settles into her stride, absorbing the sights and sounds around her, her mind setting off on a course of its own.

She thinks about the novel wondering how she was going to resolve things for Donna. Having concluded there was no way back, that the marriage was over, she'd then decided to leave a chink of hope – let the reader believe they might after all get back together. After all, there was always hope. Wasn't it the last thing to fly out of Pandora's box?

She indulges in a fantasy of her and Marcus bound for Venice on the Orient Express to celebrate their reunion and tenth wedding anniversary, before concluding it was not to be. Rather it would become another of those key moments they'd never share.

Still, she would finish the novel one way or another. The plot was good – gritty and real – the characters true to life, especially Donna. She had poured all her pain and angst into the character. She would make sure she came out on top – end in a blaze of triumph with a publishing contract, followed by a best seller and to hell with her marriage.

Her body has warmed up now, she pulls Marcus's worn cricket sweater over her head, holding it against her for a brief moment, the smell of him flooding her senses, then flings it high into the air, over the streams of runners. She glances around and sees it arc gracefully – arms splayed, as if reaching out one last time, before diving down and landing in a crumpled heap on the pavement.

***

Fran is plodding along with a band of runners in fancy dress – a man with an enormous pair of false breasts also running for breast cancer, two hairy men in shocking pink tutus, and there is the two man rhino with SAVE MY HIDE written on its rear end. The hectic strains of an Irish jig rise into the air from a pair of crackling speakers set up on the side of the road, transporting her back to the pub near the Halfpenny Bridge and the pig farmer who'd called her 'acres of a woman.' I will never be that size again, she tells herself, squinting ahead in search of a Portaloo.

She manages to strike up conversation with an ostrich, a stocky little man, who is patently hampered by the thick hoola hoop around his waist.

'That must be uncomfortable,' she says, glancing at the logo which reads, 'DON'T BURY YOUR HEAD IN THE SAND – TALK TO LIFELINE.

'I'm used to it,' he grins. 'Do it every year – took me eight hours, one year.'

Fran wishes him luck, comforted that she might not be last after all. Her heart is steady, her nerves have subsided, her only concern is the state of her bladder. It was all very well for men, she thinks, glancing towards the side of the road, where rows of them were standing, legs astride, aiming deftly into the verge. Right now she feels as if she's carrying a water balloon. Thankfully she can see some Portaloos ahead, only there is a line of rather desperate looking women waiting outside, some of whom are jogging up and down to keep warm.

If she stops now she'll lose her rhythm, or worse, seize up. That was how it had all begun, with a cramp at the top of Charlton Hill, leading to that first encounter with Gerry. She feels a stab of shame and humiliation at the memory. She groans out loud from the weight of her bladder. Maybe it will evaporate (like the love affair) she thinks without much hope. She pushes on thinking there were bound to be more Portaloos ahead.

***

Shelly calculates she must be approaching the ten-mile marker now.

So far so good, she thinks, taking a preventive slug of the sickly energy drink.

She and a woman with a body like a string bean are locked in battle – although the other woman seems to be flagging which is heartening. Shelly is aware she should be controlling her own pace, not competing with this gazelle of a woman, who keeps surging forward as if pursued by a herd of wildebeest. She checks her watch registering she has run the last mile far too fast – risking precious energy. As soon as she's shaken string bean off, she'll pull it right back, she vows to herself.

She needs to remain focussed and in control, which means not allowing her mind to wander down any of those familiar dark alleys.

'Try to remain in the here and now, or at least focus on the next mile marker, rather than dwelling on the distance in front of you,' Mr Dippy had advised.

Which also means trying not to think about the even longer road ahead, without Bruce when all this was over.

***

Fran can hold out no longer, her bladder has become a lead weight. The sight of the water station ahead is not helping, that and the fact a scout with a sweet face, is thrusting a bottle into her hand. He's even taken the lid off sending cold water sloshing down her bare legs. She groans and bites her lip, but there are some more Portaloos ahead (with the familiar queue standing hopefully outside). She slows, trying to weigh up whether it would be better to pee on herself, or become felled by a painful cramp. But the decision is being taken out of her hands and starting to trickle down her thighs. She weaves around the back of the Portaloos, pulls down her shorts and crouches down beside a police cone, groaning with relief. As she straightens up, she hears a loud cheer and looks up to where a group of spectators have gathered at the window of a terraced house to view the race, and from the catcalls coming from them, the added bonus of her naked bottom.

***

Gela who is reaching the half-way mark, is running on automatic now, fractured thoughts flitting through her mind. She's been looking out for Brian at every mile marker, hoping for a glimpse of Jamie and Matthew, but still hasn't spotted them. What if Matthew had got lost in the crowds, she thinks worriedly? She'd given him her mobile just in case, which means she can't even call him.

All her attention is suddenly focussed on a dark headed runner a couple of yards ahead. It's the legs that strike a familiar chord, long and sinuous, like the bronzed effigy of the runner poised on a plinth. He is sporting a t-shirt with HELP THE HOMELESS printed on the back. Her stomach lurches as the realisation kicks in. 'Paolo,' she breathes.

She trails him for a while, her heart accelerating, a heady mix of emotions, colliding with one another - anger, hatred, revenge. She wants to lash out at him, run him over, push him out of her path, send him reeling onto the pavement, trample on him, then leave him lying in the gutter where he belonged. Donna, her alter ego, would have done all that, and more she thinks.

She hears him swear out loud, and notices he's slowing, bending over every so often to massage his calf.

Loser, she wants to shout. Can't take the pace after all – serves you right, you bastard! She draws level, but he doesn't seem to register her – appears to be focussed on some inner pain – his features contorted into an ugly mask.

'You look in a bad way,' she blurts, unable to stop herself.

'Fucking cramp,' he mutters, without looking around.

'Serves you bloody well right,' she chants childishly, her voice shaking with emotion.

He looks at her at last, as if from a great distance.

'Angela Harvey-Wood! Well you really fucked it up for yourself, didn't you? I hear Marcus is right back where he started – just another little exec in a grey suit!'

'You're the one who fucked up,' she breathes, stopping in her tracks. 'You couldn't do it without Marcus could you? Couldn't get anybody else to back you ... you're just a nasty little con-man with a huge chip on your shoulder.'

'You don't know what you're fucking talking about,' he

sneers, 'another bloody bitch who got what she deserved!' He is limping along now like some deranged tramp that has lost his way.

'So I'm not the only one you plied with drink and virtually raped?' she fumes.

Runners are weaving past them now, somebody jolts him from behind, causing him to shout, 'fucking watch it!'

'You're blocking everyone's way,' she says. 'I'd pull out if I were you. There's another thirteen miles to go. You'll never make it!'

He swears horribly, spraying spittle into the air.

She pulls ahead, desperate now to get away from him. Shock and adrenaline cause her to surge ahead, on a new wave of energy.

'Dickhead,' she shouts back, taking a leaf out of Shelly's book.

That's the end of that chapter she thinks to herself, turning around for a last glance, but he's already out of sight, lost in the blur of moving bodies.

***

Shelly is slowing dramatically along with thousands of other runners. Conversation has been replaced by heavy breathing, as everyone concentrates on the road ahead. A man in front of her clears his throat and spits copiously onto the pavement. A young girl wobbles to a halt, and stops dead, as if shell shocked. (Another one wearing a G string, Shelly notes).

She has temporarily lost track of the miles, is aware of having passed the half-way point some time ago, after which things had gone steadily down hill. She should be feeling a lot better than this, she thinks cursing her body for letting her down.

The mental exercises and motivational chants are no longer working, being drowned out by more insistent voices: *'marathon my arse... you'll keel over... you need it up here.'*

And finally, *'a marathon is all about competing with yourself,'* The Whippet had warned, that day in some pain free life. *'Otherwise you're heading for trouble.'*

She must have used up vital stores of energy earlier on, striking people off. Now in some kind of grim retribution, a woman who looks distinctly like String Bean is passing her. She can feel an aching heaviness dragging her down, coupled with hot rods of pain in her right hip. She alters her stride, but the pain persists.

She stumbles on through a sea of concrete, feeling as if some giant obstacle is blocking her way – a wall of cement through which she cannot pass.

***

Pain is multi layered, Fran thinks, seeping into every muscle fibre and tissue, deep into the core of her, until she can no longer locate the source of it. She has become a living, barely breathing pain receptor, she thinks wildly. She feels as if she's on an endless treadmill going nowhere. She decides to intersperse some walking with running, in the hopes it will ease the agonising cramp in her calves, only the change of stride sends more bolts of pain into her lower back. She attempts her African walk – head high, hips swaying, but to no avail. What kind of masochist had coined the phrase 'fun runner' she thinks grimly. And then she sees a large banner ahead (that hated synthetic sheet, transformed into a joyful white flag) with GOOD LUCK FRAN, and there is Brian, Chloe, Jamie and Matthew standing at the side of the road, cheering and waving madly.

She breaks into a trot, trying to put her best foot forward, although both feet are in a bad way.

'Come on Mummy,' Chloe shouts, 'keep going! That's my Mum,' she yells to the pack of cheering spectators. 'Come on Fran!'

'Keep going, Fran,' echoes the crowd.

Fran forces a smile, which is more like a grimace on her

face, hears Brian call, 'I'll be waiting for you.'

'Might be a while,' she grunts.

'However long it takes,' he replies.

She nods heartened by the fact he hasn't asked if she's all right. How had she come to take him so much for granted? She loves him to bits, always has in a cosy familiar way. They had always danced to the same tune, even if the rhythm had become a bit monotonous of late.

***

Gela tells herself the end is nigh (right now, she fears it is). The crowds lining the road are getting denser, as she embarks on the final stretch.

The shock of meeting Paolo had taken its toll. After the initial rush of adrenaline, she'd started to feel weak and shaky whilst her legs felt as if they'd been liquidised. Somebody had given her a chocolate bar, which had helped, but now she's had enough – she can't think of one good reason to carry on putting herself through any more of this misery.

'You're nearly there,' somebody shouts, but enough is enough. She veers towards the pavement, looking for somewhere to sit down whilst runners stream past her.

'Come on,' says a deep male voice, 'you're almost there!'

'Can't,' she mumbles, shaking her head.

The owner of the voice is now putting his hand on her shoulder trying to propel her forwards.

'You can,' he insists, pulling her along with him. He's not young, she thinks registering white hair and faded blue eyes (he looks a bit like her beloved father) and is clearly exhausted, but not defeated – unlike her.

'There's no point,' she mumbles wretchedly. After all there would be no Marcus at the end waiting to drive her home. But the stranger is urging her along, and the roar of the crowd is getting louder. She can see the gantry ahead at last with its luminous digits registering the time – which seems meaningless now – hears him say, 'you're home now,' before melting away.

Tears of emotion stream down her face as a woman places a medal around her neck, another removes the chip off her sneaker, somebody else hands her a goodie bag. Armies of runners are limping along like wounded soldiers, swathed in silver foil, towards the meeting points.

She stands there swaying, the tears still pouring down her face, trying to remember if she was meant to go to meeting point F or G. Her brain is no longer functioning, has shut down, as if unable to register any more pain. She is vaguely aware of people congratulating one another, hugging and kissing – or locked in a sweaty embrace. A man supports his exhausted partner as she sags against him.

There's no sign of Shelly at meeting point F – Gela limps onto the verge, feeling as if her insides are disintegrating. She pulls the silver foil tighter around her, thinking she may have crossed the line but she was still in no man's land – like her hapless heroine, Donna.

Somebody is trying to grab her elbow – but she pulls away. She's beyond help now. But he's got hold of her again, his voice urgent and familiar, as he says, 'Angel, God I thought I'd never get to you.'

'Marcus?' she breathes, wondering if she's dreaming.

He looks wild eyed and strained, and is breathing heavily as if he too has run the marathon.

'I saw you at the twenty mile marker – then I lost you again, saw you briefly around twenty three then had to fight my way through the crowds.'

'I thought you were in France,' she says dazedly.

'I came back early – skipped the meeting. I was going to call, but I was afraid you'd tell me to bugger off. God, I love you,' he breathes, his voice catching. He pulls her closer and buries his head in her neck.

'I stink,' she mutters. She is aware of her mad hair, with its halo of frizz, her smudged mascara – which she'd applied at five in the morning, can smell sweat and vaseline emanating from her, hears him murmur, 'I've been such an idiot.'

'I need to sit down,' she says faintly.

He is lifting her up now, and carrying her towards the grassy patch beneath the trees.

'Need to stay near meeting point F – keep an eye out for Shelly and Fran,' she tells him.

'They'll be a while yet,' he predicts. 'You did a fantastic time. Where are the boys?' he inquires.

'They're with Brian and Chloe. I hope he hasn't lost Matthew,' she says anxiously. 'I gave him my mobile just in case.'

'They'll be fine,' he soothes. 'Brian won't let them out of his sight. I brought you some supplies,' he adds, producing a thermos of tea from a small hamper, a bar of fruit and nut, crisps – cracked pepper and sea salt she notes, a bottle of Chablis, and lastly a chocolate heart, with 'I love you,' written on it.

'Earl Grey?' he offers, pouring some into a cup.

She takes it from him, still in a dream like state. 'So you got the e-mail?' she says finally.

He nods. 'A powerful piece of prose, brilliantly done – because you're never quite sure whether the woman…?'

'Donna…'

'Yes, Donna. Whether she's the victim or perpetrator.'

There is a silence then she says, 'but you thought she deserved the benefit of the doubt?'

He takes a deep breath and looks away. 'I knew I'd made a mistake before reading your story. I wanted to come back, but that day Jamie ran away – well, I got the distinct feeling you didn't want me around anymore then you banished me to Ashlington Falls for Jamie's birthday!'

'I couldn't get through to you,' she says after a silence.

He sighs. 'I know I reacted badly. It was just Paolo of all

people – bastard! If I ever set eyes on him I'll kill him.'

'I saw him at mile thirteen,' she tells him. 'He was in a bad way – effing and blinding. I called him a dickhead,' she grins.

She digs into the crisps savouring the divine salty taste, then takes a sip of hot tea. Never before had tea tasted so heavenly, she thinks.

'Not surprised he was in a bad way,' Marcus comments, 'he'll probably be put away, now these latest women have come forward.'

'What women?'

'Did you not know he's been done for rape. It was all in the press. Didn't you read it?'

She shakes her head in amazement, remembering Paolo saying, "another bloody bitch who got what they deserved."

'I haven't read the tabloids for ages.'

He pushes his hand through his hair, which now has a few grey strands, saying 'can you forgive me? I want to make it up to you, take you to Venice for your birthday since I screwed that one up too.'

She frowns, as if considering this. 'By the way who was the woman with long black hair and pointy shoes?'

'Black hair...? Pointy shoes?'

'You were talking to her at Ashlington Falls.'

'Ah,' he grins, 'Vanessa the vampire – she's a head hunter who's been trying to poach me for a while – a real hard nosed woman. It was actually quite a good offer – managing director of a wine and spirit company in France, but I told her I was trying to move closer to home. You didn't think ... ah, no, give me a break, not my type – she's the kind of woman who sucks you dry.'

She smiles, then lies back on the grass, feeling as if she's floating above her aching body into the clear blue sky.

'That's it,' she murmurs happily, 'at last I know the ending!'

***

Shelly seems to have developed Tourettes syndrome. 'Fuck, shit, fuck shit, fuck, bastard,' she breathes as each strike sends a new shock wave reverberating through her depleted body. She had somehow managed to climb the wall and get going again, but now the reserve tank is completely empty. She must have been walking for hours ... days perhaps? She wants to punch the next spectator who tells her she's nearly there, only she hasn't the energy.

'Don't start looking for the finishing line until you're almost there.' Mr Dippy advised.

'Where's the fucking finishing line?' Shelly shouts at a marshal.

'Almost there,' he answers, automatically.

'Jesus Shell,' a breathy familiar voice behind is saying. She glances around thinking she must be hallucinating. It's Fran, limping along, hair damp and loose, skin blotchy, a faint bluish tinge around her lips.

'Shell?' she repeats, 'are you all right?'

Shelly stares at her wildly. In spite of her appearance, there is something magnificent – almost triumphant about Fran, Shelly thinks – it is the stubborn resilience of the plodder – the tortoise whose painstaking effort brings the ultimate reward.

'I can't believe I've caught up with you,' Fran pants. 'We're nearly there!' she adds, sensing instinctively she's said the wrong thing. 'Come on, we can finish together!'

Shelly shakes her head. 'Hit the wall, go,' she states, her eyes trained on the tarmac road, 'go on... leave me... you can do it...'

'I'm not leaving you,' Fran states, 'come on we can walk the last bit together. I'm knackered as well!'

Shelly shakes her head again. She wants to be left to battle it out alone, not pulled along by Fran of all people. 'Go...! I'll see you on the other side.'

'No way Shell!'

'Go!' Shelly shouts wildly, 'do you hear me... fuck off!'

'Right,' Fran says, pulling ahead, uncertainly. 'I'll wait for you at the end – if I get there that is!' She suddenly sees the twenty five mile marker ahead, shouts, 'we really are almost there... look!'

But Shelly is no longer listening.

When Fran turns around, she notices Shelly has attempted to jog again. She wants to point out there is only one more mile (plus the point two) to go, but senses Shelly is close to breaking point, that it might as well be twenty miles, at this stage.

Fran grits her teeth, wondering if she too has the strength to go on. On the other hand what choice did she have? It was either that, or keeling over like Big Mo, before the finishing post. She couldn't allow that to happen – not at this stage of the race. She thinks of Brian who would be checking his watch, every minute – making bets with Chloe, as to when she would arrive – trying to disguise his worry with bad jokes.

Come on woman, you can do it, she tells herself, conjuring up a mental image of home, and their bed with its Egyptian cotton sheets, and duck down duvet, of Brian beside her, and the blessed oblivion of sleep.

***

Shelly attempts a few stumbling steps, then peters to a halt again. There's a mad rushing in her head, a pounding in her ears – like waves breaking on the shore. She limps along blindly, feeling as if she's being sucked downward, into the centre of the earth – thrust into the firey furnace, sentenced to a life of constant agony. She can see something in the distance – a square archway, with numbers flashing above it – the gateway to heaven perhaps, shifting out of focus as if she's had too many Bullshots. She stumbles on, weaving and zigzagging, focussing on those points of light – the light at the end of the tunnel.

She is Pheidippides, running to Athens from the battlefields of Marathon to announce victory to the Athenians, before dying a glorious and heroic death, she thinks wildly.

The surface of the road has altered, turned spongy – clouds perhaps, the noise of the crowd fading as if everything is coming from a long way away. She can see a woman in a St John's ambulance uniform frowning and mouthing something into a walkie-talkie; the woman is moving forward now, trying to block her way, as she falls through the clouds and into the black void beyond – down and down, into that bottomless pit – until all is silent.

***

Brian, who has calculated it over and over, allowing Fran at least twenty-two minutes leeway is also close to breaking point.

'Where the hell is she?' he mutters, checking his watch again. 'She should have been here twelve minutes ago, even if she walked the last two miles!' He had missed her at the twenty mile marker, had then battled through the thick crowds of spectators, hanging onto the three kids for dear life, before deciding to withdraw to meeting point F.

'Maybe she had to stop for a pooh!' Chloe suggests.

'Keep an eye on Jamie,' he snaps, holding Matthew firmly by the hand, but it's too late, Jamie is running away, towards a grassy verge, shouting, 'there's Dad! He's found Mummy ... she got a medal!' Matthew is breaking away now and following. Brian sees Marcus leap to his feet, and open his arms in delight – the four of them fusing together in the dappled sunshine filtering through the trees.

***

Fran feels as if she's been evicted from her body, and is now looking down on a great moving lump of cement – the old Fran – 'acres of a woman,' who could barely run up Charlton Hill. Was it only eight months ago, that she had set off on this epic journey she thinks as she crosses the line?

'I did it,' she gasps, as someone places a medal around her neck. 'I've run a marathon!'

'Congratulations,' the woman smiles. 'It's a hell of an achievement.'

Fran feels a wild and heady euphoria, almost as intense as childbirth, she thinks – and just as painful.

She turns around hoping to see Shelly appearing, but a marshal waves her onwards, urging runners to clear the way. Fran drags herself the last few yards towards meeting point F, where she can already see Brian, his face breaking into a huge grin. Chloe is leaping up and down in excitement and there is Bruce still limping slightly, Gela and the boys, and miraculously Marcus. Everybody is crowding around her suddenly.

'Come here to me you athletic woman,' Brian murmurs, engulfing her in his arms.

'You've shrunk Mummy,' Chloe says, putting her arms around Fran's waist.

'You can lose up to two inches in height after a marathon,' Brian states with a grin.

Fran hugs Gela next. 'This calls for a double celebration,' she says, under her breath. Gela nods, her eyes filling with tears.

An official photographer appears like magic to capture the moment, causing Gela to say, 'where's Shelly, we need our trainer in the photograph. She should be in by now!'

She notices Bruce glancing at his watch with a frown.

'I saw her just before mile twenty-five,' Fran breathes. 'She was walking. I think she might have hit the wall. I tried to stay with her, but she told me to fuck off! You know Shell! She'll be here in a few minutes.'

***

'Maybe she went to the wrong meeting point?' Fran says, some fifteen minutes later. 'Even the rhino is back!' She's aware of Bruce checking his watch for the umpteenth time.

Gela frowns. 'She definitely said F because it was the closest. I've got a really bad feeling suddenly.' She has started to shiver from exhaustion. 'Maybe we should check E and G just in case?'

'I'll go,' Bruce says.

'I should have stayed with her,' Fran says worriedly.

'She wouldn't have let you by the sound of it,' Gela tries to console her.

Bruce returns some minutes later. 'No sign,' he says, looking agitated. He pulls out his mobile, saying, 'there are two messages. Didn't hear it ring – too much bloody noise!'

Everybody waits while he listens.

Gela notices a shadow pass over his face. The bad feeling has turned to fear. 'What is it?' she demands, 'is she all right?'

He turns towards them, his huge shoulders sagging, his voice barely audible. 'She collapsed... just before the finishing line! They've taken her to hospital... a suspected heart attack.'

— AND BEYOND —

It's almost the middle of the summer term, although you wouldn't think it, Fran thinks, shivering in her new plunging v-necked top. She glances down at her cleavage checking everything is still in place – a glow of pride at the sight of those two swelling half-moons, which right now are covered in goose bumps. She still hasn't got used to them, whilst Brian couldn't get enough of them. This morning they'd come back from an early morning jog – she'd managed to get him up to three miles, but he still had enough energy to make love to her in the shower. The nutrition course was going well too, had changed her way of looking at food, although she still went on the odd binge. But her weight had remained stable thanks to the daily runs, which had become part of her life now.

She can see Gela pulling into the car park to drop Jamie and Matthew off – they'd planned a shopping trip, followed by a celebration lunch. Gela's announcement they were publishing *CROSSING THE LINE* hadn't come as a surprise to Fran. The draft she'd read made compelling reading – especially as she'd recognised herself in one of the characters. Some of it was a bit close to the bone, she'd thought, especially when 'Jen' has a passionate affair with her gardener. The fact she'd been portrayed as a warm hearted, funny, yet slightly repressed character - a flower destined to bloom, had made it easier to digest. Besides she would be forever grateful to Gela for making her voluptuous and sexy, rather than fat.

Gela gets out of her car, looking dazzling in a new outfit, her hair a mass of waving tendrils. She'd given up trying to straighten it, claiming she'd thrown vanity to the wind. The fact that the tousled look was back in fashion had helped.

'You're on time!' Fran says, in surprise.

'Left Marcus to deal with the chaos,' Gela grins. 'He's got to pull his weight now I'm a real author.' The arrangement of him working from home part of the week was going well, as was the new business – a small company selling luxury beauty products, which he'd already managed to turn around. Gela had already tested out most of them.

'Shell really started a trend,' Fran says, watching a couple of mothers in shorts and trainers setting off for a run.

'She certainly managed to inspire me in more ways than one,' Gela states.

'Will you ever forget that slurry tractor?' Fran grins, 'God the amount of times I peed in my pants.'

Gela smiles. 'It was such a heightened time.'

There's a silence, as they both become lost in their separate thoughts.

'Here she is,' Fran says at last.

Gela turns and sees Bruce's Land Rover pulling into the car park with Bruce at the wheel. Shelly climbs out carefully, her hair like a copper flame in the weak sunshine. She's still recovering from those almost fatal few minutes when her heart had stopped beating. Severe dehydration, coupled with a reaction from a steroid based drug (Fran had been right) had caused her system to shut down. Tests had also revealed some blood filled cysts in her liver (peliosis hepatitis) the doctor had said grimly which meant no alcohol for the unforeseeable future.

'No wonder I felt like shit,' Shelly had exclaimed, remembering the dragging ache in her side.

Fran notices the manicured nails – no doubt to show off what Shelly called 'my rock,' a substantial solitary diamond on her third finger.

'Purely symbolic,' she'd announced. 'I'm not even sure I want to get married anymore.' Bruce had told her that the thought of losing her had 'hit him like a sledgehammer,' and that he had never fancied Marissa. (Too bloody demanding, and selfish he'd claimed). She had undoubtedly contributed to that almost fatal accident on Helter Skelter by refusing to descend earlier. 'No wonder The Ogre had done a runner,' he'd added. He'd also agreed to put The Trout and Fly in Shelly's name and let her take over the running of it.

Which meant there was no need to become Mrs Wainwright now, Shelly had said with a shrug.

'Liar,' Gela and Fran had chorused.

She hadn't gone into the details of that agonising last mile, except to say, 'I was that close ... mentally there! If only that bloody ambulance woman hadn't got in my way!'

She was still battling with the organisers to send her a medal, even though she hadn't actually crossed the line.

Now as they sit in Buffalo Joe's tucking into barbecued chicken wings and ribs, Shelly raises her glass of mineral water – she's almost got used to drinking the stuff, saying, 'well done Gel for the novel, although next time I want to be the main character!' She too, was heartened by the fact Gela had got her to the finishing line – so to speak.

Gela smiles. 'You'll always be the main character, Shelly!'

'Yeah right, the team leader! Only you two almost left me for dead,' she adds wryly.

'You told me to bugger off!' Fran reminds her.

'Besides it was never about winning,' Gela points out.

'I know. It still feels bloody good though,' Shelly grins. 'At least I beat that woman wearing the G string!'

As the laughter dies down, she adds, 'I was thinking if all goes well – once I'm back to normal of course, we could start training again. Maybe run New York?'